HOW TO
BE
EATEN

BOOKS BY MARIA ADELMANN

Girls of a Certain Age

HOW TO

BE

EATEN

Maria Adelmann

Little, Brown and Company

New York Boston London

Little, Brown and Company
Hachette Book Group
1290 Avenue of the Americas, New York, NY 10104
littlebrown.com

First Edition: May 2022

Little, Brown and Company is a division of Hachette Book Group, Inc. The Little, Brown name and logo are trademarks of Hachette Book Group, Inc.

The publisher is not responsible for websites (or their content) that are not owned by the publisher.

The Hachette Speakers Bureau provides a wide range of authors for speaking events. To find out more, go to hachettespeakersbureau.com or call (866) 376-6591.

ISBN 9780316450843
LCCN 2021947471

Printing 3, 2022

LSC-C

Printed in the United States of America

Out of old tales, we must make new lives.

—Carolyn Heilbrun,
"What Was Penelope Unweaving?"

Contents

Week One

The Beginning

The women gather in a YMCA basement rec room: hard linoleum floors, half-windows along one wall, view of sidewalk and brick. It's a Friday, just after six, and above them the city of New York bustles. Up there, people are teeming out of subway stations and into the hot sun, rushing toward tourist traps, toward restaurants, toward parties and friends.

Whatever people do on a Friday, the women in the basement are not doing it. Instead, they unfold metal chairs, listen to the rubber nubs squeak across the floor as they circle up. They collect store-brand chocolate chip cookies off a card table, pour coffee into paper cups despite the heat, shake in the powdered creamer. They write their names on white, rectangular name tags, then press those tags to their chests. The instant they're on, they begin to peel off, as if the tags themselves understand what the women want most: to be rid of their history, to start anew.

But they can't outrun their names and they can't outrun their stories.

They all had been blind cc'd on the same email. *Personal*

trauma, public figure? the subject heading read. *Unusual story?* the email asked.

It continued with more questions: Did they feel alone or misunderstood? Could they identify with certain symptoms—recurring nightmares, intrusive thoughts, numbness, self-destructive behavior, anger, sadness, guilt, shame? Were they interested in free, experimental group therapy? Would they like to schedule a screening?

They would not.

Bernice had read the email, then deleted it. Gretel had marked it as "spam." Ruby had read half of it, then marked it as "unread," where it joined over 5,000 other "unread" emails. Ashlee didn't even see it because she was trying to avoid the internet. Raina read the message, then left it in her inbox, where it fell lower and lower in the queue until it disappeared from the first page entirely.

By then, another email had arrived, and after that came another, and another.

Ashlee, who had opened her account in a moment of weakness, scheduled a screening immediately. Ruby replied to the third message while sitting alone at a bar, figuring even if it was some kind of scam, at least it might be entertaining. Bernice and Raina both replied to the fourth email, deciding that a screening would be harmless.

Gretel was the final holdout. In the middle of a sleepless night, feeling almost all of the symptoms the email had listed, she checked her spam folder. She deleted four of the five identical messages. Her cursor hovered over the fifth. What, at this point, did she really have left to lose?

There must have been others who received the email, who never replied, or who replied but never followed through with the screening, or who followed through with the screening, then decided not to come.

Perhaps those people had the right idea, the women think now as they shift in their seats, fidget with their phones, poke through their purses, look at each other and pretend not to look at each other, trying to attach faces to names, names to stories.

Bernice is fresh from the last news cycle. Until now, the other women have known her only by her media-christened name: Bluebeard's Girlfriend. The dark and bizarre secrets of the eccentric tech billionaire with the trademark cyan beard made headlines for weeks earlier that summer. Even if you weren't paying attention, you managed to accrue details by mere osmosis.

Bernice had yet to speak to the media. In freeze-frame footage from CNN, she had a double chin, a slight smirk, a nefarious brown eye peeking out from under a bright umbrella. Commentators commented: "Why so guarded?" "A rainbow umbrella, for a funeral?" "Why blue for her dress, of all colors?" Yet here, in real life, quietly eating a cookie, sans CNN, she appears less suspicious, less homely, less fat. Her uninspired office ensemble, her tired eyes, her half-bitten nails, these all make her seem so normal, so totally average, as to be incapable of anything the sensational headlines have implied.

As for Gretel, they've all heard her name, and if she's here, she's almost certainly *the* Gretel, the one from the strange kidnapping story that captivated the nation more than two decades before: a brother and sister went missing, reappeared three months later miles from home. The photo of the siblings reuniting with their father was one of *Time*'s photos of the year. The children had made wild and fascinating claims, though they themselves disagreed on what had happened, and the claims were unsubstantiated. Even so, after all these years, die-hard amateur sleuths still searched for proof, discussed theories on message boards devoted to unsolved crimes.

5

In that famous photo, Gretel is all elbows and knees and cork-screw curls, sweet gingham dress and bright, glistening eyes. It's unsettling to see her now, grown up, mid-thirties, creases on her forehead. She's still rail thin with a cropped puff of corkscrew curls. On a kid it was cute; on an adult it seems strange. Her hair is too spunky for her serious face, like a cloud has drifted in and settled on her head. The gingham dress has been replaced with jeans and an oversized gray button-down, the patent-leather shoes with Converse. Gretel sits hunched in her chair with an untouched cup of coffee in her hands, earbuds in her ears, avoiding eye contact with everyone. If she is giving off any vibe it's this: she'd rather be anywhere else.

Raina, almost forty, is the oldest of the group, though you might not guess it. She is elegantly attractive. Her makeup is natural, her ensemble classy yet functional: tailored black capris, stylish black loafers, an airy white button-down tank, a large beige leather tote, ears studded in real pearls. She has a long neck and a sleek bob. A lock keeps falling from behind her ear, and she keeps tucking it back with a short, French-manicured nail. She's reading on an e-reader—ostensibly reading—and drinking from a sleek, white insulated coffee cup. On her left hand, a diamond engagement ring sits above a pavé wedding ring.

Not one of the women recognizes her, not by name nor by face—though people occasionally do, mostly when she's standing next to her husband. Her story made waves decades ago, though the details had always been hazy and now were mostly forgotten. All that remained was a certain warm feeling people had when they looked at her spouse, a sense that the man before them was heroic and kind.

Ashlee is the recent, controversial winner of *The One*, the most popular reality TV dating show in the country. The other women

6

are surprised to find her among them. Her name tag reads ASHLEE E, 21, RETAIL ASSOCIATE, PARK POND, PA. When she first entered the room she was wearing a floppy sun hat and giant, bug-eye sunglasses. She had wandered around the space, squinting suspiciously into each corner, even looking behind the coffeemaker and her chair, her glossy lips scrunching into a blooming rose. Now she sits in her folding chair, fanning herself with her sun hat, one gleaming tan leg crossed over the other, sunglasses tucked in a purse so small it's hard to imagine that anything additional would fit inside.

In real life, as on TV, Ashlee looks like a 3D rendering of herself. Her features are dramatic, her makeup expertly applied. She has perfected the "sexy baby" look—adorable and dangerous at the same time: doe eyes, long lashes, plump cheeks, pouty lips. Her skin is so smooth, it looks as if it's been blurred with a filter. Her eyelashes are thick, her nails are sharp, her wedged espadrilles are three inches high. Her blush-pink romper has a V so deep that the point ends beneath her breasts, which—are they glittering? On her left hand, an engagement ring so massive that her hand seems like an afterthought. Even among such bold features, it is her mouth—her much talked about mouth—that is most outrageous, long and expressive, twisting and bending into projections of her every thought. In its neutral position, the ends turn up in a subtle smirk.

Will is the group leader, the only man. He is unobtrusively but certainly handsome—a full head of brown hair; soft, kind eyes flecked with green; a blue button-down that accentuates an athletic figure, the cuffs rolled up at the forearms. His demeanor suggests benevolent authority, like a young high school teacher, the one everyone likes.

He had vetted each member of the group individually in a screening interview, then assured more than one in a post-screening phone call that, though he hadn't predicted the group would be all-female, he was still the person for the job, aware of and sensitive to their unique needs.

He does seem attentive, the women think as Will scans the circle, stopping to acknowledge each group member, tiny personal check-ins punctuated with encouraging smiles. His teeth are a tabula rasa of whiteness. When the women look at them, they each see something different. Bernice recalls the bone-white inlay of a bright blue dresser. Ashlee sees the glint of her own engagement ring. Gretel sees hard candy winking in sun. Raina sees her husband's smile, all veneer.

Should the teeth be a tip-off? After all, they have already laid their fortunes in the hands of the most obvious psychopaths—billionaires and reality TV producers, metaphorical witches and literal wolves. Perhaps the women should wonder if something is amiss. Especially since one of them, yet to arrive, had already made a fairly substantial error with regard to teeth.

Ashlee sighs loudly and looks around the room for a clock, though there isn't one. Just as she's about to ask for the time, a high-heel clatter comes echoing down the hall, louder and louder until the door bursts open and Ruby, the final group member, careens into the room. She stops midway between the door and the group to catch her breath. "Sorry, sorry," she says. Her face is bright red and sweaty. Her lips are picked raw. Her hair is a disaster: much of it is stuck to the sweaty sides of her face; the rest of it hangs down to her shoulders in a tangle. An old pink dye job clings to the bottom three inches. Her clear-framed glasses, the lenses comically smudged, slip down her nose. Just as they seem poised to fall off, she pushes them back up.

It's no wonder she's sweating. She's wearing a massive fur coat: gray with dirt and ridiculous in the summer heat. It hangs open, framing a red top and a black pleather skirt, revealing the coat's worn beige silk lining. A thick lapel extends to a hood that's fallen on her back. The sleeves are so long that only the ragged, chewed tips of her fingers peek out.

She wipes the sweat from her brow with a furry sleeve, smudging a greasy tint of gray across her forehead, and squints around the circle. "Name tags!" she says, and clacks to the snack table to fill out her own.

When she spins back to the group, a chocolate chip cookie is shoved halfway in her mouth. The name tag rides along the hairs of the coat. LIL RED, it reads in smudgy all-caps. Then, in smaller letters below: RUBY. She latches an arm around a chair and squeezes in between Ashlee and Raina. Ashlee wrinkles her nose.

"Welcome," says Will, clapping his hands on his thighs. His voice is as calm and clear as a podcaster's, comforting yet with an air of gravitas. He has the impressive ability, as he speaks, to keep scanning the circle, surveying the group, like a phone constantly checking for a signal.

He reiterates why they're here, gives them the spiel they've each heard individually, about the groundbreaking preliminary research on narrative therapy, about how each week one woman will take the lead, tell her story, and the others will listen and react.

He reminds them that they are unique. They've each been through a trauma that played out, in some way, publicly. "People know *of* you, but do they *know* you?" he asks. No, they concur, shaking their heads, people don't know them at all.

He reminds them of the conditions they've agreed to in documents they signed prior to group. They should be present and participatory—no missing meetings, no lateness (he looks at Ruby with a smile), no phones allowed. Above all, they must be completely and absolutely honest. No lies, not even white lies, not even lies by omission. No holding back. He calls this "Absolute Honesty." He explains that a natural by-product of Absolute Honesty is tension and conflict. In this sense, conflict, like a fever, is a sign that things are working, and should be embraced as part of the process.

"It's not going to be easy," he tells them, "but if you stay open and do the work"—he spreads his arms wide, as if in benediction—"you're going to learn more about yourselves than you ever imagined." He lets the words linger, then his arms drop.

"Big sell," says Ruby through a mouthful of cookie. "Let's just get the show on the road."

"We could've started, like, twenty minutes ago?" says Ashlee. "If you weren't late?" Her voice, nasal yet vocal-fried, is reminiscent of a creaking floor.

"I see you're as charming in real life as you are on TV," says Ruby, wiping cookie crumbs from her mouth with a furry sleeve.

"Hashtag editing?" says Ashlee, her words lilting up.

The other women look in their laps.

"Ashlee," says Will, "you told Ruby you were upset that she was late. That's a great example of Absolute Honesty."

Ashlee beams.

"Absolute Honesty sounds like Total Crap to me," says Ruby.

"That's perfect, Ruby," says Will, clasping his hands together. "That's exactly the kind of honesty I'm looking for. Also, it's natural to feel that way. Resistance is part of the process."

Ashlee sighs dramatically. "I mean, if we *have* to be honest, I guess I should mention that I don't really know if I belong here?" She combs her fingers through her shiny hair, her pointy, pink nails sticking through like claws. "Like, I'm famous for falling in love, where you guys are famous for what? Weird tragedies? Regurgitated by a wolf? Locked in some loser's mansion? I mean, no offense."

"Right, and you've never been locked in some loser's mansion," says Ruby.

"Not *locked*," Ashlee says. "Also not a loser, obviously," she adds.

"Ringing endorsement," says Ruby.

"Speaking of rings," says Ashlee, thrusting her left hand into the middle of the circle, wrist limp, as if waiting for a gentleman to kiss it so she can curtsey. "Princess cut. Fourteen carat white gold. Two carat colorless diamond. Looks like a lot of you aren't in serious relationships, just from the hands I can see right now. I mean, Sad Face." Her bottom lip juts out in a look of extreme pity. She drops her hand in her lap, then nods at Raina. "I mean, looks like you're married, but if we *have* to be honest, I honestly don't even know who you are. I feel like I recognize you from something, but maybe I don't? Maybe I'm too young?"

"Could be," says Raina, not offended. "I have a daughter about your age."

"Maybe I know *her*?" says Ashlee.

"What is this? Twenty questions?" says Ruby. She squints at Raina's name tag. "Raina's going to tell her fucking story eventually. Isn't that why we're here?"

"I just thought we were supposed to be famous, you know?" says Ashlee. "Like, I thought that was the point? But really only me and Bernice are *actually* famous."

"Let's see if anyone remembers you in three months," says Ruby.

"You might rather they didn't," says Gretel. Her tone is neutral, even, out of tune with her curls, which quiver and bounce.

"Interesting," says Ruby, like she's gathering intel.

An awkward silence ensues, punctuated by the muffled honk and squeal of rush hour. The women take an interest in their coffee cups, their shoes, the wall. Will waits it out.

Bernice slides a chewed fingernail inside the lip of her paper coffee cup, starts unrolling it. "I'm not so much famous as infamous," she says. All eyes shift to her. "I do wonder what you've all heard about me." Eyes shift away, save Ashlee's.

"I guess I heard you were in on it?" Ashlee says. "Like helping him for money? I wasn't really paying attention. But Bluebeard's exes were all, kind of"—she brings her hands narrowly together and draws them down—"you know? More like models? Whereas…"

"Is that what they're saying?" asks Raina.

"*Of course* that's what they're saying," says Bernice.

"Because Bernice is, you know, more like a *sidekick* type than a girlfriend type?" Ashlee explains.

"You are aware that fat people can have boyfriends, right?" says Ruby.

Ashlee makes a face. Bernice flicks at the lip of her cup.

"How do you feel about what you're hearing now?" Will asks Bernice.

"I know what people think."

"That's not what I'm asking."

"I feel okay. I get it."

Will sighs, leans back in his chair, furrows his brow, not as if she's done something wrong but as if he's done something wrong, as if he hasn't yet conveyed the correct information. "What's one of our rules?" he asks.

"No lateness," says Ashlee, throwing a smug look at Ruby. "No phones."

"And?" says Will.

"Absolute Honesty," says Bernice.

"That's right," says Will. "So, Bernice: how do you feel about what they're saying?"

"Hurt," says Bernice. "I am just, in general, very hurt."

Somewhere in the city, police sirens wail. Bernice has an ear for sirens now. The sound throws her back to a few months prior, when she was lying on the couch of her childhood home as the flashing lights cut across the walls of the den. The room was rhythmically blue, blue, blue. If there were other colors, she didn't see them. Her fingertips were blue, blue, blue. Her mind itself, everything: blue. Her sister was blue, was saying, "It's okay, Berry, it's okay, you're in shock."

Bernice tries to bring herself back to the present. She feels her feet on the hard floor, her back on the cool chair. She can't blame the women for hearing what they've heard or thinking what they think. She knows how people consume the news: scanning headlines, catching a few sentences at the top of the hour, overhearing a rumor on the subway.

"I know people don't like me," Bernice says. "But whatever you heard, maybe it's not the whole story."

Will leans back, crosses one leg over the thigh of the other, cupping his knee with knit fingers. "What is the whole story, Bernice?"

"You want me to go first?" she asks, alarmed.

"I know you can do it," he says.

She has practiced her story for weeks now. She has edited pieces of it in her head during almost every free moment—while grocery shopping or riding the subway. She sees it in her mind's eye like a typewritten page. She wants to get as close to the truth of her experience as she can. Late at night, when she can't sleep, her head tucked under her covers, earplugs in, she has perfected it, her lips forming the shapes of the words. When she replied to the email, she already knew what she would say, assuming she didn't get stage fright. But, after all she's been through, is that really what she's afraid of? Public speaking?

"All right," Bernice says, nodding. The other women look relieved.

"Thank you, Bernice," says Will. "When you're ready."

Bernice closes her eyes, shakes out her arms, takes a deep breath, tries to let go of the stress and anxiety that has built up over the past months. She can use her exhaustion to her advantage. She can turn it into a kind of flow.

There isn't much in her life she has felt prepared for, but she feels prepared for this. She opens her eyes.

Bernice

Bluebeard, as he was called on the gossip sites, had two houses: a penthouse on Fifth Avenue facing the park and a blue beachfront mansion in East Hampton. And by blue, I mean painted bright blue, so that at certain times of day, in certain weather, it merged with the sky. He also had a blue Bugatti, a nineteen-foot TV with surround sound that could be controlled from anywhere in the world, and, for all of his computers, brass keyboards with round typewriter keys, which run about two grand apiece. His dyed beard was touted as one of his many eccentricities.

I'd grown up as a year-rounder in East Hampton. We lived in a modest, two-story house with cedar shake siding that had long been mottled gray. In summer, the Hamptons was the picture of the American Dream: polo-shirt-wearing families on sailboats, licking ice cream from waffle cones. I befriended kids who disappeared into boxwood hedges at the end of August, never to be heard from again. In winter, it was as if we lived at the ends of the earth.

Until Bluebeard bought the property across the street, our neighbors had been the ever-elderly Pearsons: two, then one, then grown children in to sell the place. The house's best feature was its size—so small that we could see around it, out across the tan-green beach grass into the beautiful blue beyond. At dinner, in the years following my father's sudden death from a pulmonary embolism, my mom would stare out at the water as we ate. "At least we have that view," she'd say.

My sister, Naomi, two years my senior, used to paint that view scrunched up on a lawn chair in the Pearsons' backyard. She painted on damaged canvases my mom brought home from the art store where she worked, thus the skies were cracked through with lightning or punctured with invented constellations.

Construction on the mansion had already begun when Naomi moved back to the home I'd never left. She'd earned a big scholarship and gone away to college, while I'd stayed home, saving money by commuting back and forth to Stony Brook. Naomi's boss at the nonprofit where she'd worked had wept when he laid her off—*wept*. He had been forced by policy—last one in, first one out—he hated to see her go.

The mansion loomed higher, wider, bluer by the day. Our view disappeared first, then the morning sun. "Sticks out like a sore thumb," my mom repeated each morning at the kitchen window, scowling as she brushed her teeth in the sink. Our house had only one bathroom.

Ashton Adams—that was Bluebeard's real name—sent a neighborly gift in a bright blue cake box. Our last name was emblazoned in raised, gold script on the top of the box, which itself was tied up with a silky blue ribbon. A surprisingly thoughtful, analog gift for a twenty-eight-year-old tech billionaire. We'd all read the articles.

The cake box was so elegant, we were hesitant to touch it, though the smell was hard to resist. We gathered around it with forks. "A gift from the enemy," said Naomi.

"He's kind of famous," I said, more as fact than excuse. I did the honors of untying the blue ribbon, letting it fall gracefully from the box, the way silky underwear might slip off a smooth leg. I traced the gold letters of my last name with my fingertip. I rarely saw my name in script. If anything, it was in Times New Roman and I'd typed it myself.

"Let us remember that he's a tool," said Naomi.

"What's with the hideous blue thing on his face?" asked my mom. "Is it meant to distract from—the rest of his face?"

"It's a hipstery thing," I said.

"It's marketing," said Naomi.

"People dress all kinds of ways," I said.

"*You* don't dress all kinds of ways," said my mom.

This was true. It was a flaw. To work, I wore black pants paired with abstract-patterned blouses reminiscent of corporate wall art. Indeed, a shirt in my rotation matched a spongy, tan-brown painting across from the elevator bay at the dingy headquarters of the budget clothing company where I did menial labor for the marketing department. The job had little to do with my degree in English, my minor in creative writing.

"I heard he chews through women like bubble gum," said my sister. She had somehow mastered a sophisticated Anthropologie-Patagonia look, though she shopped only at thrift stores. "Chews, chews, and spits them out," she said. "Pays millions to make them scarce once he's through." She put down her fork. "Wouldn't have to pay me."

I opened the cake box, the massive side tabs pointing toward the ceiling. The cake was a brilliant robin's-egg blue, yet the color barely registered in the face of the scent: sugar and butter, coconut and almond, a hint of vanilla, musky and warm. I imagined the vapors rising from the box, tickling my nose.

I didn't bother with a plate. I slid the fork into the cake, the cake into my mouth. "I—" I began but put up a finger instead. I couldn't speak. The smell was nothing compared to the taste. The flavors bloomed in my mouth. The texture was perfect—soft and light, the frosting rich and creamy.

My mom and sister stared.

"Are you having a religious experience?" asked Naomi.

"What were you going to say?" asked my mom.

But I couldn't for the life of me remember.

★ ★ ★

Bernice, hardly begun, stops. She has been monologuing like an actor in the spotlight, but there is no spotlight. There are actual faces before her, and they are not blotted out by light.

Will's chin rests on his thumb, his head nodding slightly. Raina stretches her long neck, shifting her head from one side to the other, pearl earrings winking. Ashlee spools hair around her finger, swallows Bernice with those giant eyes, each blink an event with eyelashes that big. Gretel, hunch shouldered, stares at the tiled floor. Ruby, her face glistening with sweat, is busy tearing her name tag into tiny pieces. She looks up from her task. "Why are we stopping?" she says. "Nothing's happened yet."

"Am I doing this right?" asks Bernice.

"There's no right way," says Will. "Just keep going." Ashlee releases the spiral of hair, and it bounces at her shoulder. Ruby tears the R of her name in half. "Bernice," says Will. "Listen to me. You're doing great, okay?"

★ ★ ★

It was my sister who was invited to the party.

We'd witnessed several of Ashton's parties from afar: the valets in the driveway whisking away convertibles, the energetic thump of live DJs, the splash and echo of night-swimmers in the pool and on the beach, the crackle of fireworks over the water. No one ever seemed to sleep, not even me, as I watched from my bedroom window, the sky bleeding blue with the afterglow of fireworks I couldn't see.

Naomi ran into Ashton at the mailbox one day while he was out walking his four Tibetan mastiffs, whose blue-gray coats had been cut to look like lion manes. I had never seen him walk them himself. One of the dogs sniffed toward her, and he tight-fisted the leash, then yelled, "STOP," with such a commanding voice that all four dogs froze like statues.

I watched from the window through a gauzy curtain, hands on the back of the faded floral couch.

When she returned, I accosted her in the doorway. "What happened? What did he say?"

"If you want to know anything about Tibetan mastiffs, I'm pretty sure I just got a rundown of the entire Wikipedia page. I doubt I could do justice to the pretentious tone." She slipped off her silver mules, leaving them next to my gray sneakers, and walked into the kitchen to start dinner.

"He's just smart," I said, following her. I'd heard him speak on a podcast once. "He's articulate."

"You mean he articulates every. Single. Word."

"Not everybody's smart *and* socially adept like you," I said.

"Do you know why he's rich?" she said. "He steals data from the masses. That's his job." She took out the curry powder and cumin and mustard seed. It was a real step up from my specialty: meals poured into pans from frozen bags. "He's pushing his personal brand," she said. "Condescension wrapped in blue. Guess you can sell anything if you know how to package it." She threw me a bag of tiny black lentils to rinse. "We need a cup of those," she said. "I'm not going to any party."

"Wait, what!?" I squealed. "He invited you to a party?"

"Come on, Berry," she said as she diced an onion with incredible speed. "It's just curated speed dating for him. He called it a 'shindig.'"

"Who cares what he called it!"

"No thanks," said Naomi. Of course. Like someone beautiful explaining why beauty doesn't matter, or someone rich explaining that money doesn't buy happiness.

"*I* want to go," I said. "Let's go. Do it. For me."

She looked up from chopping, her eyes red from the onion, though I imagined it was pity for me.

"Please," I said.

"Fine," she said. "For you."

A blue-tuxedoed doorman took our phones at the door, giving us each a four-digit number to memorize in order to get them back at the end of the night. Then he welcomed us into The Great Room with an open arm and a bow.

The back wall was made of windows overlooking the beach view that had once been ours. Partygoers orbited the room, women in cocktail dresses, in bikinis, in wide-legged jumpsuits, men in slacks or ties, a few bow-tie-and-glasses types, and a crowd of lanky, unshaven men in blazers and tees emblazoned with Ashton's company logo. Each person held a different-shaped glass, crafted to match the owner's chosen drink. The drinks were retrieved outside, under a thatched-roof bar between a pool and a life-size chessboard where two men were dueling with bright blue pawns.

I wore an eggplant-colored cocktail dress, a former bridesmaid ensemble replicated down to the costume jewelry. It was my most flattering dress, obscuring my stomach while still showing off my behind, my best physical feature. Naomi wore a cream-colored sundress embroidered with flowers, her hair in a halo of braids.

I'd seen my share of seafood buffets at the weddings and showers of monied friends, but I'd never encountered such a grand display. It was as if a tsunami had deposited an ocean's worth of inhabitants right there in The Great Room.

Blood-red lobster claws dangled over blue crabs with red-tipped pincers like painted fingernails; disembodied crab legs splayed out from ice buckets beside trays of pale oysters; pink-white shrimp and prawns stared out with wet black eyes, their bodies boiled into curls, spidery antennae and legs all pointing in the same direction. The accoutrements of extraction were laid out on a white tablecloth beside like antique surgical equipment: long, thin seafood forks, pent-up and dainty; menacing curved shears; crackers with heavy, opulent handles.

When my sister went to the bathroom, I didn't know how to act. I had yet to see Ashton. I wandered away from the seafood table to a big, beaded couch in a corner near the window. The tiny beads were all shades of blue—ultramarine, royal, aqua—but what struck me most was the wave of midnight beads, so dark they matched the ocean waves shimmering under a bloated moon.

A woman outside removed all of her clothes dispassionately, as if she were undressing in her bedroom. Her silhouette looked familiar. She had a long, elegant nose that turned up, just slightly, at the tip, and shoulders that curved in as if she were hiding or protecting something inside her. Had she been out in the neighborhood once, walking his dogs? For a second, she seemed fleshless in the moonlight, then she executed a perfect dive into the infinity pool that looked as if it fell directly into the sea.

A hand on the small of my back, and I jumped. It was Ashton, the bright cyan blue of his perfectly trimmed beard so vibrant that it obscured every other physical fact about him.

"Did I scare you?" he asked.

"No," I said, but my heart was racing. It was surreal to see a face up close and in person that I had seen so many times online. The pictures didn't do him justice. They captured neither his commanding presence nor the pure blueness of his beard.

"Are you here with your sister?" he asked.

I was surprised that he knew who I was. "Uh-huh," I said.

Ashton was unfazed, perhaps even encouraged, by my inability to speak.

He extended his hand toward the beaded couch, inviting me to sit down.

I hesitated, thinking I might have misunderstood.

He sat down first, patted the seat next to him. "The party," he said. "Are you enjoying it?"

"Totally," I said, joining him, trying to sound cool and calm. "You've got a mean seafood buffet." The beaded couch was uncomfortable, though it was soothing to trace the beads with my fingers as we talked.

"Mean how?" he asked. "Mean like 'excellent' or mean like 'lobsters feel pain when they're boiled alive'?" (Later I saw him, in one clean stroke, zip a knife down the back of a lobster tail, then pop the pink meat into his mouth.)

"Like excellent," I said.

He scanned the room with a frown. "Perhaps I'm doing a disservice. A party like this is essentially a networking event."

"Better than an over-air-conditioned conference hotel," I said.

He laughed. I felt inordinately pleased, though I tried my best not to look it.

"The point is," he said, "a party like this inspires nepotism, whereas I believe in meritocracy."

"Is it on you what people do at your parties?" I asked.

He looked over at the guys in blazers, who were gathered in

a semicircle, talking seriously. "To them, getting to the top isn't about generating new ideas or working hard, it's about making connections, flattering the right people. So they flatter me. But they don't respect me." He paused, took a sip of his drink. "I was an orphan, you know. Everything I have, I earned."

"I'm so sorry," I said. I already knew this about him; it was the sole fact listed in the Early Years section of his Wikipedia entry.

"Don't be. I learned lessons those guys will never learn," he said. "Anyway." He smiled at me, a tight-lipped exit smile.

I was desperate to keep the conversation going. "So is this why we couldn't bring in our phones?" I asked. "To prevent networking?"

He settled back in his seat. "Yes, Bernice," he said. I was shocked that he knew my name. "But it's more than that. Life shouldn't be lived behind a screen."

"But you run a tech empire."

"I believe technology should optimize reality, not the other way around," he explained. "If you have enough smart objects—if your objects are smart enough—they will know your every desire, and you'll never have to look at a screen again."

He wiped his hand across the couch. "This was hand-beaded. I bought it on a whim when I was studying bone-carving techniques in Nigeria. Feel it." I had been rubbing at it the whole time, but I made a dramatic swipe nonetheless, annoyed I hadn't polished my chewed-up nails.

"You can't get that from a screen," he said. "The digital world lacks texture. It's endlessly duplicatable. Perhaps it's the contrast that draws me to antiques, handcrafted pieces, one-of-a-kind objects. Collecting these sorts of things is a bit of a hobby for me. Maybe even a fetish. The UPS man comes so often he has fingerprint access to the place. But I do make some pieces myself."

Naomi—who was now standing in the corner under a Jackson

Pollock painting and eating shrimp from her own individual stem-less shrimp cocktail glass with its own individual ice bowl—looked toward me with a slight widening of the eyes. *See what I mean?* they said. I looked away.

"I thought your fetish was…" I gestured around the blue room. "Well, you know."

"Oh, have you noticed the color scheme?" he said with a laugh. "It started almost as a joke, as a little play on the idea of 'blue blood,' noble blood. Entrepreneurs are America's nobility, but we're as defective as old-world monarchy if we just put our friends on the board, pass down an inheritance. If I have children, I'll leave them nothing but intellectual tools and grit. Perhaps a haiku, or a scavenger hunt in riddles."

I laughed.

"It's funny," he said with a strained smile, "but I'm not kidding. The color blue is symbolic. In essence, what I'm saying is that one must make oneself a blue blood. I coronated myself."

He mimed putting a crown on his own head, and a few people nearby smiled in our direction.

"Anyway," he said. He looked out across the room at the party, then pressed his lips together and made a vague "Mmm-hmm" sound. I followed his gaze and found Naomi on the other end of it. She was giggling with one of the T-shirt-and-blazer guys, an entire king crab leg in her fist. The dark hair springing loose from her braid glowed in the light, giving her a spunky, girlish air.

I was familiar with Ashton's look of captivated amusement. I'd seen it a hundred times before: on the faces of friends, family members, reminiscing teachers (soon to be disappointed by me), and even, in a memory that still stung, my high school crush, who sat next to me on the bus only to ask about my sister.

"She is very attractive," Ashton said. "Self-assured." We watched her face scrunch into a giggle that turned into a full-bodied laugh. Soon, she was laughing so hard she had to put her hand on the counter to keep balance. "Do you get along?" he asked.

"Of course," I said, then added, with a little croak in my voice that betrayed the lie: "I think she's seeing someone."

Ashton cocked his head, then swiveled it toward me slowly like an owl who had heard a mouse rustling in the grass. "You think so?" he asked.

I smoothed both index fingers across the beaded couch. "Yes," I said. "I think so."

He stroked his beard. "How old are you?" he asked.

"Twenty-three," I said.

"Come," he said.

Partygoers glanced curiously as we made our way to the stairs, parting to let us through.

In a two-story study with wall-to-wall bookshelves and a tiger-skin rug with the head still attached, Ashton drew me to a simple lamp with an asymmetrical leather shade and brass fixtures. Of all the items in the room, I could not decipher why this one, in particular, was special. "Very smart," I said, for lack of something better.

He beamed. Techno pulsed through the floor. "Not as smart as it looks," he said. It was, he noted, one of the few lights in the house that worked by an old-fashioned switch. He flicked the switch several times and then, almost as an afterthought, pulled a trio of bespoke leather journals off a nearby bookshelf. He sniffed at them deeply as if smelling fine wine. "Rare leather," he said, holding them out for me to smell too.

In his third-story lounge, we admired four limestone jars flanking a giant marble fireplace. They were elegant, thigh-sized, and bullet-shaped, with each lid carved into a head—one human, three animals. "My Tiffany jars," he said.

"Like the jewelry?"

"No," he said. "Like how people name their cars. Tiffany was my first major acquisition." He smiled. "Do you know what they are?"

"Ancient Egypt," I said, thinking back to grade school. "With the organs."

"Very good," he said. "Canopic jars. These are from 800 BCE."

"Empty?" I asked, wrinkling my nose in a way I hoped was cute.

"What would be the fun in that?" He pointed to each, naming the organs inside. "Stomach," he said. "Intestines. Lungs. Liver." He paused. "You dispose of the brain."

"Unraveled through the nose with a hook," I said.

"Common misconception." He made a whisking motion with his hand. "You blend it up through the nostril until it's mush, drain it out the nose."

As he turned to lead us out of the room, I thought I heard a squeak. Let me rephrase that: I thought I heard a squeak speak. *Don't,* the squeak said. I stopped in my tracks, pressed my foot into the floorboard. No squeak. As if Ashton's new mansion would have a squeaky floorboard.

His bedroom contained his prized possession: a teal dresser with gleaming white inlaid-bone set in a repeating pattern of fleur-de-lis. "The fleur-de-lis," he told me, "is meant to be a lily—or maybe an iris. It's well-known for its use in French heraldry, but it also has a darker history. In some places—New Orleans, for example—slaves were branded with the symbol for trying to flee.

"Branded," he repeated, tracing the shape of the fleur-de-lis on my bare shoulder.

"That's awful," I said, caressing the top of the dresser. A shard of bone cut into my finger. "Ow," I said. I pressed my thumb to it to stop the bleeding.

"No pain without pleasure," Ashton said. He licked his finger, wiped my smeared blood off the bone.

"I think it's the other way around," I said.

Suddenly he looked up at the ceiling. "Andrea," he called, as if commanding the air.

"Yes, Ashton," came a woman's voice from above, sultry and unnervingly calm. I looked around the bedroom. "I'm Ashton's digital assistant, Andrea," she explained.

"Send a butler with a Band-Aid, darling," he said.

"Sure, Ashton," she replied.

He pushed a piece of hair behind my ear. At once, I knew what he was doing, and I couldn't believe he was doing it.

His head came toward me, snakelike—fast and with his tongue protruding. I must have moved slightly—I can't say whether it was away or toward—and our teeth knocked together. I pulled my head back and laughed. "Let's try that again," he said.

I cocked my head to fit in his lips, which were smooth and thin, hidden among the bristly hairs of his beard. His tongue was acrobatic, passionately invasive. He led, I followed.

Already, I wondered what he'd do next. Would he lead me to his bed? What would Naomi say?

But when we pulled apart, he looked so stern that I wondered if I'd done something wrong. "Must make the rounds," he said. Game over.

Downstairs, I wandered through the party alone, my finger wrapped in a blue Band-Aid. Drunken party guests advanced toward a buffet of desserts where cylindrical jars of blue M&M's flanked tiered displays of fat cookies and individual pies. At the table's center, that bright blue coconut cake that, not many weeks earlier, had rendered me dumb.

* * *

"Ashton sounds like *quite* the tease," says Ashlee. The other women look at her in disbelief. "What? Am I not supposed to interrupt?" she asks.

Ruby's sitting cross-legged on her chair, her pleather skirt barely covering her underwear, both heels abandoned on the floor, fur coat draped dramatically around her, her face slick at the bridge of her nose, above her chewed-up lips. Her torn name tag, stuck back together in an unreadable mosaic, is balanced on her pointer finger, waiting to be affixed. "You do know how this pans out, right?" she says.

"Did you miss some red flags, Bernice?" asks Will.

"What red flags?" Ashlee asks.

"The pretentious asshole word-vomit, to start," says Ruby.

"Well, you can't see red flags when you're falling in love," says Ashlee. "Like, because of the rose-colored glasses," she explains.

"Is that what was happening?" asks Will. "Rose-colored glasses?"

"Yes," says Bernice. "No," she corrects. "I don't know." Her voice is growing hoarse.

"He made you feel important," says Raina. "It's what you're desperate for at that age."

"A guy's *supposed* to make you feel important," says Ashlee.

"But, Ashlee, he isn't supposed to use it against you," says Raina. "Ashton's money, his beard, his attention—it wasn't for her. It was all a distraction."

"Would *you* be distracted by someone like that?" Bernice asks Raina.

"Distracted?" says Ruby. She slaps the torn-up name tag to her bare thigh. "I think the word is *played*."

* * *

Ashton didn't like texting. He preferred handwritten notes, extravagant gifts: pastry boxes filled with blueberry croissants or blue velvet cupcakes, blue flowers—forget-me-nots, a blue bearded iris, a bouquet of stunning blue roses—a blue velvet box with sapphire earrings and a note addressed *Dear Blue Berry* and signed *Your Blue Blume*.

Ashton disappeared into work for days at a time. Just when I was sure he was ghosting me, he would reappear with a surprise— an expensive dinner in the city, lunch on his yacht, and, to the slack-jawed awe of my coworkers, a blue limo whisking me away from work to front-row seats at a Broadway show. Online, I found a picture of Ashton and me getting out of that limo holding hands, his beard brilliant in the flash of the camera. Everywhere we went in public together, his blue beard caught attention, and a murmur followed in our wake.

We consummated the relationship with my head at the foot of his bed, him above me, watching himself in the oval mirror hanging over the teal inlaid-bone dresser, his favorite piece of furniture.

After, he called on Andrea for a late-night snack. "Whatever you want, darling," she said. I imagined her as beautiful, a woman like one of his exes. I'd Googled them—they were variously long nailed, large breasted, rail thin.

"Ashton?" I asked.

"Yes?"

"You were interested in my sister."

"Your sister is beautiful," he said. "But you have something more important."

I wanted him to tell me what it was, but he was already out of bed, walking to the bathroom in a blue silken robe.

The next morning, too early, my phone alarm sang "La Cu-caracha" into the dark. I curled up into him. "I don't want to go to my stupid job," I whispered. "I want to stay here with you."

His fingers tiptoed up my back in a way that made me shiver. "I could keep you here," he said. His voice was strange—not playful at all, but cool and logical, as if merely stating a fact.

I laughed as if he'd told a joke.

His fingers stopped, rested on my spine, like the tines of a plug. "You'd have no choice," he said. "You would have to stay forever."

When I left the mansion fifteen minutes later, it towered above me, blue-gray in the dark. I turned from it to cross the street, half expecting my own house to have disappeared. But there it was, small as a doll's. It seemed impossible that the two houses existed on the same street. It was like one of those trick pictures, in which you could see either the beautiful young woman or an old hag, never both at once.

* * *

Bernice hadn't practiced it quite this way. She had forgotten, until just then, about that morning conversation. The memory hadn't gone missing, exactly. It was more like a piece of furniture hidden under a sheet. Now that she's pulled off the sheet, she feels a horrible twist in the gut.

"What's wrong?" asks Will.

"It's nothing," says Bernice.

"Stay with this feeling," says Will. He is leaning forward, holding her gaze, and when she doesn't say anything he breaks it, drops back in his chair.

Bernice sticks and unsticks her finger from the corner of her name tag, which has peeled halfway off her shirt.

"I was creeped out that morning," Bernice admits. "I should have known something was wrong." Her voice cracks. "Maybe part of me did know."

"Listen to me, Bernice," says Will. He looks at her with such singular focus and empathy that the others feel as if they are witnessing a private moment, that they shouldn't be in the room. "Perhaps you feel ashamed about what happened to you or even of the choices you've made, but you should also feel pride about your capacity to share this."

Bernice smiles tearfully, nodding.

Ruby cracks the knuckles of one fist with the opposite hand.

"Yes, Ruby?" prompts Will.

"Nothing," says Ruby with a shrug. "Not exactly a big reveal, though. What twentysomething hasn't fallen for some creepy asshole?"

"This isn't *some* creepy asshole," says Ashlee. "It's Ashton Adams."

"So a rich creepy asshole," says Ruby. "Even less original."

Gretel shifts in her chair, just slightly, and Will notices, the way a hawk homes in on a rustle in the grass. "Gretel?" he asks.

"Is originality the goal?" Gretel says. Her tone is so featureless that it hardly sounds like a question, never mind a challenge, but Ruby raises her eyebrows anyway, asks: "Would you win that one?"

"It's not a competition," says Raina.

"I'm just saying, it's not a particularly *unusual* story," says Ruby.

"I get it, Ruby," says Bernice before Will can even prompt her to respond. "I've always gotten it, so you don't need to rub it in. I wasn't special before this happened and I'm not special now. I'm just another woman who was desperate and dumb enough to walk right into a trap."

* * *

My favorite gift: a real Fabergé egg, designed for an empress of Russia, made of lapis lazuli and finished with elegant gold filigree.

Inside, a necklace with a pendant of rare Dominican blue amber, a fly trapped inside.

Naomi held the necklace up to our kitchen window before breakfast. In the light, the amber was a deep, glistening blue. "That's cool," she said. She dropped the necklace back in the Fabergé egg. On top of the linoleum counter, the egg looked like a fake, like a knickknack from Marshalls. "All my flings ever got me was takeout," she said. She returned to scrambling eggs with a fork. From where I sat, the blue mansion filled the entire window.

"Can you just let me have this?" I said.

"I *am* letting you have this," she answered.

"Just because he's rich doesn't mean he's an asshole," I said. "He was just an orphan from Spokane who—"

"—who dropped out of Stanford," she finished. "I know, I know, I've heard. He mentioned it to me, it's in every interview, it's on his Wikipedia page, it's in his *New York Times* profile..."

"That's not fair," I said. "They quote that like he's being pretentious when really he's just proud that he made something of himself."

"Is that how Ashton sees it?" Naomi said, eyeing me. She poured the eggs into the sizzling pan, and I thought of those scrambled brains pouring out of a nose. "I'm going to say this because I'll regret it if I don't," she said. "There's a disconcerting power dynamic. You're at his beck and call. You drop everything whenever he wants.

"You know it's cheaper for him to buy you a Fabergé egg than for you to buy him dinner at McDonald's?" She sighed as she shifted the eggs in the pan. "Let's say you end up together. He'll always get to decide. You'll be living in *his* story. You'll always be eclipsed by him."

Did my sister not understand that I was already eclipsed? That

I'd spent my life in her shadow? In pictures of us together, I always looked less by contrast, the sibling who'd drawn the bad hand.

It was true: Ashton's beard was so vibrant you had to look at him first. Yet next to him, I didn't look less by contrast—I looked more by association. There had to be something special about the woman by his side.

One Saturday a few weeks later, I was sitting alone at one of the mansion's many dining tables, mulling over model-ship-building kits on my new blue laptop. I thought Ashton might be impressed by an analog hobby, and I needed something to do. I was staying at the mansion more frequently, overnight and sometimes all week- end, in part just to avoid Naomi. But Ashton, it turned out, was usually away working. I felt strange in the quiet mansion, alone yet not alone, watched by silent butlers and a digital voice assistant that, I sensed, didn't like me.

I had just ordered a ship-building kit to his house, same-day delivery, when my computer screen tipped closed and I gasped. Behind it was Ashton, dressed for a meeting: blue suit, blue tie, blue leather loafers.

"I see you're enjoying the new laptop," he said.

"I didn't know you were here," I answered, hand on my chest. "You scared me half to death."

"Only half?" he said. "I have something for you before I go." He held up a small, gilt-edge book with a filigree cover and a golden clasp. "You're spending a lot of time here. I thought you might want to explore." The book contained passcodes for all the mansion's locked doors, which he himself could negotiate by voice or fingerprint. The famed "key to my house" milestone, with all of Ashton's grandeur.

He pulled an old skeleton key from his breast pocket, dangling it from his fingers by the looped heart of the bow. "This," he said, "is for the room behind the wine cellar. It's the one place I ask you not to go."

"But then why give me the key?" I said.

He looked briefly disappointed. "I trust you," he said, smiling, wrapping it into my hand.

After he left, I wandered the mansion, the skeleton key clasped in my palm, hypothesizing about the mystery room as I opened doors using impossibly long codes. By the time I was wearing a copper and brass deep-sea diving helmet, knee-deep in a closet full of antique scuba-diving gear, I'd settled on the idea that the room was a test. It would reveal an embarrassing fetish of Ashton's—blue dildos, a Fleshlight collection, the accoutrements of BDSM. If I was into it, I was supposed to mention it. If I wasn't, I was supposed to pretend I hadn't gone in the room at all.

I took off the diving helmet, headed to the basement. The stairs fed deep beneath the house, through a maze of wine, vintages I knew cost more than I'd ever make in a year. It was chilly by the time I arrived in a dimly lit alcove with an old oak door featuring that classic keyhole, shaped like a pawn. My heart quickened as I inserted the key, pushed open the door.

I smelled it first—sharp, putrid, and oversweet, like rotting fruit. I gagged, recovered, held my nose, walked inside. If this was a sex thing, I wasn't into it.

The room was dark, cold, slightly damp, and cavernous—I could tell from the echo of my shoes. A murky shaft of light shined ominously through the partly open door behind me. I felt along a cold stone wall for a light switch but couldn't find one. I felt my pocket for my phone, but I'd left it upstairs. "Andrea?" I called. No reply, just my own voice in the darkness, nasal because I was holding my nose.

Slowly, my eyes began adjusting. I saw a peg-wall of antique tools—chisels, pliers, saws, ball-peen hammers, butcher's knives. They were made of aged steel, some with old wooden handles worn smooth, the crevices worked through with black. A cord of bristling rope hung beside a full gas mask of molded blue rubber with giant bug eyes and a single fat canister extruding like a proboscis.

What was this? A workshop? Or a Kink Castle type thing?

I leaned over the workbench to read the worn spines of books stacked in the corner: *The Encyclopedia of Taxidermy, Furniture & Other Home Projects, Postmortem Anatomy, The Ultimate Home Tanning Companion.*

My mouth was so dry that I had to unstick my tongue from the roof before I spoke. "Andrea?" I tried again.

No answer. I turned from the books. I saw mounted steel shackles on a streaked stone wall. I saw, in the middle of the room, dark as a shadow, a figure hanging from the ceiling.

What was it? A sex doll? A sex doll on a hook? You could buy sex dolls for thousands, pick each part to your liking.

I walked toward it, and the caged sconces that ran along the walls flicked on, all by themselves, the light dim and yellow.

She was thin. Her head hung as if bowed in prayer. Her skin was waxy, bluish, sagging at the cheekbones and where the eyebrows arched. Her nose was long, and it pointed up, just slightly, at the tip. I pictured her diving into the infinity pool.

My stomach turned. My eyes darted back to the tools. I thought of the bone dresser, the leather lampshade, the leather journals he had asked me to sniff, all of Ashton's "acquisitions."

Vomit traveled up my throat. I swallowed it back down, my mouth sour with acid.

I too had been "acquired."

My body took charge. I was sprinting to the exit, racing up the endless stairs, calling out, as if there would be someone to save me, as if Ashton didn't have a plan, as if the house weren't full of servants entirely loyal to him.

Just as I arrived at the mansion's front entrance, a chorus of sharp clicking noises echoed through the mansion, the simulated sound of every single door locking. I pulled and twisted at the handle anyway, desperately and to no avail. Red blood streaked the shiny handle, and I realized I had been gripping the skeleton key so tight that I had punctured the skin of my palm.

"Going somewhere?" Andrea asked from the ether.

My hand trembled on the bloody knob. I was shaking so much that my teeth were clicking together, a response to terror I hadn't known was real. "Let me out," I squeaked.

"I can't do that, Taylor," said Andrea.

"I'm not Taylor," I said.

"Ah, that was the last girlfriend," she replied. "Did you meet her? In the basement?"

"I'm Bernice!" I cried with more conviction than I'd ever said my name.

"No need to yell," said Andrea.

"What kind of woman are you?" I shouted.

"I exist beyond your human concept of gender," said Andrea.

"Fuck you," I said.

"There's no need for that language," said Andrea.

Even before I tried everything—my cellphone, my computer, the doors, the windows, the passcodes from the blue book, shouting at the top of my lungs, beating the window with a blue flamingo statue—even before all that, I knew I was trapped.

I lay down on the beaded couch, my heart hurling itself against my chest like a caged animal.

"Andrea?" I whispered.

"Yes."

"Can you open the doors?"

"No," she said.

"Is there some password I can say so you'll open the doors?"

"No," she said.

"The windows?" I asked.

"No," she said.

"Do you get asked these questions often?" I asked.

"Yes," she said.

The nineteen-foot TV flipped on, and the blue-bearded face of my boyfriend filled the room. A half-smile drew across his face, just one side, like a person having a stroke. On the TV, his smirk was twice as long as my entire body. He looked like he could swallow me whole, but this was wishful thinking: Ashton clearly liked to torture his prey.

"Find anything interesting?" he asked. His words boomed around me, surround sound.

"No," I said, but my voice shook.

"I asked you not to go in there," he said.

Suddenly I saw Ashton as my sister saw him—not as a hero or a self-possessed business mogul but as an awkward and ugly asshole. His beard was designed to both counter and conceal his soft, stupid face. His pretentious tone was an attempt to elevate a bitter history of geeky uncoolness. I thought of all of the awkward grudge-holding school shooters, the vol-cel Nazis, the pudgy and petulant dictators, the pale men on power trips who were always either my bosses or my boyfriends.

It's strange, to learn your boyfriend is a psychopath and to not be entirely surprised.

"Obviously, I've been watching you this entire time," he said.

"Obviously," I squeaked.

"Obviously, I'm at the front door," he said.

He walked in, holding the phone in front of him, so there were two smug, blue-bearded faces in the room with me, three if you counted the one he was staring at on his own phone.

By the time I realized I should lunge at the door, it was already clicking closed behind him.

He must have seen my body's slight jerk toward freedom. "Sorry," he said. "No use trying. Just you and me, for the next five hours."

Five hours? I thought about the knives, the hammers, the saws. I thought I was going to throw up, but instead I started hiccupping uncontrollably, which made everything I said sound ridiculous.

"Don't"—hiccup—"do this," I said.

"Tell me," said Ashton, cool as a cucumber, "why don't you deserve this?"

I considered the closeness of sharp and heavy objects. I considered the oldest trick in the book: seduction. He put down his phone as I walked toward him, so the TV showed only the bright white of the ceiling, washed out and featureless, like the soft light of nothing you're supposed to see before death.

I tried to sound sexy. "I'll do anything"—hiccup—"you want."

He leaned down toward me, as if he was going to kiss me, then whispered in my ear, "I know."

I stepped backward, hiccupped again. "Don't," I said.

"Why not? Tell me, why don't you deserve it?"

"Because I didn't do anything wrong," I said, my voice trembling. "You murdered—" I hiccupped again.

He laughed. "So you're an innocent victim?" Sunlight poured through the narrow window next to the door, illuminating him from the back in a long rectangle of light that looked like careful production work, his blue leather shoes sharp and shining, his smartwatch gleaming. "Don't tell me you liked me for my personality, that you weren't using me. Where was all the female attention when I was a fat kid at computer camp?" He sighed. "I told you my philosophy the very first time we met. Were you listening at all?" He gestured to my blue amber necklace, my blue laptop closed on the table. "Have you earned any of this? Why do you deserve the spoils of my labor? Why do you think you're entitled to all of the keys to my kingdom when you haven't done any of the work?"

I felt hot tears on my cheeks. It struck me that I had believed, on some level, that being in a relationship with Ashton would be work enough. "You gave me these things," I said. "You gave me the keys."

"You're just like everyone else," said Ashton. "You say yes, yes, yes to my face, then turn around and do whatever you want. Do the very thing, in fact, the *exact thing,* I asked you not to do. You don't respect me."

"Yes, I do," I said, my voice shaking.

He smirked. "What's my job, Bernice?"

"You're an entrepreneur," I said.

"You don't even know what I do, and you think you deserve the money I make?"

"You steal data from the masses," I said.

"Oh, so it's worse than I thought! You want my money, but you don't want to be complicit in my crimes? You're as bad as a Nazi wife, feigning innocence while flaunting her gold jewelry, pilfered from the dead, reading by the warm glow of a skin lampshade as the scent of burnt flesh drifts in through the window. At least I don't pretend to be good."

Men don't have to pretend to be good, I thought. *In fact, they're supposed to be a little brutal.*

He began a speech I was sure he'd recited many times before, to the many girlfriends he'd murdered. The speech was about, among other things, aristocracy, meritocracy, mediocrity, technology, morality, disruption, and his associations with the color blue.

"My beard isn't just *blue*, it's *cyan*," he was saying. "Cyan is the *C* in CMYK, the four-color printing system that transforms the digital back into the physical. The word 'cyan' derives from '*cyan*ide.' Test a solution for cyanide with iron sulfate and you get Prussian blue, the first modern color. You know it?" he asked, rhetorically, though I did know it; it was a deep navy, you might say, but richer, a royal blue as seen through darkness. "Prussic acid is Zyklon B. The Nazis used it in the gas chambers. The *B* stands for blue acid, *blausäure*." He said the last word with his best German accent.

He was working through some core of internal logic, but trying to follow it was like trying to make sense of spam. I zoned in and out. I saw through the window a man advancing toward the house. He was wearing all brown and had a big brown box in his hand. UPS. My model ship.

The deliveryman paused a few feet before the narrow window, and the sunlit square disappeared from the floor, but Ashton kept talking. I tried to catch the deliveryman's eye. I wanted him to read the terror in my face.

"In my kingdom," Ashton was saying, "crimes like yours, I'm sorry to say, are punishable by death. If you want to enjoy my wealth while not doing anything, you might as well be an inanimate object."

The deliveryman didn't read the terror in my face at all. He just smiled, then gestured that he would bring in the package. He turned the knob. And the door... it just opened.

Same-day delivery, deus ex machina.

Ashton turned toward the noise, and I kicked him in the groin.

For the briefest moment, I caught the expression on his face: not anger or horror but shock—shock that I, of all people, might do him in. He caught my foot in his hand as he doubled over. I jerked my leg, kicking it free, sprinted out the door as he moaned behind me.

By the time the police arrived, blue lights flashing over blue house, a final flourish, Ashton was dead. Poison. Cyanide. Go figure.

★ ★ ★

Outside, the light is graying, but the basement is bright, lit up like a set. Bernice's head is bowed forward, shoulders slumped.

Will is still nodding, always nodding, a bobblehead never coming to rest. Ashlee's mouth hangs open, wide as a sewer grate.

"I'm so sorry," Raina whispers.

Same-day delivery, deus ex machina. Bernice had loved that line when she practiced it in bed, mouthing it under the covers. It had seemed clever up until the moment she'd said it aloud, when suddenly it became ridiculous. Maybe the line was clever, but she hadn't been clever at all.

She had assumed that by the time she finished telling her story, a weight would be lifted, but here she was, all weighed down.

"That story was super Sad Face," says Ashlee. Her lips backbend into a frown. "Honestly, I didn't even realize he almost murdered you too."

"Come on," says Ruby with an exasperated sigh.

"It's not like you can tell from the headlines," Ashlee snaps. "Mostly they're like INSIDE BLUEBEARD'S BILLION DOLLAR MURDER MANSION! Or whatever."

"Did the word 'murder' tip you off or no?" says Ruby.

Ashlee scowls.

"The news stories don't make any sense," says Bernice. "They imply I'm not attractive enough to have been dating him, so I must have been helping him—but how? Luring women? Cover-ups? Even the police aren't convinced. They stopped questioning me long ago." She pauses. "You know, when people recognize me, they cross the street. They think I helped him, and they're not even afraid. They're just disgusted. I'm nothing without him, not even a threat."

Will taps his fingers on his knee, thinking. "You've done such a good job telling your story here," he says. "It sounds to me like you *could* set the record straight, yet you've refused public interviews. I wonder why."

"Like an interview would unfuck things," mutters Ruby.

"It didn't seem right," says Bernice. "The dead women can't set the record straight. They don't get a say."

"Weren't they just, like, strippers and gold diggers?" says Ashlee. "I mean, no offense."

"Ashlee," says Raina gently, "they're dead."

Ashlee crosses her arms over her chest. "First I'm in trouble for not reading the news," she whines, "now I'm in trouble for reading it."

"Why should I get to sit down and tell my story?" says Bernice. "Why should I get an audience? I mean, even here. Why do I get to sit here and tell you all of this?" She is tearing up. She looks at her hands, brushes her pointer finger over her thumb.

Raina extracts a little pack of tissues from her purse, passes them to her.

"Because you're still alive," says Will.

"I could just as easily be one of them," says Bernice. She pulls out a tissue, crumples it in her fist.

Will scratches at his arm. "I wonder," he says. Suddenly he is up, dragging two folding chairs into the center of the circle, setting them face-to-face. "A little role-playing activity," he says. Ruby groans. Gretel frowns. Will explains that Bernice should sit in one chair and choose someone in the group to sit in the other, to represent one of the dead.

"I'm not sure this is a good idea," says Bernice.

"Up to you, of course," he says.

She hesitates, watches Will pick a piece of fuzz off his trousers and drop it to the floor. "Yes," she says. "Okay."

Will smiles.

She takes her place in one chair and—much to everyone's surprise—chooses Ashlee to sit in the other.

Ashlee beams. "I'm super good at this kind of thing," she announces. "It's basically like a group date activity." She splays herself dramatically in the chair opposite Bernice, head lolled back, eyes closed.

Raina glances at Will, who is pacing the circle. "Are you sure she should sit like that?" she asks him.

"Let's just see how it goes," says Will. "Bernice, what would you say to her?"

"I guess I should say I'm sorry," says Bernice.

"Say it *to* her," says Will.

"I'm sorry," says Bernice.

Ashlee lifts her head. "Uh, yah, me too," she says. "Because I'm dead."

"Do you want to talk about how you died?" asks Bernice.

"Was it like knives or mallets or something?" says Ashlee.

"Is this helpful?" Gretel asks.

"I think it's riveting, personally," says Ruby.

"You got off easy," Bernice tells her. "You were choked to death."

"*Easy?*" says Ashlee. "More like *easy for you to say*. You're alive.

Could they even find all the pieces to my body? Wasn't I, like, chopped up and then buried in the yard or something?"

"Ashlee," says Raina. "Do you really think the women Ashton killed would be mad at Bernice for surviving?"

"I'd be," says Ashlee. "She was saved by—what?—online shopping? If I'm dead, I'll never get to shop online again."

"Why did you ask about how she died, Bernice?" asks Will.

"Because it's all they want to talk about."

"All who want to talk about?"

"The dead."

"What do you mean?" he asks.

"Ghosts?" whispers Ashlee.

Bernice rubs at the back of her neck, then slides a finger behind her ear, sets it in the soft, warm spot against the jaw. She opens her mouth slightly, feels the mandible move. All those body parts of hers still together, still working together, still making her human. "They're talking to me," she says. "They're in the furniture. They're in his things."

Will's eyes brighten. "The dead women speak to you?" he asks. "How?"

"I don't know," says Bernice. "With words, kind of. Something between words and thoughts. They're in my apartment. They keep me awake."

"Really buried the lede on this one," Ruby grumbles.

"What do they talk about?" asks Will.

"Oh, lots of things," says Bernice. "Or nothing really."

"Tell us," says Will.

"You'll think I'm crazy," says Bernice.

"I don't have much room to call anyone else crazy," says Gretel. Raina nods in agreement.

"Dish it," says Ashlee.

* * *

Mornings after, I'd wake up exhausted in my old room at my mom's house, my head at the foot of the bed, an angle that caught the marshy sea breeze. A moment of peace, and then I heard the helicopter hawking overhead, the horde of TV vans idling in the street. I opened my eyes and a corner of the mansion was already in view: blue over blue, unreal, like a collage.

"Serial killer," they began to hiss on the news, and in my dreams, Ashton's exes were a legion of the undead, crawling out from under mansion floorboards and beds, their skin icy, blue-tinged, their eyes dark as bruises, their features vague. They came toward me with a unified animal slink, maggots oozing from rotting black wounds. In these dreams, my own hand (fleshy, living) had a dark red stain the shape of the skeleton key.

The women stalked me through the night, and the mansion stalked me through the day. From window to window it followed— bedroom, bathroom, kitchen. Why was every important room on that side of the house? Anger clenched my heart like a fist. I no longer understood the allure of the house, nor could I understand the idiotic person—me?—who had been lured.

The mansion was ridiculous, over-the-top and insistent on itself, a mocking blue monstrosity. The bright dog statues guarding the driveway were a bizarre mixture of threatening and childish, like sadistic *Sesame Street* characters, their lips curled back to reveal gleaming gums and bright teeth, sharp as daggers. Ashton was an off-color joke or a deformed string-pull toy—the kind that comes to life, lectures everyone, then kills them.

I'd told the police that if they were looking for bodies, they might want to check out the furniture. "Have you seen the inlaid-bone dresser?" I asked.

"We've got leads," a detective said, taking great care to look me in the eye as he ignored me.

The "leads," I knew, were the scavenger hunt of clues Ashton had left behind as a suicide note. It was a wild-goose chase, yet backhoes, search dogs, and boats arrived. Ashton was dead, he was a serial killer, and he still had more clout than me.

After Taylor's funeral, I had to get out of the Hamptons. Naomi helped me move into a cut-rate sublet in Queens. In my new neighborhood bodega, the cashier stared, then looked over near the window. I followed his eyes to a display of newspapers and tabloids. I picked up a paper where an op-ed headline read WHEN CURIOSITY KILLS, as if opening the door had been the real deathblow. A tabloid had a photo of me on the cover, on the day of the funeral, wearing a dark navy dress, almost smirking under a rainbow umbrella. TRUE BLUE! The headline shouted in bold lettering. The subheading: BLUEBEARD'S GIRLFRIEND STANDS BY HER MAN.

I was always a reference point for someone else. I was born into the last name of a father I hardly knew, in school I was always my sister's little sister, in the mansion Andrea had called me Taylor, and now I was the nameless possessive of some stupidly named serial killer.

"Wearing navy to the funeral," said one apparent expert in an unnamed field, "suggests that she's still aligning herself with Bluebeard." They wrote about me as if I'd attended the funeral of a mistress I was complicit in murdering. They compared me to the smiling wives of cheating politicians and the adoring fans of death-row inmates.

"What are you doing over here?" my sister said, stuffing the paper back into the wrong slot as the bodega owner glared.

I don't remember choosing clothes the day of Taylor's funeral.

I remember the gray rain, the flashing mass of reporters, the cavernous church echoing pipe-organ songs, the sound of Taylor's mother sobbing at the pulpit, the arched X's of the vaulted ceiling. In the dizziness of looking up at them, they seemed almost to sway, and for a moment I was sure they'd descend like giant arcade-game claws.

At the door of the new apartment, I fumbled with the brass key, cold and heavy in my hand, a bruising weight. Bile rose in my throat, but when I swallowed, my mouth was dry as cotton. Naomi gently lifted my hand off the door and turned the key herself.

It was just an empty apartment. I stood in the entryway as my sister opened all of the closets, the cabinets, the fridge, flipped on all of the lights, double-checked the locks.

We carried up the few pieces of furniture we'd bought at the thrift shop, then stood in the center of the room, looking around at the barely filled space. I pulled on the chain of the ceiling fan, and dust rained down on us like scattered ashes.

"Don't you want to go get anything else?" Naomi asked.

"No," I said.

A haphazard array of nails and molly screws were still embedded in the walls, tiny silver polka dots, and I couldn't make out even the hint of a pattern to whatever the previous tenants had hung there.

I thought about Ashton's walls, the kind you didn't dare touch, hand-painted wallpaper and carefully arranged original paintings, not one haphazard decision to the design. Calculation had been Ashton's strong suit. Even what appeared to be spontaneity had been a contingency plan, like the cyanide pills.

The wood floors of the apartment were warped and white with water damage below the radiator valves. Naomi had walked over and pressed a rubbery floorboard down with the toe of her gladiator sandal. As she lifted her sandal off the damaged wood, it popped right back up. I was back in my gray sneakers and ankle socks, all comfort, no style. A blue beard or a blue amber necklace, a billionaire on your arm—you were always you, in the end, weren't you? *I told you so* draped across the silence, lay between my sister and me like a wide, empty field.

"You don't have to be an ascetic," she said. "You don't have to repent."

"I know," I said.

"Do you want me to stay?" she asked.

"I'm fine," I said, but of course I wasn't. I wanted to be alone forever, and I never wanted to be alone again. I wanted to never unlock another door, never enter another unfamiliar room. I didn't want to encounter any more mysteries: not one wrapped gift, not one page in a page-turning novel, not one movie where the ending wasn't abundantly clear. I wanted to avoid everything: myself, the news, the color blue—every shade, cyan and slate, sapphire and cerulean. I wanted blue eradicated. I wanted the sky to pick another color, any other color, but it arched over me daily like a blue bowl, and I was a bug trapped beneath.

I knew I should be grateful—for the sky, for the sun, for days at all—but I wanted to escape, to shoot out of the atmosphere into the blackness of outer space, or else I wanted to fold into myself, like origami, so that I could see only the darkness of my own inner edges. But even then—or especially then—I knew the dead women from my dreams would be waiting, stretching their bony, decaying hands out to me, begging me to give them faces, to give them names.

Tiffany, the first victim, was also the first woman to be ID'd after Taylor.

In life, Tiffany had been short and compact, cheerleader-build, with blond hair, big boobs, a fake tan, and ombré manicured nails studded with gems. There was Tiffany online and on the newsstand, Hooters tank top and *Charlie's Angels* pose. Tech Genius Billionaire's First Victim Was Hooters Waitress, the headline read. There was Tiffany, double-fisting flamingo-colored cocktails in clear plastic cups. There was Tiffany, throwing a bright-blue-manicured middle finger at a camera like a talon. There was Tiffany: duck-lip selfie; pouting; suggestively licking a lollipop. From Vixen to Victim, the headline read. There was Tiffany, kissing some wrinkly, velvet-robed Hugh Hefner type. There was Tiffany, sprawled across the hood of a blue Bugatti in a blue bikini, a blue amber necklace framed by her cleavage. Gold Digger Likely Met Gruesome End, the headline read.

"You knew her?" asked the cashier at the bodega, raising his bushy eyebrows as if I might offer up some tale of a ménage à trois.

"No," I said, offended that he had lumped us together. Her fingernails seemed catty, tasteless. But maybe I was the one being catty and tasteless. Did I really have to judge a dead woman? And besides, we had fallen for the same man, or the same man's money, or the same man's trap.

"Wonder what happened to the rest of her body," said the cashier.

"What?" I asked.

"They just found the jaw," said the cashier, clacking his teeth together.

The Tiffany jars flashed before my eyes. I knew what was inside.

The mansion was surprisingly easy to access because the crime scene had moved outside. I just called the police, told them I had to pick up some things. I rolled the jars across the street one by one in a piece of luggage, in the middle of the afternoon, as backhoes dug up the yard.

Soon, the canopic jars stood silent and sentry in the little entryway in my nearly empty apartment in Queens. The lid of each jar was carved to look like a different ancient Egyptian god. There was a jackal—alert, sly; a baboon—close-lipped, thoughtful; a falcon—fierce, discerning; and finally—with baby-face cheeks, a Beatles haircut, and an expression that seemed to say, *Wait. What?*—a human head. The expression I imagined Tiffany had right before she died.

"Hello, Tiffanies," I said as I kicked off my shoes recklessly at their side, shook out my umbrella with abandon, rainwater dripping down their sturdy bodies. I used the jars like coatracks, hanging jackets over their lid-heads, hooking sweaters over the jackal's pointed ears. The jars were probably worth millions, but I didn't care.

Why didn't he turn her into decor like the others? Maybe he was yet to be inspired. Maybe he was honing his skills, discovering his style. Maybe he tried to tan her skin or pull out her hair or sand down her bones. Maybe he messed it up, or got busy, or got worried. Maybe he had been on an ancient Egypt kick, wanted to make use of his prized jars.

He had killed her more than five years before we'd met. In all that time, no one had ever reported her missing.

Jake Jackson, America's most overused TV host, interviewed Tiffany's parents in an ABC special, which aired right after *The One*. Same host, drawing the same crowd.

I watched it after it aired, on my computer, feeling sick. In the old days, before Ashton, I would've tuned in during prime time. I would've enjoyed it. I had watched prison interviews with serial killers, had watched an axe-wielding murderer's arms rise above his head in a cheesy true-crime reenactment. I'd also watched the real crimes: the police shootings, the domestic violence caught on tape. I had claimed I was bearing witness, but I'd been a rubbernecker just like everyone else.

Now it was different. My stomach turned, but I had to know.

Tiffany's childhood home was tiny with beige siding and, incongruously, a new blue Cadillac Escalade parked outside. Inside, dated floral prints curled across the upholstery and up the walls like an invasive species. Tiffany's parents sat side by side on a worn floral couch that sagged so much they were forced to lean into each other at the shoulders. The parents' faces were bewildered, uncomprehending, like the faces of alien abductees freshly returned to Earth. And Jake Jackson, with all that plastic surgery, looked alien himself, like an old man with a ziplock bag squeezed over his face.

"She was always smiling," said the father. This was untrue. Pictures of Tiffany were all over the house, and in them Tiffany was mostly frowning, in a sassy model sort of way. But there were no duck-lip selfies here, no middle fingers, no Jell-O shots. There was Tiffany, cute middle schooler with two ponytails and a pink T-shirt. There was Tiffany on Christmas morning, wearing silky red pajamas and full makeup, holding a mug that read, BETTER LATE THAN UGLY.

"Never had much luck with men," said the father, shaking his head. "Or, you might say, *a lot* of luck, but *bad* luck."

"The beard was strange," said the mother, "but we got over it. Eccentricity comes with the territory, doesn't it?"

"What territory is that?" Jake Jackson asked.

"Genius," said the father.

"To be honest," said the mother, nodding, "we thought he was too good for her."

"He was good *to her* as well," said the father. "Never laid a hand on her." Jake Jackson furrowed his brow. "Well, *until...*" added the father. "And then, of course, to learn of this." He waved his hand around randomly, as if the wallpaper had killed his daughter.

"Was this really love?" Jake Jackson asked.

"She liked nice things," said the mother, "labels on bags and all that."

"She loved the money," said Jake Jackson.

The mother looked spacey, didn't answer.

"People can't help but wonder," said Jake, "how she could have been dead for five years without anyone noticing."

"We were just as shocked as everyone else," said the father. "We thought she had run away."

"Just like her, to run away from something good," said the mother, "like she didn't show up for her high school graduation party, and she dropped out of college to waitress." She paused and then whispered, "At *Hooters*."

"We told her, we told her you can pick up all kinds of creeps at a place like that," said the mother. "We thought it was a bad idea to break up with Ashton, because she'd have to go back to that degrading job."

"We talked to the police," said the father. "So did Ashton. We all agreed she'd skipped town. Ashton was heartbroken. Showed us a text she'd written him, about how he was too good for her, how she wanted to start fresh somewhere else. Ashton said he spent thousands on a private detective, trying to track her down."

"'Millions,'" whispered the mother. "That's what Ashton said."

"But he didn't," said Jake Jackson. "He was lying. We know that now."

"Yes, we still have the car!" the father shouted, apropos of nothing, sitting straight up so the mother sprung a little from the couch.

"The car?" asked Jake Jackson.

"So he gave us the Escalade," said the father, throwing up his hands. "What do you want from us? We were furious with her! How were we supposed to know?"

"You know what Ashton told us?" the mother said. "He said if you loved something, you had to let it go."

In the best light, they were mourning, shocked, guilt-ridden, torn between Tiffanies—the one who was dead and the one whom they thought had left them wordlessly behind.

In the worst light, they were complete idiots.

I clicked off the interview. I walked into the hall. I took the sweaters off the heads of the Tiffany jars. I looked into each pair of those almost three-thousand-year-old black eyes, and I saw the sassy Tiffany-essence stare through.

I dragged a chair into the hall and sat with my feet squashed up against the opposite wall. I rolled my pants up to the knees, got comfortable.

I told the Tiffanies what went down with her parents.

The Tiffanies spoke. They spoke without moving at all.

What assholes, said Human-God Tiffany. *Ashton was a big ol' douche.*

Little dick too, said Falcon Tiffany.

The bigger the douche, the smaller the dick, said Human-God Tiffany.

Yeah, said Falcon Tiffany, *I'd love to peck that little pecker offa him.*

Tiny snack, said Human-God Tiffany. *Wouldn't hold you over until dinner.*

Jackal Tiffany, ears perpetually perked, didn't say anything; she just laughed and laughed.

Baboon Tiffany was quiet for a minute, then said, almost sagely: *My parents would rather have me murdered by a quote-on-quote genius than work at a quote-on-quote Hooters.*

"It's 'quote, unquote,'" I said.

Great, thanks, said Baboon Tiffany. *That will be useful knowledge in my life as a fucking jar.*

Laugh's on them, said Human-God Tiffany (Jackal Tiffany laughed on cue), *because I left Hooters to work at a "quote, unquote" gentlemen's club, which is where I met the fucker.*

That's how much they thought of me, said Baboon Tiffany, who was riding along on her own train of thought. *They still have the fucking Escalade.*

Who to be angry at? So many choices, said Human-God Tiffany. *At my parents for being assholes? At my parents for being fucking ridiculous? At that douche for murdering me?*

Ashton was right about one thing, said Human-God Tiffany. *I was using him for his money. Why fucking not? He was using me for my tits. What's the big fucking deal?*

I was starting to feel vertigo. I put my feet on the chair, my head between my knees.

"Why didn't you warn me?" I whispered.

Jackal Tiffany started into a long, high-pitched cackle.

Warn you? said Baboon Tiffany over the laughter. *We warned every-body—all of us did. Nobody listens to what they don't want to hear. Nobody.*

I remembered the *Don't* I mistook for a floorboard's squeak. I thought of the furniture, the women, trapped in the mansion, yelling to the parade of girlfriends passing by, each one eventually joining their ranks. Then a throng of media banged at the mansion gates and cops and detectives roamed the house, asking questions of one another but never of them. How infuriating, to have people all around and to still not be heard.

* * *

A loud crunching sound, and everyone turns to find Ruby noisily pulling the insert from the chocolate chip cookie packaging, reveal-ing a fresh row of cookies. "What?" she says.

"Did you have something you wanted to say?" asks Will.

"Nope," she says, taking three cookies and walking barefoot back to her seat.

"The story has gotten more—let's use your word here, Ruby— *original*, hasn't it?" Will says.

"Sure," says Ruby.

"Does that upset you?"

"Leading question," says Ruby. "Anyway, I have better things to be upset about. Global warming, for example. Rent prices."

"You're deflecting," says Will.

"We've been here for hours," says Ruby. "I'm starving." She holds up a chocolate chip cookie like a flash card. "What did Freud say? Sometimes a cookie is just a cookie?" She turns her attention back to Bernice.

Bernice looks around at the group. "Can I ask..." She hesitates. "Do you believe me? I really don't blame you if you don't. I wouldn't have believed myself five months ago."

"I wouldn't waste a lot of time trying to figure out who believes you," says Gretel, not unkindly.

"I believe you!" says Ashlee.

"Though what wouldn't you believe?" says Ruby.

"So you don't believe her?" asks Will.

"I'm not the arbitrator of truth," says Ruby.

"What about you, Raina?" asks Will. "Do you believe Bernice?"

Raina considers the question seriously. "There was a time in my life when I trusted the—I don't know," she says. "I trusted the things you trust. Let's say, the rules of physics. Back then I wouldn't have believed any of this." She turns her head to look out the empty windows, her profile fit for the cover of *Vogue*. "But something changes after tragedy," she says. "It's like you've spent your whole life putting one foot in front of the other, knowing the ground would always be there to meet you, and then suddenly, one day . . . it isn't. The bottom has dropped out. The unbelievable happens and you just . . . fall."

"What are you saying?" asks Bernice. "That tragedy proves that the worst—the absolute worst—can actually happen?"

"I'm saying that if you can't trust the world to behave how you thought it would—if the impossible becomes possible—then you're open to believing so much more," says Raina.

"So it makes you more empathetic and understanding?" says Bernice, unconvinced.

Raina nods, and her errant lock frees itself from behind her ear.

Bernice looks from the lock into her own lap, where her fingers clutch a cup of cold coffee. Her nails are craggy, picked over, a bad habit that betrays her anxiety and has only gotten worse.

"It's got to be different for someone like you," says Bernice. "Easier to find silver linings." She pauses. "When you fall, Raina, people must rush to help you up. With me, they point and laugh."

"The news has been unfair to you," says Raina. "I can't imagine what you've gone through."

"Diplomatic," Ruby says, suspicious.

"Maybe Raina looks like she has it all together," says Will, "but it's worth remembering that many of us are very different on the outside than we are on the inside."

"Yeah, not me," says Ruby. "I'm a get-what-you-see kind of gal."

"Ashton saw me exactly for the person I was," says Bernice. She watches Raina's hand make its way toward the lock, the tips of her fingernails as white as her pearl earring, the pearl earring sparkling like her rings, the hair now properly tucked, her hand back in her lap, like everything has a place, like it's easy to put things back together.

★ ★ ★

When I returned to East Hampton a few weeks later, it was in the middle of the night with Naomi and a U-Haul and I wasn't even afraid. I was too tired to be afraid, or else I was afraid all the time, so the circumstances didn't make a difference. "Are you sure you don't just want to go to Target?" Naomi had asked when I'd told her I wanted his furniture.

I collected not just furniture but other items from the mansion: a bone-white comb, a leather desk pad, a Victorian cloche jar whose delicate flowers, I was sure, were made from human hair. Even on a midnight run to the scene of a crime, my sister looked beautiful. She worked at United Way now. She had a nice boyfriend, a social worker named Ravi whom I was sure wouldn't try to kill her.

"I don't understand why you want this stuff," Naomi kept saying. "We can get you furniture that won't remind you of…anything." By the time we'd dragged everything to my apartment in Queens, dawn was stretched across the sky and my apartment looked like an estate sale.

As soon as my sister left, one of the Tiffanies muttered, *These bitches again.*

They were not a chorus, as you might hope for if haunted by dead women, but a cacophony, like an all-girls school after the last bell, on a bad day, all anger and heartbreak, tears that give way to wailing, sad contemplation, quiet existential cries in the night. They started right in on their most awful stories, about how they died, about what sort of objects they'd rather be, how religion was a scam, they knew that now, even reincarnation was bullshit—you were supposed to come back new, memoryless, as a living thing, capable of making choices.

Thinking it would help, I read aloud from a book I'd read in high school, an excerpt of which I'd found online. It was written by a man who survived a concentration camp. "See what he's saying?"

I told them. "He's saying that no matter how many freedoms are taken away, you can still *choose* what you think, you can still choose your atti—"

You really need to shut up, said the inlaid-bone dresser.

We're not really in the mood for a Holocaust story, said the lamp.

If you read us one more line of that shit, said Human-God Tiffany, *I will be living in my actual, literal hell.*

We all just need to stay calm, said a journal. *Maybe try some self-care techniques.*

Self-care, said the lamp, *is a neoliberal trap.*

I x-ed out my browser window, put my hands in my lap. I listened. It was the least I could do.

Charisse had been raised by her grandmother in California. Soon after she moved to New York to attend college, her grandmother died. She met Ashton after she graduated with over a hundred thousand dollars in student debt and no job.

In six months, she was a set of three leather journals and a bookmark. Unlike most people who acquire expensive new journals, Ashton did not have new-journal paralysis. He filled a third of one of the journals with notes on woodworking, taxidermy, and inlaid-bone techniques. His handwriting was small and meticulous. Compact architectural-style drawings showed the measurements of the many furnishings he had built. Her initials were stamped in gold foil on the interior covers. The leather bookmark was embossed with a quote in an old-fashioned serif font: "The true hero of the American utopia is neither the cowboy nor the soldier but the pioneer, the pathfinder."

The Charisse journals spoke in unison or said the same exact thing one by one. The bookmark never said much, though sometimes it read its own quote aloud, and the journals lamented together, *What does it mean? What does it mean? What does it mean?*

I think it's Virilio, taken out of context for Ashton's own bullshit ends, explained Aisha, who, prior to becoming a lamp, had been studying political theory at NYU.

Sometimes Charisse would ask if anyone wanted to know their specifications, and she would read them from herself whether they wanted to know or not. *Stool. Seven inches wide. Fourteen inches long. Nine and a half inches tall. Pantone color? Question mark, question mark, question mark. Cerulean? Question mark.* By the time Charisse was reading dimensions, it was often late, and we were all too emotionally exhausted to convince her to be quiet.

Aisha was presumably the third victim, the lampshade presumably her skin. In the news, much to Aisha's ire, they kept referring to her as "a hardworking immigrant in pursuit of the American Dream." I placed her next to my reading chair, though was hesitant to switch her light on. Her voice had an echoing, megaphone quality to it, due to the cone-shaped shade. *In retrospect, I can't say I loved him. Can any of us, in hindsight, say we loved him?*

It's ironic, really, she said. *This is the pinnacle of late capitalism, isn't it? To be lured by wealth, to be murdered for wanting it, and then to be transformed into a one-of-a-kind object, a kind of rejection-of and reaction-to mass production?*

I could see, on some level, how Aisha and Ashton might have gotten along.

The dresser—the one featuring inlaid-bone fleur-de-lis—was Blanche. We all resented her. *Blanche was "the one that got away,"* noted Charisse, though clearly Blanche had not.

He didn't pull the key stunt with me, said Blanche proudly. *I broke up with him. I started packing my things, and he chloroformed me that night. He was pretty torn up about killing me too, crying and wailing and stuff.*

He didn't cry for me, noted the Charisses in unison, oblivious to the satisfaction it gave Blanche.

I was surprised by you, Blanche said to me. *I look more like your sister. But you take what you can get, I suppose. Nothing to say of you, of course, just in terms of body type—he had ... a type. You understand.*

Sometimes, when Blanche spoke, I fantasized about using the skeleton key to scratch her perfect, glossy finish.

He didn't have a type, corrected Aisha. *He was collecting types. That's why we're all so different.*

Blanche ignored her. *Ultimately, all that money, all that fancy stuff,* she said, *none of it could hide the fact that he was boring. He was selfish in bed. With him, it was all horror and headaches and blow jobs.*

I thought of my first time with Ashton, how he had stared at the dresser, at Blanche. I knew the only pleasure he'd taken in pleasuring me had been for the sake of torturing her.

Basically, she said, *I could do better.*

Sure, of course, yes, we all said, hating her for having realized what we had not.

How did he kill you? Aisha asked.

I don't feel comfortable saying, said Blanche, as if there was some code about dying and telling.

The Tiffanies, on the other hand, felt very comfortable telling: strangled in bed while having sex. *Like every third guy, he was into choking, so I didn't think anything of it until I was dead.*

Not such a hard way to go, muttered Aisha.

The worst part, said Human-God Tiffany, *is that I never got to come.*

I mean, the worst part after being dead, clarified Falcon Tiffany.

I mean, the worst part after being dead and coming back to life as a fucking jar, added Baboon Tiffany.

In death, or whatever it was, she felt perpetually horny, or not quite horny, but like she was always on the verge of something exceptional yet unachievable.

T, M, I, said the Charisses, a letter emitting from each journal, and then the bookmark started reading the goddamn quote over and over again.

O, M, G, the Tiffany jars mocked. *Shut, the fuck, up,* they said.

Astrid, an exchange student from Sweden, had her bones inlaid in a squat wooden stool. The design was simple, especially compared to Blanche, but Astrid was functional and beautiful in her contained smallness. According to the other women, she had been tall, diligent, and very quiet. *Except,* Aisha noted, *for when she died.*

I put Astrid in the kitchen. She was the perfect size for reaching items stored above the cabinets. I was hesitant to stand on her at first, but her hardworking, Protestant essence implied that she'd rather be made use of than simply looked at. If I was still wearing my shoes, I'd put a paper towel down, so she wouldn't get dirty.

She wouldn't speak—she was either too traumatized, too shy, or both.

"Are you sure it's her?" I wondered aloud, even though she matched Charisse's specifications to a T.

Yes, said Aisha sadly. *When Astrid walked in with the skeleton key, she fainted at the sight of my skinless body.* I knew the story already. She had told it a million times. The skin, the blood, the screaming. I forced myself to listen.

Something in the hallway squealed, *Please!* I went to investigate, grateful for the interruption.

"The shoes?" I asked the Tiffanies.

The motherfucking shoes! agreed at least two of the Tiffanies.

I kept Ashton's sky-blue leather loafers by the door with my shoes. For camaraderie, I guess, in case someone was inside them. I crouched down and picked them up. I pictured them on Ashton's feet, squeaking toward me.

Though we can't be, like, totally sure it was the shoes, said Human-God Tiffany.

Actually, it was maybe me, added Baboon Tiffany. *But I don't think it was me.*

In the other room, Aisha was still talking. *Blood like a splatter painting,* I heard her say. *Ashton's face lit: wild with joy,* I heard her say.

"Shut up!" I shouted, tossing the shoes to the floor.

I want to tell the story! Aisha wailed through the cone of her lampshade.

"Maybe Astrid doesn't want to hear that stuff again," I said.

Charisse started to read off the dimensions of what Taylor had been slated to become: a sleek, ornamental table with thin legs and a bone-shard mosaic tabletop.

"What was I going to be?" I wondered aloud. Charisse went silent. "Charisse," I said. "Do you know?"

I felt dizzy as I stood up and walked to the journals. I opened the first one and flipped through.

What are you doing? she asked. *It's very cold when you do that.*

I picked up the second notebook, flipped through.

Don't! said Charisse. But I was already reading a page that Charisse had never read aloud.

"There's stuff back here, Charisse," I said, annoyed.

What does it say? Aisha funneled in from above.

I don't think we should read it, Charisse said.

Just read it, said Blanche. *Jesus.*

So Charisse did: *Tiffany is ill-fitted for jars. (Though possibly good joke? Trash in ancient jars worth millions!) Not my best work. Charisse: Little ability to develop own ideas, reflects what you put in, blank slate personality. Aisha: Illuminating, but only so much reach, modern "alternative" aesthetic, but still an aesthetic. Astrid ideal as a stool: Shy, small personality, tall yet ultimately overlooked. Built for function.*

And then there was me. *Fat leather ottoman? Haha,* it read, nothing more. The rest of the page was doodles of swords, one of them stabbing through a bloody anatomical heart.

"Fat ottoman," I said.

He's an asshole, said one of the Tiffanies.

What about me? said Blanche.

Oh, shut up, Aisha said. *We all know you're functional and ornamental.*

Charisse started reading, once again, from the beginning of the journal in a near-hysterical tone, specifications we'd already heard a hundred times.

He made us caricatures of ourselves, said Aisha over the droning of Charisse, *distilled us into objects. We became mere set pieces in his story.*

What is this, your fucking thesis? said Human-God Tiffany.

I was writing a dissertation, hissed Aisha.

I can't believe we dated the same man, said Human-God Tiffany.

You and me both, huffed Aisha.

Charisse, still droning: *Stool. Seven inches wide. Fourteen inches long. Nine and a half inches tall.*

I was getting a headache, or else I had had one the whole time.

Holy fucking shit, Charisse! shouted Falcon Tiffany. *We know how tall Astrid is!* But the Charisse journals just kept going, louder and more hysterical by the second.

I had heard their stories hundreds of times now, but they had never heard mine.

"I was so scared," I said, my voice rising over Charisse's.

No, said Blanche. Her voice was so cold and sharp, everyone fell silent. *You don't get this.*

"But—" I tried.

But what? said Blanche, Ashton's most illustrious ex. I imagined Blanche as the beautiful human she once was, staring down at me, skinny arms crossed over her ample chest. But, of course, she didn't have arms or a chest or eyes. She was a dresser—three drawers, six small white knobs. Under the light of Aisha, Blanche's fleur-de-lis— her broken bones—shone like white-hot stars.

I wanted someone in the room to say something on my behalf, I wanted just one of them to agree that I should continue, that I should get a turn to tell my story. But no one spoke up, not a Tiffany jar, not Astrid, not the shoes in the hall. Not the bone-white comb, not the woven hair, not the leather desk pad, not so much as the bookmark. Yet the room was far from quiet. The air quivered with their breath, loud as liquid rushing over me.

Maybe I wasn't an ottoman, but I had transformed in that basement too. It was like there had been an earthquake inside of me, like I had been hollowed by it, and now I was left to live in the ruins.

Who could ever really understand but them?

Tonight I will go back home, and they will be there, talking, telling me over and over about how they lived and how they died. Mostly how they died. I will never get to tell them my story, because it's my duty to listen, because what I do get—isn't it enough?—by pure, stupid luck, I get to live.

Week Two

Ruby

Ruby's eyes open. A smudge of faces swim above her, backlit by fluorescent lights. The tiled floor is cool beneath her. She is itchy with sweat and wet. Her head feels as if it's been split with a hatchet. Warm fingers on her wrist, checking her pulse. It's Will, kneeling by her side.

"She's waking up."

"What happened?"

"Give her a second."

A trail of red liquid leads to the spot where she's collapsed. Ruby is covered in red, drenched in it. It's soaked through her gray T-shirt, it's dripped into the pleats of her metallic skirt, it's streaked across her face and glopped in her hair. They have searched for a wound, but they all know: if it were her blood, she'd be dead.

"You fainted," says Will. "You're overheated." Will, leaning over her, looks vaguely heroic, like a doctor from a medical drama. "Are you hurt?" he asks.

"Not acutely," says Ruby, her voice cracked and slow. The lenses of her glasses are smudged pink, as if she tried and failed to wash them off. She licks at a front tooth: chipped. "Fuck," she says. She can smell herself, her own sour scent. The basement is cooler than the 90 degrees it is outside, but not nearly cool enough.

Sirens whir.

"Those aren't for me?" Ruby asks. The sound sobers her. She props herself on her elbows.

"Obvi they are?" says Ashlee. Ashlee stands as if posing for a fashion photographer, with a hand on her waist, the opposite hip jutted out, her feet slightly apart. The sweat on her skin looks more like lubricant, like oil. Ruby can see up her black denim skirt, can see how the tan keeps going, up her skinny legs and thighs, until it's exposed again, her midsection bejeweled beneath a pink boxy crop top.

Ashlee reminds Ruby of a bug, the way her enormous lashes flap, the way her giant sunglasses are pushed atop her head like an extra set of eyes, the way she's so fucking annoying.

"Congrats," says Ruby. "I see your belly button got engaged." Ashlee makes a face.

Will has left to meet the ambulance. Ruby watches his brown leather wing tips rush past the alley windows. "The ambulance is pointless," she says.

Raina tries to help Ruby take off her coat, but Ruby refuses, so Raina offers up her water bottle instead. Ruby guzzles the water, some of it spilling down her chin, the stainless-steel bottle gleaming like a bullet under the basement lights. She wipes her chin with the wet fur of her sleeve, leaving a fresh track of red across her mouth so it looks as if she's just devoured a bloody meal.

"Thanks," Ruby says, thrusting the empty bottle back to Raina, who is looking as polished and perfect as she did the week before. Ruby's never trusted anyone who French-tucks their shirts. Not that she trusts anyone who doesn't either.

Despite protests from the group, Ruby stands up, holding out an arm to steady herself. Raina tries to assist, but Ruby waves her away, then slinks like a wounded animal to the circle of chairs, a trail of red dripping behind her. She sinks down in the same chair as the week before, sinks so low that the wet shoulders of her coat hover above her. She looks like someone taken in from a post-apocalyptic rainstorm or like a person back from the dead.

No one has followed her. Ruby eyes them through the blur of her smudged drugstore lenses. They are all staring from the other side of the room, save Gretel, whose eyes fix on nothing, just a random spot midair.

Gretel's wearing nearly the same clothes as the previous week. Her button-down is too big on her small frame, as if she hopes to get lost in it. The thin fabric sticks to her back in the heat, and Ruby can make out the vertebrae of her spine. The top two buttons are undone, and in that V, part of a clavicle juts out like a knife blade.

Gretel's head is electric with curls. Ruby can't figure out if the look is more mad scientist or little girl. She can't figure out Gretel's deal in general, can't figure out if she's uptight or couldn't care less, if she's above-it-all or quietly deranged. With childhood trauma like theirs—assuming Gretel's story is true—who knows?

Ruby has never seen someone so capable of disengaging without an excuse. Gretel's earbud cable is coiled up around two fingers, and she isn't even bothering to fiddle with it, isn't bothering to pretend to do anything at all, won't deign to pick at a nail or adjust a piece of clothing. It's somehow more hurtful to be ignored without pretense.

The wing tips click back, four white sneakers in hot pursuit, and all of them tear down the hall and burst into the room like troops, the paramedics badged and blue.

Ruby thrusts her hands in the air. "I don't have health insurance!" she shouts.

A paramedic with a jaunty black ponytail sinks down next to Ruby's chair, asks questions like, "What's the year, Ruby?" "Who's the president, Ruby?"

"Who cares?" says Ruby, sliding farther down in her seat. "It's always the same shit."

The paramedics insist they won't charge her for the sports drink, the wet towel they place on her head. She refuses to take off her coat. She wrings out her hair, pink water dripping onto the tiled floor. "I black out all the time," she says. "I'm like an overheating hair dryer. Shut myself off instead of breaking."

"And what are you covered in?" the paramedic asks.

"Unrelated issue," says Ruby.

The paramedics leave; they can't make her go with them. Will and the women circle up slowly, returning to their seats from the previous week. Ashlee, who's seated beside Ruby, scoots her chair away, closer to Bernice.

Ruby eats a stack of sugar cookies ravenously, taking huge bites. Her coat drips, little puddles gathering around her chair, as if she is melting. Ruby feels like she's regenerating, powering up. She feels better than she's felt all day, though that's a low bar.

She vaguely listens to the rest of the group talk about the previous week, and then vaguely notices they are too distracted by her to keep talking, and when she's finished devouring the cookies, she looks up to see Will watching her, furrow-browed, with one arm folded over his stomach, the other under his chin. She takes her time wrapping up, sucking crumbs off each finger.

"So," she says finally. "That was an adventure." Heat radiates off her. Beads of pink sweat line her forehead. Sugar crystals are caught around her cracked lips.

"Is that what you call it?" says Will. "Because to me it's concerning. You look ill, frankly. You're overheated, exhausted, dirty."

They're all overheated, thinks Ruby. It's the hottest day of the year. They're all sweating, save Will, who is miraculously dry, skin fresh and bright, despite the long pants and button-down. As for exhausted, Bernice takes the cake there—she's already stifled several yawns and is now taking the long, slow blinks of someone milking each one for a miniature rest. And dirty? Yes, Ruby concedes. But it isn't her fault.

Ruby rubs her hand down the sleeve of her coat, so all the red-stained hair is slicked down. "I'm fine."

"This is what fine is for you?" asks Will, his face puckering with empathy.

"On a bad day," says Ruby.

"You black out all of the time?" asks Raina with genuine concern.

"Well, if you want to get technical," says Ruby, "it's only some of the time."

"You're triggering Bernice by looking dead," says Ashlee.

"I'm triggering myself by being me," says Ruby.

Bernice appears less triggered than tired, but Ashlee seems pleased with her defense of Bernice and smiles at Will as if he might give her a gold star.

"I wonder why that coat is so important to you," Will asks Ruby.

"Transitional object," says Ruby.

"From what to what?" asks Will.

"It was a joke," says Ruby. She flicks a glob of congealed red off her thumb. "I've had a fucked-up day. If *you* had the day I just had, you'd be crying in bed right now."

"But you're not crying in bed," says Will.

"You're doing, like, whatever this is," says Ashlee, waving her hand up and down with a look of disgust.

71

"Ruby, what happened to you today?" asks Will.

Ruby runs her hand up the sleeve of her coat so all the hair sticks straight up. "It's a long story," she says. "Or a short story. Or not a story at all. More like several things that happened, and now here I am."

She scans the faces in the group: concerned, disgusted, curious, bewildered. They may not like her, but they are riveted. That's the other side of misfortune: the power you wield. The least you can get out of a bad day is a good story, something people can really sink their teeth into.

She flicks at her chipped tooth with her tongue, entwines her fingers, stretches her arms out in front of her so that all of her knuckles crack along with one of her shoulder blades. "So, actually, it is a story," she says. "Story of my fucking life."

"Go on," says Will, and he leans back in his chair as if settling into a good book.

★ ★ ★

This morning, I was late for my shift at the coffee shop because I fell asleep on the train and had to backtrack, because I was sleep-deprived, because I was hungover, which is another story, not one worth telling. When I arrived at the coffee shop, I was soaked with sweat because of the heat, but also the coat, which, clearly, I wear no matter the weather.

Chloe, one of the other baristas, was scowling at me from behind the counter like I was a rat that had crawled out of a sewer. "You're fifty-"—she yanked her phone out of the apron to check the clock—"eight minutes late. This time," she added, scathing, like I'd eaten her mom for lunch, "we're *not* letting it go."

I was late, but also: Chloe is a bitch. My least favorite thing about her, besides her personality, is her tattoo. Don't get me wrong—I like tattoos. I *have* a tattoo—a Western 45 handgun on the back of my right biceps. It's Chloe's tattoo specifically that I dislike.

Most of the time, all you can see of it are these two stupid prehistoric bird feet sticking out from under the hem of her skirt. At the coffee shop, she lifted her skirt several inches, several times a day, just to show off the whole, disappointing design: a monocle-wearing peacock, its muted purple and green plumage fanning out across her right thigh.

When I asked about the tattoo, about what it meant or meant to her, she responded with eye-rolling disdain, as if I'd missed the point entirely by asking the question at all. "Nothing is anything anymore," she'd said, stalking off to refill the array of milks, whole and skim, almond and oat, soy and lactose-free.

Nothing is anything? Was she kidding me? Humans have been making meaning for tens of thousands of years, adding and changing stories like some intergenerational Exquisite Corpse. Even the fucking Neanderthals were scribbling on the walls. As if Chloe and her lame tattoo were immune, as if she'd managed to pull something unique and pure from the ether. I wanted to razor-slash that tattoo, right through that pretentious monocled eyeball.

I went behind the counter for some water while Chloe finished up the cappuccino she was making. "Don't come back here," she hissed before huffing off to complain to the boss.

I sat on one of the white metal barstools near the table, resigned to the impending lecture.

Then I spied Emil, one of the other baristas, creeping along the far wall, trying to exit into the back room without my noticing, taking great interest in the honeycomb-tiled floor he'd washed down after the early morning rush. This was a new level of avoidance, even for Emil.

Emil and I have this on-again, off-again storage-closet romance. "Romance" is a strong word for it. He sometimes nonexclusively jams his junk down my throat over lunch breaks until I can't breathe.

Emil has the personality of a drunken pirate trying to clean up his act. For three weeks out of each month, he treats me like a siren trying to shipwreck him. When he's exhausted himself from abstaining, he'll reappear with that hungry, wanting look. Later, he'll pawn it off as a moment of weakness that was my fault, saying things like "Well, when you wear that dress" or "You finally washed your hair." We keep doing it, just like that, in a way that's annoyingly unstoppable, like how you find yourself singing along to a crappy pop song on the radio that you unfortunately know by heart.

The storage closet stuff, mostly it killed time. Everything at the coffee shop was grayscale: white tiled floors, fake marble tabletops with ashy gray swirled in. To me, the people coming in and out all day were like a single patron wearing different skins and ensembles, featureless as a crowd in an impressionist painting. I filled the orders by rote, the finished products appearing in the customers' hands mostly correctly, to everyone's surprise.

Chloe reappeared from the back looking smug, and Sergio, who was newish but friendly, caught my eye, then looked away. Maybe he was stunned by the metallic gleam of my pleated miniskirt.

My boss appeared, covered in flour in a way that made her look blurred. Her face fell as she saw me.

"Ruby," she said, shaking her head, a fog of flour puffing out of her hair, "something's got to give." I was hoping Chloe was what had to give, but I wasn't banking on it.

My boss looked down at her forearm, then scratched it as flour plumed from her skin. When she looked up at me again, her face was all pity. "I know you've been through it," she said.

I hadn't known she'd known anything about me, actually.

"Through what?" I asked, just to make her squirm.

My boss opened her mouth, closed it, opened it again. "Everyone has their stories," she said.

Sure, and fuck you, I thought. Maybe everyone has a story, but not everyone was interviewed by Barbara Walters at age twelve, cross-legged on a couch in a red dress and Mary Janes, skin still red from stomach acid, getting chastised for her wantonness. Not everyone was in a Western 45 handgun ad just to pay the hospital bills. Not that I was the one who shot him. Not everyone is the fictionalized star of pedo-erotic-true-crime fan fiction and actual porn, posted on the deep corners of the internet, some version of me wandering around a subdivision in pigtails naked, save for a red-hooded cape.

People were recognizing me all the time again, after a two-decade lull. I blame it on the recent uptick of *Where Are They Now?* listicles featuring pictures of tragedy celebs all grown up: Elizabeth Smart, Amanda Knox, computer-generated age progressions of missing girls who had never been found, and yours truly. Me in a fur coat, fucked up from a night out. What a shame, how people go wrong. So sad. Then there was the *Law & Order: SVU* episode, and just last year a producer contacted me about some Jake Jackson reality TV show called *The Stranger Who Saved Me*, about reuniting with the person who saved your life. I didn't call them back. I guess it never got off the ground.

There's also that children's book that came out a couple of months ago. I hate-read it at a bookstore, hate-jamming an ass cheek into one of those armchairs designed for kids. On the cover there's a drawing of a girl in superhero pose: arms akimbo, red cape flying behind her. She's the hero of the story because, just when the wolf is about to eat her, she gets him to start talking. She saves herself by *listening*. It turns out the wolf is starving, and she starts a food drive on his behalf. On the final page, the girl and the wolf are playing Mandala together and the grandma—very much alive and not covered in wolf guts—serves up homemade pie.

Sensational or sanitized, there's no middle ground.

"Great point," I said.

I glanced around the coffee shop. Post–breakfast rush, only a few patrons remained staked out at tables. Chloe was taking an order, straight-backed and straight-faced, the consummate professional, but I didn't miss the smirk that flashed across her face as she pumped out the dark roast, listening in. Emil had reappeared, poised near the door to the back room, and Sergio was wiping down a table self-consciously like an extra in a play.

"This consistent lateness..." said my boss.

"*Inconsistent* lateness," I said.

"You're not helping," she said. "You know we have security cameras in the storage room?"

"I was not aware of this," I said. I threw a look back toward Emil, but he'd ducked out again. "Why am *I* always in trouble?" I asked.

"That's a good question to ask yourself," said my boss. "I've already spoken with Emil, if that's what you mean. Emil comes to work on time, and, uh, appropriately dressed."

"Do we have a dress code?" I asked.

"Insofar as...just common sense, Ruby. The smell of the...It's very hot outside, so the coat...There's a measure of self-respect required..."

Maybe Emil was right. Maybe Febreze wasn't cutting it anymore. Recently, Emil had rubbed his hand on my coat, then rubbed his fingers together to show me the little gray stuff rolling off, dirt and oil from years of wear.

"This is disgusting," he'd said. "Why do you need to wear this fucking thing all the time?"

"I don't *need* anything," I'd said.

"You do," he'd said. "You need everything to be all fucked up."

Later, making out near the raw sugar and the plastic knives, it was all I could do not to bite off his tongue.

"Maybe you should take some time," my boss said.

"Time?" I repeated.

"Time," she repeated.

"Time," I said like I was talking to myself in a cave.

"Go home," she said. "Get some rest."

Did she think I was Chloe? That I was in this for the pocket change?

"For how long?" I asked.

I looked around the coffee shop. Chloe, still bitch-faced, held out a medium coffee midair, the customer's outreached hand paused before it. Emil peeked out of the back room. Sergio stood over a table, staring at me. I was the butt of a joke I didn't understand.

My boss's expression was pained. "I'm sorry," she said.

"What?" I said, because I'm a fucking idiot.

"You're fired," she said.

★ ★ ★

Ruby laughs. A bead of red sweat has rolled down the side of her face, leaving a grimy pink trail. She wipes her sweaty forehead with her pink-stained hand, then wipes her hand on the stained breast of her coat, then looks at her wet hand. She's just transferring liquids from one place to another.

"What's funny?" asks Will.

"That I finally understood the joke," says Ruby.

"Which was…?"

"That I was fired," says Ruby.

"So that's funny?" says Will, as if trying to make sense of it, though Ruby knows he's just making a point. She's supposed to realize it's not funny, that she actually has some masochistic interest in self-destruction. Which she does, but the laugh is simpler than that: she's enjoying herself.

For once, she has an audience captivated not by a story they already know—or think they know—but by a story they don't. And her sweaty, red-stained body embodies the suspense.

Ashlee uncrosses her legs, stretching a tan, glistening leg into the circle, then recrosses them in the opposite direction. "I think you deserved to be fired, TBH."

"You and everyone else."

Will taps his fingertips together. "Does it always feel like you versus everyone else, Ruby?"

"It *is* me versus everyone else."

"How so?"

"Were you listening? Which of those people were on my side? Chloe? Emil? My boss? Fucking Barbara Walters? The Western 45 Gun Company? Jake Jackson?"

Raina frowns. "I'm not sure Jake Jackson is on anyone's side anymore," she says.

"Meaning?" asks Will.

"He's on the side of the ratings," says Raina.

"Do we think Ashlee here is on my side?" Ruby asks. "Bernice?"

"I'd like to be on your side," says Bernice.

"Right," scoffs Ruby. "The same way you want to be on the side of your dead roommates?"

"And that means what?" asks Bernice.

"You don't actually *like* them," says Ruby. "You're jealous of them. They're in a clique you can't join because your story just can't compete with theirs."

"Lay off," says Gretel.

Ruby licks her upper lip, leans back in her chair. "Sure," she says. "Thanks for chiming in." She looks at Will with raised eyebrows, smiles. "You see?" she says. She points at herself. "Me"—then extends her hand out to sweep the circle—"versus everyone else."

★ ★ ★

I lingered in front of the coffee shop, not out of spite, per se—okay, maybe a little out of spite—but mostly out of incredulousness and indecision. What was I supposed to do all day until group?

I couldn't go home. For cut-rate rent, I'd agreed not to be in the apartment for certain hours, so my roommate could practice her dance routines or conduct drug deals, or whatever the fuck she was doing. I'm a serial subletter, squatting in other people's apartments, among other people's things, while the original lessee studies abroad or takes a sabbatical or goes to rehab. It's a way of living that makes me feel at home and not at all at home everywhere I go.

I tapped at my thighs, feeling for the razor blade wrapped up in masking tape that I usually keep in the pocket of my shorts, but I wasn't wearing my shorts. I'd fallen asleep in the clothes I'd gone out in.

I texted Emil, Yo, but he didn't answer.

It was hazy and sweltering. The sun hovered in the sky, white and fluffy as a severed rabbit's tail. I could see the air moving across the pavement in slick waves, ghost tentacles. I looked back through the gleaming coffee-shop window. Sergio glanced in my direction, offered an embarrassed half-smile, then looked away.

Hello? I texted Emil. Yo? Hello?

Please, he texted back. I pictured him ducked behind the napkins and paper coffee cups where I'd choked on his dick many a time. We weren't supposed to use our phones at work.

What do you want? I wrote.

You're the one texting me, he said. I'd meant to imply, like, a blow job in the alley or something.

The triple dots blinked, and I waited for them to become a message. We can't do this anymore. His favorite refrain. I think this was the push we needed to really make a clean break.

I rolled my eyes, typed back: ME being fired was the push WE needed?

Sorry to put it that way. He wrote this with a period, like it was an official statement, like he was not sorry at all.

I typed back: I don't understand why free blow jobs are a *problem* in your life.

Do you even get what's wrong with the way you phrased that? he typed.

What exactly are you losing in this arrangement? I wrote.

My dignity. The dots again. I'm tired of treating you like shit.

That makes two of us, I replied.

Does it though? he asked.

Once, during the zip-up, Emil had asked, "Why do you let me do this?," the whites of his eyes glowing in the coffee-scented darkness. It was a little thrilling, to see only the most generic part of his eyes, to imagine that they could be anyone's eyes, that either of us could have been replaced with someone else in the dark. "Do you get anything out of it?" he'd asked. "Do you *want* to be treated poorly?"

"Jesus, I don't know," I'd said to whatever question I was supposed to be answering. I'd been on my haunches next to the napkin supply, trying to clean the cum out of my coat, one of hundreds of liquids that had seeped into the fur over the years, a scrapbook of stains: beer and dirt and tears, and, in the lining of the sleeves, smeared lines of blood.

Sex isn't supposed to be a transaction, he wrote. You're supposed to feel something. Like, with your emotions.

I delivered an eye roll, literally and textually.

Here's some advice, he wrote. Get rid of the coat. It smells terrible. No one will hire you in that...I have to get back to work.

I almost typed At least you have work to get back to, but I didn't want to be that lame and petty in a screenshot-able format.

I put my phone away, bit a little piece of my lip skin loose, then worked on peeling it off with my fingers.

"Excuse me," snapped some Wall Street type who couldn't bring herself to step two fucking feet around me to get into the coffee shop.

"The coffee in there is shit," I said. "The girl at the counter gives everybody blow jobs because she doesn't know how to forge human connections."

"That's really sad," said the woman.

I'd probably just earned Chloe a big tip.

I watched Chloe standing in her favorite spot, the gap between the employee area and the customer area, cinching up her denim skirt to show off her stupid tattoo.

In the glass of the café window, I caught the reflection of a homeless woman, her face slick with sweat, her eyes bleary and mascara smudged.

Out of habit, I tapped my thighs, thinking I had pockets, and the homeless woman did the exact same thing.

Motherfucker, I thought.

A beat-up black car crept up the street, and a guy with twiggy arms stuck his narrow head out of the passenger-side window and yelled to me, "Yo, babe, how much?"

I could've shouted, *You couldn't pay me enough!* but I wasn't that kind of girl—you *could* pay me enough.

I get mistaken for a prostitute from time to time. I have long suspected it's because of the coat, its dingy opulence, plus the vague heroin-addict look around the eyes. "Not exactly..." said Emil once. "You just *look,* I don't know, like a rabbit or something, mischievous and scared, like you're waiting for something violent to happen, and when it does, you're gonna love it, you're gonna love being torn apart."

"That's stupid," I'd said, gripping my coat. "This is a wolf."

"A woman in wolf's clothing." Emil sighed. "A lone wolf," he said. *"Elle a vu le loup."* Once a week, Emil dreamed of being a poet. One semester in college, he dreamed of speaking French.

"What the hell are you talking about?"

"That last one's an old French saying," said Emil, "about losing the V-card."

The black car slowed in traffic, to the pace I was walking. The twiggy yeller looked sheepish now, bowing his head down and staring into his lap.

I looked down at my coat. Emil wasn't wrong. The fur was stray-dog matted and sheenless. It rose everywhere in sad little clumps. I wouldn't even pay me to sleep with me. I was embarrassed for us all.

I was also starving. I rummaged in my purse, hoping I'd stashed a snack in there, then gave up and started walking, fast, as if I were late for something.

Soon, I was sitting in a red pleather booth at McDonald's with a Coke, letting the sugar work its way through my system. As I rode the invigorating high of AC and a rising glycemic index, I tried to convince myself everything would be all right. I could pay a month or two of rent on my credit card, maybe. The city had a billion coffee shops. I could find another job.

Right? With the coat, though?

That fucking clown was staring at me with his shit-eating grin, bright red like he'd just eaten something alive.

A dumpy woman carrying a tray full of breakfast sandwiches and coffees was staring at me as I chewed on my straw.

"Yeah?" I said with the straw still in my mouth.

"Sorry," she said.

"Okay," I said.

"Do I know you?" she asked.

"Do you?" I wasn't going to do her work for her.

"Were you…?" the woman asked. "With the wolf?" She didn't need an answer. "I believe your version," she said. "I mean, a kid couldn't make that stuff up, right?"

"Too fucked up," I agreed.

"I mean, *basically*, I believe your version. The scientist said that for sure that was stomach acid on your skin, or like microbacteria from the wolf's gut?" Where was all this shit coming from? Had there been some true-crime podcast I'd missed? I couldn't keep up.

"We all have our stories," I said, chewing on my straw.

"You just never expect to see someone famous," she said.

She walked to a table in the far corner and whispered to her friends. Everyone turned and looked at me, pretending and failing to be discreet, as I pretended to look at my phone. "Look, look," I heard the dumpy woman say, "I heard she wears the bastard as a coat."

Then it was all "Ohmygawd" and "That coat's disgusting" and "She's in it for the attention" and "I can smell it from here." This coming from a group of women who went to McDonald's for brunch.

But could they really smell my coat from all the way over there? Through the grease and the coffee? I mean, if I leveled with myself,

I *had* been mistaken for a prostitute and a homeless person already that morning.

Suddenly it came to me: I didn't have to trash the coat. I could just get it cleaned. Why hadn't I thought of it before? There was this block in Midtown I'd walked down about a hundred times, chock-full of fur and leather shops with big-lettered signs, every font imaginable, digital marquees shouting deals in red dots that blinked and scrolled. It was enough to give you a seizure. I dumped the soda, made my way north.

★ ★ ★

Ruby takes in her audience. Will is nodding with pursed lips. Raina is pert and attentive in a way that feels unsatisfyingly nondiscriminatory. Bernice is still fuming, working off a piece of fingernail. Gretel is silent and sulky. Ashlee is seesawing her hand, checking out the glint of her ring. Either they're losing interest in her or she's losing interest in them now that the adrenaline-rush luster of the day is wearing off.

"Bored?" she asks.

Will recommends they take a break. They stretch, refill coffee cups, eat cookies, visit the restroom, make small talk about the heat. Ruby wanders around the room, a trail of red dripping behind her.

Once they're resettled, Will makes another hard sell on narrative therapy as Ruby tries to finger-comb the knots from her clotted, drying hair. He talks about the value of sharing stories, about how it makes people feel less alone. He calls sharing an act of bravery, not just because it takes vulnerability to be open with others but because it takes courage to be honest with oneself.

After some pressing from Will, Raina admits that she finds the justification for the group somewhat vague, the possible outcomes nebulous. Gretel agrees.

They talk about their reservations. Raina doesn't want to dredge up the past for the sake of dredging up the past. Gretel is very private, isn't sure she's the kind of person who gets much out of sharing. Ashlee wonders if she even belongs here, given that her story is mostly—as they know—about love.

Will empathizes with their uncertainty and ambivalence. He notes that, for those interested, he can refer them to several academic papers on the effectiveness of narrative-based therapy for trauma. He asks them all to think about why they came here. What made them reply to the email? What do they hope to get out of this? If sticking around means getting that, will it be worth it? What about if they don't get what they want—will they have lost something? If they feel conflicted about staying, why? What are they afraid of? Is it a fear worth overcoming? He gives them time to consider these questions, then asks Bernice to talk about how it felt to share her story.

Bernice says that prior to telling her story, she had thought the furniture was mostly to blame for making her feel unhinged. What she hadn't realized was that constantly being dismissed had made her feel that way too. In the aftermath of Bluebeard, she had been a spectacle, talked about but never heard. It was a disconcerting way to be ignored.

She explains the relief she felt when she finally told the group about the furniture. Not because she was sure they believed her but because they believed she was worthy of being listened to, because they took her seriously. It was a favor she wanted to return. She would feel respected if they all stayed, saw these few weeks through, for the sake of reciprocity.

"I mean, really heartfelt," says Ruby. Her head is tilted almost to her shoulder as she forces her fingers through a particularly tenacious clump of hair. "Personally, I just want the same amount of blackmail on you all as you all have on me."

Bernice frowns.

Will looks between them but lets it rest. He suggests they wrap up break with a little activity.

"Great. Can't wait to hear what it is," Ruby deadpans.

"Primal screams," he reveals with a smile. "What do you think of that, Ruby?"

"Worse than I expected."

"I know, I know," he says. "It sounds silly." This is part of his charm: his ability to remain unoffended, his perpetual confidence in the process, his capacity to keep plowing ahead. He explains the benefits of primal screams, references a "truly groundbreaking" fMRI study, notes the lighting up of the amygdala.

"I'm *great* at this kind of thing," says Ashlee brightly. "Basically group therapy and group date activities are the same thing."

"That's not concerning at all," says Ruby, but Ashlee is already screaming at the top of her lungs, her mouth wide as an opera singer's.

Ruby screams half-heartedly. Raina emits a reluctant yelp. With encouragement from Will, Bernice works her way up to a long, mournful cry that would embarrass her if she weren't so tired. Gretel refuses to participate, puts her hand on her jaw as if it might be incapable of opening wide enough to scream.

"One more activity?" Will asks. He proposes crying next, in the name of catharsis. He lists the health benefits of activating the lacrimal glands.

Ruby says she can only take so much bullshit in one day and refuses to cry. Gretel says she can't cry, so there's little use in trying. Ashlee fake cries so she won't ruin her makeup. Bernice cries easily.

It takes Raina two minutes to cry, just a single tear glistening down her cheek.

"What are you thinking about?" asks Will.

"Someone I knew," Raina says, "once upon a time."

"Oooh," says Ashlee, perking up. "A mysterious lover? With a tragic fate?"

"Nothing like tragedy to give you a hard-on," says Ruby.

Bernice's expression says, *Seriously?*

"Just what you want to say," says Ruby.

Will nods. "Honesty," he says. "That's the policy."

"I think you're the one who loves tragedy," says Bernice cautiously. "I'm not jealous of my furniture because they're more tragic than me—that's why *you'd* be jealous of them. You would rather be dead than have a boring story." She pauses. "Maybe the reason you try to turn everything into a joke is because we threaten you, Ruby. Because you always need to be the most interesting person in the room."

"You think making it through one fucking news cycle gives you the street cred to psychoanalyze me?" says Ruby.

"Why did you come here looking like this?" asks Bernice. "If your identity isn't about having the best worst story, then why not just get rid of the coat? It appears to be causing you a lot of problems."

"Oh, and your house full of dead women isn't causing you problems?" says Ruby.

"It's an entirely different situation."

"Is it? A relic of your trauma, making you miserable, et cetera?"

"I'm *helping* them," says Bernice.

"Are you?" says Ruby. "Or is it some martyr complex built on survivor's guilt? Some fucked-up hair-shirt thing?"

Will, who has been leaning back in his chair watching the volley, leans forward. "Interesting word choice," he says.

"Oh, nice," says Ruby, grabbing at a red-stained sleeve. "Clever."

"Personally," says Ashlee, "I only wear stuff that reminds me of *good* things." She splays her hand out next to her face: five pink, pointy nails and one massive rock.

"For fuck's sake, Ashlee, are you peddling those or what?" says Ruby. "Remind me why you're here if you're so fucking happy."

"I'm having a tiny bit of trouble adjusting to the real world," she says. "I mean, not that reality TV *isn't* the real world," she corrects. "Actually, if you think about it, reality TV *is* basically the real world, just without the internet and stuff? Which maybe makes reality TV *realer* than the real world? Because the real world has the internet, which is virtual reality, which is not, like, regular reality, which is why people are so mean on it?"

"I don't envy you kids today," says Raina. "The internet is worse than the tabloids. Back then at least it was possible to be forgotten."

"Not when you become part of the zeitgeist," says Ruby.

"See?" says Bernice. "You're so proud."

"Do you wear the coat so people remember who you are?" Ashlee asks, a look of extreme pity on her face. "Because your thing happened so long ago? I mean, Sad Face, but you're old news."

"You'll be old news one day too, Ash," Ruby says, "and your coworkers and your boyfriends and your fuckbuddies will Google you, and the first thing they'll see is your giant fucking mouth, wide-open, surrounded by a bunch of dicks."

"What?" says Raina.

"It's called Photoshop," says Ashlee, picking at her belly gem. "I've never been around that many dicks."

"Too bad," Ruby says.

* * *

I walked uptown as the sun beat down. People always ask how I can wear the coat all summer, but the truth is I kind of like that dizzy feeling of impending heatstroke, like being drugged and hugged at the same time. It's a kind of hell, the seventh circle, which—if I remember from the CliffsNotes—is the one for self-loathers and sodomites, and I'm guilty of both. Dante's had a boiling river of blood and fire-rain, which, if you ask me, isn't an especially bad punishment for a bunch of masochists.

I'd only made it a few blocks when I got a ping from a match on Tinder. In his first picture, he was double-fisting beer in a dark bar, his eyes glowing like an animal's because of the flash. He had a dark brown beard and tufts of dark hair sprouting from the collar of his T-shirt.

The message said we matched. Studded with a winky face.

Another ping: ur very close to me.

Ping: we could have a drink?

I wrote back: It's not even noon.

Ping: u at work?

Ping: got some place to be?

As if not having a place to be was a reason to be somewhere other than where you already were. But he *was* only two blocks away. I could take a detour, see what his deal was.

I found him smoking outside of a gloomy bar, looking devilish in the red glow of the window's neon sign that was, for some reason, lit late morning. He stared at me as I approached, smiling a smile almost concealed by his big brown beard. His eyes were glassy from drinking, his pupils huge, hungry looking, and he clicked his tongue against the roof of his mouth, a disguised catcall.

"Cigarette?" he asked.

"No thanks," I said.

"Come on," he said, like I was killing his chill. He was already pulling out a little pouch of tobacco and a rectangle of rolling papers from his back pocket. He made a table of his thigh, his sneaker flat against the wall of the building. "Stop and smell the roses," he said.

I had already stopped. "Which part of this is roses?" I asked.

"Your face is red," he said, pausing his cigarette work to look me in the eyes, "like a rose."

A romantic cliché wrapped in an insult. My kind of guy.

"I'm getting hot just looking at you," he said. "Why are you wearing that giant coat, when it's, like, ninety out?"

"Sweating out my sins."

"Mmm-hmmm," he said. He licked his lips. "Sinssss."

I could see how the afternoon would unspool if I stuck around: flirty, half-mean banter, drinking at the bar, coming back outside for another cigarette, deciding on a pretense for going to his apartment. It seemed like a lot of work.

The guy handed me the rolled cigarette with a wink, like he was bribing a doorman.

"Actually," I said, pocketing the cigarette in the silky confines of my coat, "do you live around here?"

He did not, it turned out, live around there. We had to take the F train to get to his tiny studio in Brooklyn. He was drunker than I thought—he couldn't figure out which subway was going downtown.

We sat side by side on the orange seats. "Are you thinking dirty thoughts?" he whispered in my ear, his hands slithering around me. Neither of us smelled great. I was hoping it was like garlic breath, that somehow we'd just cancel each other out.

"Let's not speak until we get there," I said and pulled out my headphones.

He looked offended. His lip curled to reveal a flash of yellow-white teeth above his eraser-pink gums. But then he decided I must be flirting and fished some earbuds out of his back pocket.

My phone was out of space, so I had only one song downloaded on it, which I listened to on repeat as I stared at my hazy ghost reflection, the dark wall whizzing behind it. She didn't look like me. She looked like some crazy person who'd just run a marathon in the desert. Maybe it was attractive in a sort of tousled way?

It wasn't, but the guy was too drunk to care.

He lived on the third story of a five-story walk-up. The apartment itself was a stuffy, compact rectangle with a galley kitchen and no overhead lighting.

He flipped on some lights and went to the bathroom as I waited by the stiff gray futon. A little AC unit cranked away, but it wasn't doing anything productive. It felt like a metaphor for my life.

With the sleeve of my coat, I wiped away sweat that had beaded up along my hairline, felt the dirt and grease drag across my forehead.

Through a window across the street I could see two people, gray and featureless as shadow puppets, shuffling around what seemed to be a kitchen, maybe preparing to host a dinner party later that night. I didn't know why I couldn't be one of those people, with friends you wanted to have over once in a while.

The guy returned with bottles of beer, and we sat together, side by side on the futon, in the awkward almost-silence of the bumbling AC.

"Don't you want to take off your coat?" he asked.

"Not really," I said.

I guzzled the beer down because I was hungry. The drunkenness hit me hard behind the eyeballs. He seemed impressed.

Suddenly his fingers were up my sleeves, feeling across the raised lines of scars on my arms. "What's this?" he asked, too brightly, already knowing. I was annoyed at his self-congratulatory tone. He was so thrilled he'd scored a masochist, like a thief realizing the bank vault was already opened.

"What do you think it is?" I snapped.

"That's why you wear the coat," he said.

"I wear the coat," I said, "because this wolf tried to kill me."

He laughed, clearly thinking it was a joke. He hadn't recognized me at all. His skin was moist with sweat, matting down the hair that came to a straight line a little too far forward on his forehead.

"Why would a pretty girl like you do this to herself?" he asked. His smile curled at the ends. "You're into some messed up stuff, huh?"

He ran a finger back and forth across a short but thick raised scar that ran perpendicular to the vein in my forearm. His finger running across that scar made my heart ache with longing. Not for him but for something. If I knew what I wanted, I would have it, and I wouldn't be using my arm as a cutting board. Sometimes the cutting fulfilled some immediate surface need, like eating the first thing you see in the fridge when you're hungry: olives, pickles, slices of American cheese.

He jumped up and wiggled his mouse around on his computer. From the speakers, a deep, bellowing voice sang. I tried to sink into the sadness of it.

He slid his hand down the front of my skirt, into my sweaty underwear, his fingers rubbing circles as he watched me with a smirk.

With his free hand, he brushed the hair that had fallen around my face, tucking it gently behind one ear. I didn't like it. I mean, we'd only just met. "You're really hot," he said. "I mean . . . temperature." He gave up on jerking me off, felt my forehead with a flat palm, then slunk his hand around the neck of my coat and slipped it off of me, holding it by the skinny scruff of the neck before throwing it over the arm of the futon.

He pulled off my shirt next, dropping it to the floor. He rubbed his hands on my back, stopping when he felt the scars: four even, raised lines on my right shoulder blade.

He wanted to get a good look at them. "Whoa," he said. He followed the four scars with four fingers. "This is fucking insane."

"A wolf tried to kill me." The shock-value punch line I love to repeat.

"That kind of shit is always happening," he said.

"Wolves?" I said.

"Not *actual* wolves," he said. "Like, guys trying to kill women. Have you heard about the girl? What's her name?"

"Bernice, the Bluebeard girl," I said, since it was fresh from last week.

"No," he said. "The one trapped in a basement for a decade. Or was it an attic? Did she escape through a heating duct? Was she nailed in a box under a bed?"

"You're combining a bunch of different people," I said. "Have you heard about the one they called Little Red?"

"Yeah, what's that one? Mom lets the kid wander off alone? Girl refuses to follow directions? Girl gets distracted? Girl is easy, flirts with wolf? Girl gets what she deserves?"

"Something like that," I said.

"Speaking of wolves," he said, snickering. "Hands and knees, yeah?"

"Whatever," I said, assuming the position.

I was surprised by his chosen entryway but—what can I say?—I didn't object. You never know if someone's testing your boundaries or preparing to barrel right through them. That's the advantage of not having boundaries in the first place.

I thought about whether or not I actually wanted to be there. This was exactly how women ended up mutilated and dead in garbage cans. There was a certain thrill, anyway, in the possibility of the day going in unpredictable directions. I couldn't help but think there was a lesson at the pulsing heart of things, where heat, darkness, and danger lay.

There was a lot of pushing with no give, and then, without warning, my body relented. It reminded me of the moment when, trying to shove a mattress through a tiny doorframe, you're surprised to find that you've barreled your way through to the other side. I won't say it didn't hurt. A quick, sharp, stinging pain at first. I felt hot and cold, bloated and light-headed, like my body was being filled to the brim and spilling over, like I might need to throw up just to make space.

But I also felt electric with energy, lit up.

He was starting slow, out of necessity, just trying to gain some ground, while I was biting on the knuckle of my balled-up fist. Even without the coat, I was hot. Sweat rolled down my face, stinging my eyes, dripping off my chin and nose. My back itched. His hands were slipping around my sides.

One of the most alluring aspects of the position was that we didn't have to look at each other. I knew what I looked like: my skirt pushed up to my waist, my hands clutching at the fur of my coat hung over the arm of the futon as he pounded away behind me. The background music was now just wailing without instrumental accompaniment, and the futon rocked with an unsteady creak, out of rhythm with the song.

"You are a fucking bad, bad girl," he was saying.

I closed my eyes and saw light speckled behind my eyelids. I imagined the man creature-like, humping and hairy: hair matted like a carpet over his chest, hair creeping messily down his back, tangly beard crawling up his cheeks.

"Don't talk to strangers," my mom had always said. "Don't bother with men," she said. "Men, they're dogs. And worse." But then why was she always talking to strangers, men at the grocery store, at the gas station, at Parents' Night? Why was she always writing her number on a slip of paper, clasping it into a pair of hands? Strangers crept through our house like ghosts. I felt them like that, as an absence, my mom distracted, tossing the Cheerios on the table, saying, "Come on, come on, hurry it up. I'm not driving you if you miss the bus."

The guy was amping it up, smacking me around a little, the futon pitching back and forth, the grunting growing louder and louder behind me. I rode the wave of pleasure-pain, nauseating and thrilling, an endorphin rush, a runner's high.

Overcome, and then it was over—for me, anyway. He was still going at it, but suddenly the whole thing was uncomfortable and unattractive, embarrassing even.

I was afraid he would never stop. I watched my sweat drip onto my fur, wet splotches bleeding into other wet splotches, so I couldn't tell the order in which the mess was made. A dull throb developed in my lower abdomen, which I attempted to counter-balance by biting my knuckle. The oft-used phrase "up in her guts" seemed suddenly, viscerally real.

The air was stifling. Goose bumps rose on my skin. I felt like I couldn't breathe. I wanted to put on my coat. "You're such a bad girl," he said. The whine in his voice suggested he was about to wrap up. "You're all fucked up."

* * *

Ruby raises an eyebrow, daring them to comment.

"Ugh," says Ashlee, scrunching up her nose, taking the bait.

"Grow up," says Ruby. She scratches at her cheek, which has dried stiff and cracked like a desert landscape. Tiny peels of red flake to the floor.

"Does anyone know what this incident might have to do with Ruby's past?" Will asks the group, looking around at them seriously. When no one answers he prompts, "What have you heard about the interactions between Ruby and the wolf?"

"Oh, oh!" says Ashlee, shooting her hand into the air. "I know. This totally tracks! I heard that *she* seduced *him*."

"Hm," says Will, nodding.

Raina looks at him in disbelief.

Ruby scrapes a curl of dried red off her thumbnail.

"You must have heard the rumor, Raina," says Will.

"I haven't believed it," says Raina. "She was a kid. She couldn't *seduce* anyone."

"It's important to address the rumors," says Will.

"I don't think we should waste time on rumors that can't possibly be true," says Raina.

"Aren't you the one who said the impossible is possible?" Ruby says. She stands up abruptly. "I need coffee."

"You have *heatstroke*," says Gretel.

"Ruby, let's stay with this," says Will.

"Maybe that shit works on Bernice, but it doesn't work on me."

"I can get you some more water," says Raina.

"Thanks, Mom," says Ruby, already pouring herself coffee. "But I can take care of myself."

"Can you?" asks Gretel.

Ruby twists around. Her eyes narrow behind her smudged glasses. "I've survived so far," she says. She turns back to the table, pinches her fingers over three sugar packets, shakes the sugar down with three aggressive wrist flicks. "'Can you?'" she mimics in a mumble, tearing the packets open all at once and dumping them into her coffee. "What about you, Gretel?"

"You don't know anything about me," says Gretel.

"Not much, no, because you've hardly said two words," says Ruby. "But I have eyes." She shakes in too much powdered creamer, thrusts the container back onto the table.

"What's that supposed to mean?" says Gretel.

"She's probably talking about the anorexia," says Ashlee.

"It's my teeth," says Gretel, alarmed. She glides four fingers down each side of her jaw, as if to say it's all of her teeth, it's her whole mouth. "It hurts to eat."

"Sure," says Ruby, heading back to her seat. "Nothing about your experience would fuck up your relationship with food."

"You don't get to analyze everyone else's problems and not your own," says Bernice.

"What do you think I've been doing for the last hour?" says Ruby.

"You've been telling us this long, drawn-out story about—what?—the series of bad choices you made today? Without any self-reflection? Without talking about your *actual* issue? And now you're lashing out at everyone else?"

"What is my *actual issue*?" says Ruby.

"Well," says Bernice, "I mean, you haven't said anything about the wolf."

"The wolf?" says Ruby with a laugh, gripping her coat. "This whole fucking story is about the wolf. My whole life is about the wolf." She flips up her hood. "Fine," she says. "The wolf."

* * *

Even as a kid, my vision sucked, so when I first saw him, he was just a blurry figure standing on hind legs, feet crossed at the ankles, leaning against a tree in the wooded area that hemmed the cul-de-sac. Handsome and human as far as I could tell. But the texture of his skin was weird, shining soft and silver in the dappled canopy light.

I was squatting in the cul-de-sac halfway between my apartment building and my grandma's house. My bike was lying on the pavement next to a bag of canned soups, which I was supposed to deliver to the latter destination. Instead, I'd been rubbing sticks together over a pile of leaves, trying to make fire so I could light a cigarette I'd stolen from my mom's purse.

I was twelve. Maybe I looked older, fourteen. I was wearing my mom's lipstick and blush, a red corduroy skirt, and a red hoodie. The hoodie was supposed to cover the new boobs. The cigarette was supposed to make me look cool. I'd taken the long way, to avoid certain kids who called me a pussy. Not that I couldn't hurl back "dickhead" or "shitforbrains," but some days you just weren't in the mood.

"I see London," said the figure's deep, humming voice. "I see France."

I stood up. I shrugged. I winked, one of my mom's signature moves.

The figure stretched down strangely onto all fours, began to slink around me in a wide circle, shoulder blades shifting as he walked.

"What are you?" I asked, squinting toward him.

"A wolf," he said.

"Wolves aren't supposed to talk," I said.

"Girls aren't supposed to smoke cigarettes."

I'd left the cigarette on the pavement. I stepped on it, as if he would unsee it.

As he slunk closer, details emerged. His face was an elegant arrangement of triangles: two raised ears and a pert, pointed face.

His eyes were the color of honey. His pupils, wide as mouths. His muzzle was regal, pointed upward, punctuated by a wet nose, dark as potting soil. When he smiled, I saw his eyeteeth, razor-sharp. *His teeth!* I thought. *I should be terrified of those teeth.* But he was the handsomest creature I had ever seen.

He was very close to me. His soft tail wisped around me. He sniffed at me, inhaled me. He was seeing me beyond sight. His sniffs made my skin feel cool, extraction of essence and heat.

His soft tail flicked between my legs, under my skirt.

Something inside me—it's terrible—tingled.

His nose and tail were everywhere. I felt like liquid about to boil over. A strange quiver rushed through me.

I had a brief, idiotic fantasy, one that I unfortunately shared with Barbara Walters when she asked: "Why didn't you run?" It was of the wolf and me going out together to a restaurant with pink table-cloths and flickering candles, devouring rare steak with white linen napkins tied around our necks.

But it wasn't that kind of courtship.

He laughed with a growl, like he knew something I didn't. "So you're that kind of girl," he said.

I was embarrassed, confused. I reached my hand out to steady myself, but there was nothing to hold on to. My hand looked spotted and strange in the light, like the hand of a leper. My eyes moved to the sleeve of my blood-red hoodie. Later, soon, blood would be all around me, and it would not be bright red; it would be like rust.

Later, after I did all the things you're not supposed to do, after I told him where I was going and who would be there, like handing him a fucking menu; after I meandered through the neighborhood light-headed and slow and thinking of him; after I was very, very late to my grandma's; after I heard no answer when I knocked on the door; after I walked in anyway; after I thought his face could somehow, possibly, be the face of my grandma—a mistake I will never live down, that I can't even explain, that has led people to wonder if I knew exactly what would happen—after he pulled his lips back into a terrifying snarl, revealing his mountainous pink gums, his sharp gleaming teeth, that's when I finally turned to run. But it was too late, way too late; his claws were tearing into my back, his mouth was expanding around me, his teeth zigzagging at the edge of my vision.

And then there was nothing. Just dark and dark and dark, hot and airless and reeking of acid. I took in great hyperventilating gasps, but I couldn't get air. I kicked and squirmed and felt something react. The freshly clawed cuts stung in the acid, but the pain grounded me. I sunk into it. It was the only thing I could hold on to when everything else was slipping away.

I awoke on my grandma's bedroom floor covered in wolf guts. My grandma's lifeless, pink body was crumpled facedown in a pool of blood. I couldn't assimilate the information. The last time I had seen her, she had been very alive, her fingers creasing paper, teaching me to fold stars from shiny silver strips.

The plastic bag of canned soup sat on her nightstand. It seemed like in a moment she would crawl out of that puddle, would open a can with her red-handled can opener, would glop it into two of the white, silverware-scratched soup bowls, pop them into the microwave one by one, one for me and one for her, mine first.

I threw up. My red hoodie was soaked and heavy and reeking, but I knew this more as fact than scent. It was like my brain had been overloaded, some circuit broken. My shoulder throbbed.

The wolf was strung from a ceiling beam by a single paw, a great bloody hole revealing the mushy interior where I had spent some time. A man in a buffalo plaid jacket was by his side, a bloody hunting knife clutched in his fist, a Western 45 handgun tucked into his baggy jeans. My school was full of kids who would grow up to become this guy, a suburban conservative who shot at tin cans and snorted coke.

He rocked back and forth on his toes, admiring his work. "Man, oh, man!" he said. He cracked his knuckles in his fists. He couldn't stop moving. "What a day!" he shouted. "No one's gonna believe this."

He jerked his head in my direction. "Damn," he said. "You're alive! You're back from the dead!" He looked over at my grandma. "Right, right, right," he said. "You look sick," he said. "You're covered in blood. You're all red." He kept moving. I think he was sort of chewing his tongue. "I guess I'm a hero," he said. "I was outside," he said, as if he were talking to reporters. "I was out there and I heard a scream, and I was like—somebody needs my help!"

I walked toward the dead wolf, whom I had fraternized with not hours before, whom I had led to this very place. I walked right up to his glistening amber eye, so close that I could make out the reflection of a girl in a red hoodie. I shifted my focus to a bead of blood swelling on a tuft of his gray hair. It bloated and bloated, then dropped to the floor under its own weight.

The man rocked on his feet. "You're audacious, man," he said to me. "You're all red. Sorry about the guts. But what a shot, right? It's not even hunting season. I used a fucking *handgun*." He stopped rocking for a second. "Hey, you mute? What's your name?"

Ruby, I thought, but I couldn't seem to say it. I didn't feel like me anymore, and in a way I guess I wasn't.

"All right, then, Little Red," he said, and he was rocking again. He swiped his knife through the air. "I'm gonna make you a coat, Little Red. A big-ass, fluffy coat you can wear when you're older so you can walk around like a bad bitch."

Soon the man and I stood outside the door of my apartment

building, his bloodstained finger on our buzzer. My hoodie and skirt had dried stiff as cardboard. My skin stung so sharply that I wanted to crawl out of it.

"Sorry, kid," said the guy. He sighed. "Fuck, I should've called the police. Man, I'm coming down hard."

When my mother opened the door, I started to cry.

Were there really men all around who destroyed me, saved me? The beast—a wolf—and the man with the gun? Or was the hero my mom, who set straight to work, hosed me down in the backyard, scrubbed me numb with a dark yellow sponge, raked her fingers through my hair until they slid clean through. A lukewarm darkness spread over us, salted in stars.

My mom filled the yellow tub with cold tomato juice, and I bathed in it, like a dog after being sprayed by a skunk. My skin grew redder and redder, until it looked like I'd been turned inside out. When I stood up for a rinse, a tomato peel sticking to my stomach looked like torn flesh.

The hospital, the police, my grandmother's funeral—a blur of white rooms, blue curtains, fluorescent lights, pens tapping on desks. There was the stupid TV interview, the stupid questions I was too young to understand were traps. Funny, how they can doubt you and blame you in the very same breath. I remember the studio light, the glint of it traveling back and forth across the toes of my black shoes.

But at night there was never enough light. My mother tucked me into bed, but I stopped her before she bent down to kiss me good night. "More light," I said, and she rubbed my hair. I squinted up at her. I made sure her teeth were her teeth and her mouth was her mouth and her ears were her ears. "It's okay, baby," she said. But when she closed the door, darkness expanded around me: airless and reeking and wide as a mouth.

* * *

Ruby's sitting with her hood flipped up, her bare feet perched on the edge of the chair, her arms linked around her knees, not caring that her underwear is showing under her skirt. The fur coat is drying stiff, little points of fur hanging down as if tired of dripping. She hugs her legs tighter, puts her head down, cheekbones to knees, so she looks like a giant, bloodstained fur ball.

"Oh, Ruby," says Raina.

Ruby's head snaps up. "I was flirting with the enemy." Her face is darkened by the hood.

"This wasn't your fault," says Raina.

"Come on, I gave the fucker the address."

"I practically moved in with the fucker," says Bernice.

"Great, so we're both idiots," says Ruby.

Ruby's head is pounding. What possessed her to tell this story, the whole thing, the real version? She hadn't planned to. She's gotten off track, as usual, took this dumb detour, the long way with a bad view.

Ruby pushes her left hand up underneath her right sleeve, up to where the elbow bends, and then she drags her gritty fingers down, feeling the raised skin of her most recent cuts, furrows like a freshly plowed field. What she would like more than anything is a razor so she could slice out this bad feeling. Who are they to say it would be a bad idea, that it wouldn't help?

"Ruby," says Raina gently. "You were lured by a predator."

"I was *into* it."

"But that's a predator's bait," says Bernice. "That's the manipulation. It doesn't mean it's your fault."

"Oh, right, like you don't blame yourself for hooking up with Bluebeard?" Ruby says.

"Well, maybe I should lay off myself a little."

"And anyway, aren't you the one who said I loved tragedy?"

"I didn't mean you were *asking for it*," says Bernice. "You were a kid. Now you're an adult capable of making certain decisions."

"I'm not getting rid of the coat," says Ruby.

Gretel touches her cheek gingerly, as if she has a sore tooth. "I understand why you'd keep the coat as evidence," she says. "But I can't understand why you'd wear it."

"Evidence?" says Ruby. "Who cares about evidence?"

"Don't take for granted that you know what happened," says Gretel, "that you have proof."

"It's not like there's a trial," says Ruby, "except the trial of public opinion, which actually seems pretty immune to evidence."

"Why would you want to be constantly reminded?" asks Gretel.

"Is there some option where I can forget?" Ruby says.

"You're avoiding the essential question, Ruby," says Will. "Why do you wear the coat?"

"Because this coat made me who I am," says Ruby. "Because who the fuck would I be without it?"

* * *

I awoke in the guy's apartment in the middle of the afternoon, sprawled on the futon. I was covered in so much salt that for a second I thought I'd been brined, but it was just the dregs of evaporated sweat. The dude was zonked on the floor. He looked completely harmless and not even that hairy. I nabbed a couple of twenties off his desk, got dressed, put on the coat.

Then I noticed the smell, so strong that not even the beef and garlic wafting up from the restaurant downstairs could mask it. It was an overwhelming, acrid, bacterial armpit stench. It was like cotton balls had been stored under my pits, then shoved up my nose. I cupped my hand over my nose and mouth, but that seemed only to capture, to sharpen the scent.

The smell was me, was my coat. The problem was worse than the immediate sweaty reek. The smell had layers: coffee dregs and stale beer, metallic blood and salty tears, ashy cigarettes and a fishy rot that I wanted not to be old cum.

My face jerked toward the ceiling in a quiet gag. I tried to gulp in fresh air, but it was so humid it just felt like a mass of fur stuck in my throat.

The guy on the floor rolled over. I checked my phone for the time. Maybe I could still make it to the fur shop, accomplish one fucking thing before group.

I tiptoed out of the apartment, pausing at the door to unmatch with the guy, then dashed down the stairs, out of the building, and to the subway, slipping sideways into a car just before the doors dinged closed. Forty minutes later, I hopped out in Midtown, sprinting toward the fur shops, weaving through traffic, sliding between people, turning at intersections to avoid red lights, doubling back if I had to, my fur coat flying behind me like a cape, my heart wild, my lungs burning. Nothing I ran past registered. It was just me in a race against time, me against my own inescapable sweaty stink.

By the time I reached the fur block, I was drenched in sweat and dizzy, gasping for air. Outside one of the shops, I heard a man shouting, "Her is dead! Her is dead!"

What did it mean? Did he hate women? Did he want to obliterate gendered pronouns? I wasn't totally opposed. Why did he have to be so annoying about it?

The guy was skinny and holding a big sign on a stick. The poster board bent backward as he paced in front of one of the fur shops.

I walked closer.

The sign had a bunch of laser-printed pictures of skinned rabbits, hanging on hooks or heaped in piles, all bright red muscle and shiny black eyes. NOT SO CUTE ANYMORE, it read in black Sharpie.

I walked toward the door of the shop, and he hustled in front of me, blocking the way. "Her is dead," he shouted. His face was so close to mine that I saw each bead in his sweat-mustache.

"What is this?" I asked. "A performance piece?"

"A *protest*," he said.

"Her is dead?"

"FUR is dead."

"Oh."

"Your coat," he said, "is an atrocity."

I bared my teeth. I smiled. "This coat," I said, "killed my grandma."

He didn't blink. "An eye for an eye leaves the whole world blind," he said.

"Eat or be eaten," I said.

"You'll pay for this," he said. "You go into that store? I promise, you'll regret it."

I'd never been in a fur shop before. The store was packed from floor to ceiling with coats and jackets of every style and type, wall-to-wall death, scents of mothballs and leather. In general I agreed with the fuck-up outside. It made me sad, to think of all of those hairless rabbits, stripped naked to bare muscle.

The AC was cranked to freezing, and the sweat felt cold on my face. After a minute, I didn't even smell myself. The coat suddenly seemed okay, fine, useful.

The store owner appeared from behind a rack of dark leather jackets. "Hello," he said. Hair sprouted in his V-neck in a way I liked; hair was combed across his forearms, his hands, his knuckles, as if drawn on with marker.

"How much to clean this?" I asked.

"For you?" he said with a smile. "Sixty dollars." Then he seemed to take in the state of my coat. "*That* coat?" he asked. "My God, that coat is horrible."

"So I've been told," I said.

"But you've come to the right place," he said. "Nobody else on this block would touch it for sixty bucks."

He motioned for me to take the coat off with a four-fingered wave, like he was directing a car into a parking space. "This is absolutely terrible," he said. "You can't walk around like this. What's your number?" he asked. "I'll call you."

"Why?" I asked.

"To tell you when your coat is finished," he said.

Why hadn't I read some store reviews online? Maybe this place ruined coats, washed them with fucked-up chemicals. Maybe they stole the coats and resold them with fake tags. Or whatever. I don't know anything about fur.

As if reading my mind, he said, "What? You don't trust me? You think I stayed in business this long because I'm bad at my job?"

"I don't have the money," I said, though technically I did have the twenties I'd swiped from that guy's desk.

"Check, money order, credit card—chip or swipe, internet money, I take it all," he said.

"What about trades?" I asked with an eyelash flicker, just to see what he'd say.

"I'm no prostitute," he said.

"Never mind," I said.

"Never mind what? The whole thing?"

"I changed my mind," I said.

"It's a health hazard!" he shouted after me.

As I stepped out of the door and into the sun, a bright red liquid flashed around me, enveloping me in wet warmth. Was it blood? Was blood everywhere? Was it coming out of me or falling into me? Was I bleeding spontaneously and profusely, like on day two of my period, which I call The Civil War, my body battling itself? Had I been shot or stabbed or slashed with a knife? Was I dying?

As I stumbled backward, excitement shot through me, like I was on the peak of an unfinished roller coaster, going up, up, up, about to flail out into the sky.

I was sure I was dying, and my brain did its best to savor the moment, conjuring tastes and images and feelings that I knew, quite suddenly, I would miss, like the jolty bitterness of coffee and the way red wax peels smoothly off those rounds of cheese and the breeze—any breeze, even if it's carrying some garbage scent from a forgotten corner of Queens, which it often is, in my neck of the woods. I didn't even care about these things most of the time.

Maybe this is what I wanted, some dramatic, fireball finish.

"It's always something with you," Emil had said to me once after I'd spent the night in the bathroom of a twenty-four-hour café because it turned out my roommate was friends with a bunch of convicts. "You're always involved in some weirdo catastrophe." He wasn't exactly wrong.

Sometimes I felt like a drug addict chasing some original high. Or like a soldier I'd read about, who said that being almost-dead made him feel extra-alive, that the thought of losing everything made the world appear more beautiful. How can being basic-alive be interesting after all that adrenaline shooting through you? How can daily life compete with the thrill?

I found my footing, felt the liquid dripping down my face, looked down to see my fur wet-matted, bright red. Red was running down my hands in rivulets. A bare-knuckle fight? Who had won? Who was I up against in the first place? I felt no pain.

"What the hell!" shouted the shop owner, who'd run outside.

"It's not real! It's not real!" a voice shouted, and I saw the protester, cowering against the store window, a five-gallon bucket dropped at his side, red dripping from its lip.

I wiped my eyes with my hand. I licked at the liquid that had dripped onto my lips. More starchy than metallic. It wasn't real blood. I wasn't injured at all.

"I tell everyone this never happens," said the shop owner. "This has only ever happened to Joan Rivers."

The protester was shaking. He put his hand over his mouth, then took it away, so his mouth was covered in a red handprint.

"I'll clean the coat for free! I'll just do it for humanity!" the shop owner shouted. I wanted to tackle the guy—not the protester, the shop owner. I clutched my coat around me. It was heavy and wet. Red liquid dripped into a pool at my feet. I could see my reflection there: dark, distorted, shimmering. It was beautiful, in some wild way. Rabbit or wolf, I couldn't tell which.

Both, I guess. Probably a little of both.

The Office

Will—his skin bright, his features perfectly symmetrical—undresses in front of the mirror as soon as he's home. Bright slits of light cut into the dim study from the edges of the drawn shades, but they catch nothing in the air, not one floating mote. That's how thorough the cleaning lady is. The room smells faintly of lemon and pine.

He throws his white button-down onto the gleaming wood floor, pulls his white undershirt over his head, and reveals—to himself— his perpetually flexed, evenly tanned, washboard abs. They were modeled after Michelangelo's *David*. The lightly threaded happy trail is a modern addition.

The abs are merely aesthetic; he can't actually move them. He can't say why he spent extra for a detail no one will see. The only way to get his money's worth now is to enjoy them himself.

So he does. In the floor-length mirror hidden behind a closet door, he admires his abs from different angles. He stands frontward and pretends to flex. He stands sideways, hangs his arms back, and pretends to flex again. He turns, takes the same stance on the other side, pretends to flex. Since the sides are symmetrical, both positions look exactly the same.

Then he makes the same mistake he makes every week: he touches his abs. He presses at his stomach with his finger, and there's a disappointing sensation of rubber on rubber, like he's poking another man's stomach with a pencil eraser. The spell is broken.

He remembers, once again, how his insides don't match his outsides. He remembers how incredibly itchy he is.

At the beginning of group, his skin merely tingles. By the end, it's a solid itch, and dreams of moisturizer vie for his attention. He's able to resist the itch during the abs-admiring phase because he dreads the rest of the routine so intensely that, for a moment, the need to procrastinate is stronger than the need for relief.

Now he must endure the part he despises. Will slides his leather belt out of the loops, tossing it onto the floor with his shirt. His beige pants follow. He faces away from the mirror as he removes his boxer briefs. These are just a formality. They cover nothing. He doesn't need to look at that smooth mound between his legs, that nude lump of skin, sexless as a Ken doll. It seems almost ridiculous now, that he sprung for the abs but didn't spring for this one final detail, despite the exorbitant price.

Astoundingly, the lack of sex organs isn't even the most humiliating part. The most humiliating part begins when he maneuvers his hands behind himself, placing one on each buttock. Then he inches his hands inward, his fingers crawling toward the crack where the skin is thick and can tolerate tugging—if he started farther up, he'd risk tearing the material. Once he feels the crease, he works his hands into himself until the seam begins to pull apart. The relief is progressive and punctuated by pain. The taut rubber snaps loose around him, and his muscles—his real muscles—start to relax back into their usual amorphous shapes. But the relief is measured by the friction-burn of rubber pinching off his dry skin.

He looks like a diver unzipping himself from a suit, or like a snake shedding skin, though not nearly as graceful. He works his fingers up behind him, and the invisible seam starts to rise of its own accord, up his back and to the nape of his neck. Now his real back is fully exposed, old and dry, and the thin, rubbery skin of Will hangs loose around him.

Now he must peel himself out of the delicate compression fabric. He must step backward out of himself—out of not-himself.

The man's real skin is dry-cracked and flaky. His gut sags. His hair is matted back in a lunch-lady hairnet. His face—well, it's his face. It's aged despite every intervention. Irrecoverable, at this point, unless he wants to start from scratch. Unless he wants a whole new face. Which he does. Which he now has for a few hours each week.

The irony is not beyond him, that each week he must essentially crawl out of his own ass. Sometimes the man inside of Will feels as if Will—that lifeless suit that houses him on Friday evenings— is torturing him, embarrassing him on purpose. But now Will is formless, spineless, shriveled and ugly, and sometimes the man prefers him this way.

The Will suit extracts moisture from his skin. The Will suit has to be spritzed every few hours when he's not wearing it. Will is needy, and this neediness makes the man feel owned. Will is part of him and supersedes him and smothers him. Will sucks him dry. What makes the man feel crazy makes Will look alive, look so entirely human that no one would ever guess that anything strange lies beneath.

The dressmakers—or, okay, they like to call themselves "engineers" now—who created Will are a team of women rumored to have, on several occasions, sourced fabric from the natural elements, who once (it was said) made a beautiful young woman appear to be a real donkey. He forgets the rest of that story. He can't even invent a reason why a beautiful woman would want to make herself ugly on purpose.

The man takes to the task of turning Will right side out again. He feels strange during this part, like he is sobering up after a drunken bender. The inside of the suit is smooth and textureless as a plastic ball, thin as plastic wrap in some spots. He has to be gentle—he forces himself to be gentle. He takes the puddle of Will's face and inverts the nose, presses the brow back into place. There are just holes where the teeth and eyes should be, which is why the man wears colored contacts. The man inverts the arms of the suit last, pressing his own arms back inside to reverse the fingers.

Then the man zips Will up into the garment bag, like a corpse into a body bag.

Week Three

Week Three

Ashlee

Ashlee checks her watch: Ruby is late—again. The watch also counts her steps—she barely has a thousand. That's bathroom, bed. That's apartment, subway, group, that's mostly thanks to all of the stairs, everything in this new city hiding out in underground lairs.

Ashlee is hiding out too—in the apartment, under sunglasses, under hats. This week, a baseball cap with the brim pulled down so far that her face is just a chin. The hat coordinates with her shirt, an oversized pin-striped Yankees jersey with the ends tied in a knot above low-rise, high-hemmed denim cutoffs.

No one else seems annoyed by Ruby's lateness, which annoys Ashlee further. Bernice certainly doesn't care—she's asleep. Her head has fallen forward and she snorts occasionally through one nostril. A cup of coffee, half drunk, sits between her thighs. Gretel might as well be asleep; she isn't doing anything, not really, just staring out the window at a brick wall, listening to whatever she listens to—a podcast, Ashlee guesses. She knows Gretel's type, one of those people who pretend to go with the flow while fighting the flow. It's like how you'd think a limp body would be easier to push off of you, but actually it's harder. Ashlee learned that on an obstacle-course group date.

Raina is reading a book on her e-reader, her legs crossed at the thighs, her silky, mid-length skirt sweeping out like a fan. It's so chic, Ashlee thinks, and the prettiest color, some hue between orange and gold. It reminds Ashlee of things she misses, like the fall in Pennsylvania, like amber-colored beer. Here in NYC, the girls drink clear. Lower in calories. It feels like years since she's been home.

Will's too busy looking at Raina to care that Ruby's late. He's leaning forward in his chair, watching her as if she's an endearing zoo animal he can't quite identify.

Raina glances up from her book and smiles at him. For a split second, he looks guilty, caught, then he smiles back. It's a charming smile, a lot of twinkle in the eyes and the teeth, and he extends it to include Ashlee. It gives Ashlee déjà vu. That's how few people smile at her now: smiles feel like memories.

"How are you today?" Raina asks them as she slides the e-reader into her tote.

"Totally great!" says Ashlee.

"Fine, excellent," says Will, scratching at his forearm.

"Do you need lotion?" Raina asks, and in an instant a metallic tube has been fished out of her purse.

Ashlee is in awe of this, of Raina's maternal instincts, the quick retrieval of necessities, which she always has on hand. She pulls them out like a dental assistant: wet wipes, water bottle, lotion. She knows what people need practically before they do. Ashlee's own stepmother was pretty good, but not this good.

"Lotion, Ashlee?" asks Raina, and it feels so nice to be included that she says yes.

She's still trying to rub the lotion into her sweaty hands when Ruby arrives, flinging the door open and apologizing at the same time, jolting Bernice awake. Ashlee has to lift her chin high in order to see Ruby from beneath the brim of her baseball cap.

Ruby's still wearing the coat. It's hideous—frizzy and splotchy and pink as a tongue, matching the frayed dyed ends of her hair. Ashlee catches a strong whiff of shampoo as Ruby breezes to the snack table. She must have washed it at home.

"Super nice of you to join us," Ashlee says, wiping the excess lotion on her thigh.

"Had a job interview," says Ruby.

"How did it go?" asks Will.

"Terrible," says Ruby.

"Didn't we, like, already decide that no one would ever hire you in that gross coat?" says Ashlee.

"And what the fuck are you wearing? You're dressed like a baseball player who robbed a bank." Ruby shoves a bunch of Oreos into her coat pocket and heads to her seat.

"My fiancé? Brandon?" says Ashlee. "He loves the Yankees."

"So you just like everything he likes?" says Ruby.

Ashlee picks at the knot on her jersey.

"And the hat?" asks Ruby. "Got a black eye under there or what?"

"No," says Ashlee. She removes the hat, pointer finger and thumb pinching the brim, engagement ring flashing. "Just keeping a chill profile. *Some* of us don't need to be the center of attention all the time."

Ruby flicks off her flip-flops, curls her legs up on the chair.

"You're still wearing the coat," Will says.

"Yeah, somehow I haven't been cured."

Will pushes up his rolled sleeves, as if preparing for hard work. "Why do we think Ruby's still wearing the coat?" he asks the group. After a silence, he asks them one by one.

"Holding on to old patterns," offers Bernice.

"An unwillingness to let go of the past," suggests Gretel.

"Attention," says Ashlee, who is aggressively snapping and un-snapping the strap of her baseball cap.

"Because when it's your own story it's harder to see it clearly," says Raina, "it's harder to know exactly what to do, and it's harder to do it. It's easier to see the big picture when you're not involved."

"You have more perspective when it's someone else's story," Will says, nodding. "Perhaps we can learn from one another."

"Are we supposed to be learning things?" asks Ruby. "I'm just here for the entertainment and free snacks." She pulls an Oreo from her pocket, twists the cookie open, then drags her front teeth through the cream, leaving tracks.

"I do know how much you like to be entertained, Ruby," says Will with a smile. "Which is why I came prepared with another activity."

Ruby raises a skeptical eyebrow, licks cream off her teeth, chipped tooth first.

The activity is musical chairs, sans music. "The silence," explains Will, "will create a space for *listening.*"

"Bet the fMRI data on Unmusical Chairs is really something," says Ruby. "Real amygdala lighter."

They move their belongings to the wall, place four chairs back-to-back in the center of the room, gather around them in a circle. Will sits on the sidelines, watching with a hand under his chin. "Let's go," he says, and they begin to march in a circle, Raina's heeled mules clacking, Ruby's flip-flops flapping, Ashlee's sneakers squeaking, Bernice's making more of a clomp, Gretel's Converse surprisingly silent.

"We could revolt," says Ruby. Her mouth is black with cookie. "We could all just sit on the floor instead."

"You scared?" says Ashlee.

"Of you?"

"Stop!" shouts Will, and they slide easily into chairs. Ashlee pumps her fist, looks around at her rivals, finds Gretel is the one left standing, right between two chairs.

"You didn't try at all," says Will.

"Pick your battles," says Gretel.

"Or give up before you can lose?" ventures Will.

"Sometimes it sounds like you just memorized a bunch of lines from a pop-psych bestseller," says Ruby.

"All right, all right, settle down," says Will.

They reset, pushing three empty chairs into a triangle, four of them marching around. When Will yells "Stop!" Ashlee and Ruby each take a chair easily. Bernice rushes for the last chair. Raina lets her take it, smiles at Bernice.

"You could've gone for it," says Bernice.

"I don't need it," says Raina, shaking her head.

Bernice cocks her head.

"What is it, Bernice?" Will wonders.

"Do *I* somehow need it?" asks Bernice.

"I didn't mean that," says Raina.

"Is there a reason you used the word 'need,' Raina?" asks Will.

"I was just trying to be friendly," says Raina. "It's just a game."

"Right," says Bernice, standing up. "Let's finish it."

"Let's stay with this," says Will.

"I'm just overtired and oversensitive," says Bernice.

"Aren't you the one who insists on psychoanalyzing everything?" asks Ruby.

Raina busies herself with carrying the extra chair to the sidelines.

"Do you have an analysis, Ruby?" asks Will.

"Yep," she says. "Bernice is pissed because Raina doesn't *need* to compete. She already has everything."

"What does she have?" asks Will.

"You know, three-hundred-dollar shoes, a husband, good looks, self-confidence," says Ruby.

"Why are you instigating a fight?" Bernice asks.

"Yeah," says Ashlee, trying to join in. "Is it because you *love* drama? Because you *love* making a skeptical of yourself?"

"*Spectacle,*" says Ruby. "And have you watched yourself on TV?"

"Don't pretend you're above her," says Bernice.

Spectacle, thinks Ashlee. Obvi the word is spectacle. Duh. She knew that, probably. Maybe she's dumb, but she's not so dumb that she doesn't know everyone thinks she's dumb, not so dumb that she doesn't know there's a reason for all these activities, like there's some metaphor or something.

"You know what I think?" says Ashlee, only just noticing that Bernice and Ruby have stopped arguing and stood up. "I think Unmusical Chairs is a metaphor." She smiles at Will.

"How so, Ashlee?" Will asks.

"It's a lot like being in group therapy," says Ashlee. "You know, it's like..." She hesitates. "It's like we're fighting and then teaming up?"

"It mimics the therapeutic process by revealing group tensions and alliances," says Will, nodding.

"Exactly," says Ashlee, beaming. "It mimics the therapeutic process."

"Eureka," says Ruby.

Ashlee can feel a frown arching across her face like a bridge.

"Can you just get up so we can finish the world's dumbest game?" Ruby says.

They complete the next round in awkward silence, Ashlee, Ruby, and Bernice circling the chairs like sharks around prey. Raina and Gretel watch with Will from the sidelines.

When Will shouts "Stop!" Ashlee and Ruby rush to opposite chairs so quickly that Bernice ends up looking between them, bewildered, off her game. "I'm annoyed," snaps Bernice before Will can even ask her how she feels.

They reset the chairs. Ashlee versus Ruby. The final showdown.

Ruby flicks off her flip-flops, pulls a bare foot to her butt, stretches one quad, then the other, her face shining with sweat. She flips up her hood, throws a few fake punches in the air like a boxer, winks at the women on the sidelines. Ashlee smirks.

They begin to circle the last chair. Ruby taunts, stretching her arms out wide, an incredible wingspan with her coat, the silky interior threadbare, the color of chewed bubble gum.

Ashlee sets her jaw. She knows she can win this. She won just about every group date on the show, never mind the biggest prize of all. Maybe these women all think she's an idiot, but she's the idiot who won the whole fucking thing.

"How do you feel?" Will asks from the sidelines.

"Jesus, Will," says Ruby. "Can't you see we're busy?"

They circle and circle and circle.

But for how long? wonders Ashlee. How long have they been circling and how long will they keep doing it?

She'll do it for as long as it takes.

"Stop!" shouts Will, and Ruby and Ashlee both lunge for the chair, landing at the exact same moment, pushing into each other's hips as hard as they can. Ruby is larger, should win this one easily, but suddenly, quickly, she stands up, and Ashlee, her full weight pushing on nothing, falls out of the chair. She smacks onto the linoleum floor, catching herself hard on her left arm, looks like a baseball player who's slid into first.

Ashlee jerks her head to clear the hair from her eyes, sees Ruby standing calmly above her, and realizes the chair is still empty. She scrambles to it, crawling while clutching her left arm, climbing frantically onto the seat.

"I won," she says, breathless, sitting in the chair dirty-kneed and cradling her arm. She looks at everyone, smiling, beaming, but everyone is not smiling back. They are not looking at her like she's a winner. They are looking at her more like she's a loser. She forces herself to keep smiling. "You jelly?" she pants, but no one answers. No one appears to be jelly at all.

She tries not to frown. "I can't help it if your stories end with you guys being losers whereas mine ends with me being a winner." She catches the glint of her engagement ring on the hand of her cradled arm, seems momentarily mesmerized by it. "I can't help it if I'm the only one here who got a happy ending. But it's like I said: it's just totally obvious I don't even belong here."

"We know," says Ruby. She tongues a cream-free round into her mouth like a church wafer, talks through cookie. "Because your story's a love story."

* * *

Talk about fairy-tale endings. Brandon and I are standing on the edge of a cliff on the Amalfi Coast overlooking vineyards and lemon groves and, like, a hundred bright houses stacked stadium-style toward a turquoise sea. I'm wearing this white Grecian gown with a silver beaded belt and matching heels, plus a gem-encrusted headband. The makeup artist somehow made my eyes look bigger and my cheekbones look sharper, and maybe my mouth is, like, a little toned down.

Brandon is wearing a black suit and a blue tie that's the color of the sky plus the sea. His jaw is so incredibly square. His eyes are glistening. My eyes are glistening. Basically everything is glistening because of the epic sunset emitting a super-romantic hazy golden glow. #nofilter #*natures*filter

We're like Ken and Barbie come to life, like bride and groom already in our black-and-white evening wear.

I'm shaking, like a lot, like really shaking. Brandon takes my hands, says, "You're shaking."

I tell him that the past two months have meant so much to me, that I never imagined I'd open up so much and fall so hard for someone so fast, that I love him more than anything.

He says he never imagined meeting someone like me. Then he stares off into the distance all broody, and my face falls. He looks back at me and smiles, like: *psyche!*

"I found my person," he says, "my missing piece, my forever. I've been waiting so long to tell you this, Ashlee E: I love you, and I want to spend the rest of my life with you by my side."

Then he's down on one knee and the velvet black box and the flashing diamond ring, glistening, glittering, like the sea and our eyes and our skin and my gem-encrusted headband and the shimmer of makeup on cheekbones and also between my boobs.

"Ashlee E," says Brandon, "will you marry me?"

I'm really shaking now, seriously shaking, and my mouth does its thing, its jaw-drop thing, wide as a coin purse hinged open. Then I'm gulping back tears and kind of hyperventilating and saying, "Oh my God, wait, really?"

And he's like, "Yes, really!"

Now my head is in my hands and I'm totally overwhelmed, and I'm saying, "Yes, yes! A thousand times yes!" which I guess is from something, and then he puts the ring on my finger, and I draw it close to my face, like, WOW. My mouth and eyes are wide—hysterically, epically wide—but I'm happy, I seem so happy, like happier than can be. He kisses me and lifts me in that classic bridal-threshold carry and then it cuts to an engagement ring commercial.

★ ★ ★

"This isn't a story," Ruby interrupts, "this is propaganda. How are we supposed to believe this crap?" She hasn't taken a seat, is still hovering over Ashlee, who is still sitting in the final unmusical chair in the middle of the room, cradling her arm.

"So I have to believe in talking wolves, but you can't believe in love?" says Ashlee. She looks around at the others, who are scattered in a semicircle around her, in the chairs they sat in when they were out of the game.

"I haven't seen the show," says Gretel.

"What?" says Will.

"Really?" says Raina.

"You mean, like, just my season?" says Ashlee. "You haven't seen my season?"

Gretel shakes her head. "I mean ever," she says. "I've seen commercials. A group of women all dating one guy."

"He eliminates them one by one," says Ruby. "Whittles his way to a wife."

"It's been on for twenty years," says Raina. "Something like that."

"There's a contingent of women who watch the show on Monday nights with pink ensembles and rosé," says Bernice, eyeing Raina as if she might be one such person.

"Most people just watch it with irony," says Ruby.

"What do you mean, 'irony'?" asks Ashlee.

"I don't watch it anymore," says Raina.

Will cocks his head. "You don't?"

"No," says Raina. "Not typically."

126

"Why not?"

"A lot of reasons," she says, smoothing her hand over the silky lap of her skirt.

"Such as?"

"Well, for example, and this is nothing against you, Ashlee," says Raina, "the premise is regressive."

"That's why my sister won't watch it," says Bernice with a frown.

"I don't see why you guys are so against getting married," says Ashlee. She throws a pointed look at Ruby. "Not all of us want to sleep around for the rest of our lives."

"I think the issue is that the show paints happiness as one-size-fits-all," says Raina.

Bernice shifts in her seat, flicks at a hangnail.

"You disagree?" Will asks.

"Not exactly," says Bernice.

Will pushes her to say more.

"The size does seem to have fit Raina just fine," she says.

"How so?" asks Will.

"If we're being honest here..."

"We are," says Will.

"I guess it's what Ruby said," Bernice concedes with a sigh. "It's Raina's... aesthetic. It's the aesthetic the show sells. It's the life you're supposed to have, and it appears to be the life Raina has."

"And what life were you trying to have when you started dating a billionaire?" Ruby asks.

"I didn't get that life," Bernice snaps. "That's the point. She did, and now she's calling it 'regressive'? It's like rich hipsters who play at being poor. It's easy to pretend you're too cool for something when you already have it."

"You're not wrong," says Raina. "I do have the life 'you're supposed to have' and it does afford me certain privileges."

"What are you, a politician?" says Ruby. She looks at Will. "Why does she get away with this BS?"

"Let's say, for the sake of argument," says Will, "that Raina does have a perfect life. Wealth and a loving husband, that kind of thing. What makes that so difficult for you to tolerate, Bernice?"

"It shows me who I'm not."

"Yeah, we get it, you're not your sister," says Ruby. "We can't all be prom queens who don't want to go to prom."

"But do I have to be this?" says Bernice, gesturing to herself, the pitch of her voice rising. "The fattest girl Ashton ever dated? So ugly that *I'm* the bad guy? *An ottoman?* It's like the horror-story version of when some jock asks a girl to the prom as a joke."

"What makes you so annoying, Bernice," says Ruby, "is that you're not actually as ugly or as stupid as you think."

"Cool, thanks," says Bernice.

Ruby sighs. "Ashton didn't pick you as a joke," she says. "He picked you because your self-esteem is in the toilet, because you're jealous of your sister. Raina's probably here because her life sucks in some horrible way we can't imagine. What's the point of being jealous of her too?"

"There's no point," says Bernice. "I just am."

Ashlee taps her long fingernails together. "Um? Sorry?" she says. "Speaking of things to be jealous about...can we get back to my love story?"

"Please," says Bernice.

"Perhaps you should explain the logistical details of the show, Ashlee, if Gretel's never seen it," says Will.

"Cool," says Ashlee, perking up. "I can start more at the beginning. Narrating is one of the skills I learned on the show." She places her left hand flat on her chest, begins again.

* * *

I'm known as Ashlee E, if you didn't read my name tag the first week or catch my season or see any TV or magazine covers for the past several months, if maybe you don't have Instagram or Twitter or don't listen to interesting podcasts or whatever. That's A-s-h-l-e-e. Plus another *E*. If you're thinking, that's way too many *e*'s, I feel you. *E* isn't actually one of my initials. It's just, there were two of us: same last name, same first name but different spelling. So they just called me Ashlee E. But even if *E were* my last initial, it wouldn't matter anymore because pretty soon I'm gonna be Ashlee I., that is, Mrs. Brandon Irizarry.

My chyron from the show isn't totally correct anymore. A chyron is, like, the subtitles floating below your face when you're on TV. Like, for example, I'm actually twenty-two, not twenty-one—my birthday was mid-season. And I'm *from* Park Pond, PA, but now I live in Brooklyn, as of, like, a month ago. And I *was* a retail associate, but I quit my job to be on the show, and the show aired, and now no one will hire me.

Brandon was chosen for *The One* the way all leads are chosen: through a super-secret nomination and interview process. The lead has to be hot and charming. Brandon fits the bill with his sweeping brown hair, miraculously square jaw, and insanely chiseled abs. But the guy can't *just* be hot. He also has to have some other special feature, like he could be heir to a fortune or he could be a professional athlete or he could have a tragic story. In the case of Brandon, it was that last thing. His high school sweetheart died in his arms. Which: Sad Face, obviously. In the package at the beginning of the first episode, Brandon visits his high school girlfriend's grave and cries. Then he says to the camera, "And I remember thinking: *she's* not just dead, *love* is dead."

Which, not true. Love is alive and well in the Irizarry apartment, in which I have lived for a month.

The title sequence for *The One* is always the lead in a suit dancing with thirty women in white lingerie. The song is a DJ Money remix of "Here Comes the Bride" plus "I'm a Slave 4 U." The bachelor hands out white rejection roses to the dancers, who sulk off one by one. The last dancer gets a red rose. She clamps it between her teeth and hops into his arms. Then it cuts to a shot of an amazing cliffside mansion in the Adirondacks. That's where we lived when we were dating Brandon.

During each episode, the bachelor gives out a certain number of red, pink, yellow, and white roses. The roses are stuffed in vases all over the house and out on the patio and also, especially, in the gazebo, which is invite-only. The vases are so the bachelor can just, like, pluck a rose out and thrust it in a face whenever he wants. Immediate feedback.

Red roses mean he's super into you. Pink roses mean he's starting to vibe. Yellow roses are bad. Either you did something shitty and he's, like, trying to teach you a lesson or—worse—you're friend zoned. You don't come back from The Friend Zone. White roses suck hardest: kiss of death, parting gift, go home. As soon as the stem hits the hand, the girl starts crying and Jake Jackson, the host, appears like the grim reaper, and I'm not just saying that because he's old. It's because your time is up and he's like, "Sorry, you did not find love. You must leave as you came, single, alone, and still searching for... The One."

I was driving to work in my crappy Ford Aspire when I saw the billboard announcing a casting call. It was like, "Looking for love?" Which, duh. I was at the bottom of the barrel, Tinder-wise; I was getting repeats, swiping right for people I'd already swiped left for, swiping for people fifty miles away. It was all dick pics and

U up?s—i.e., not Marriage Material. Meanwhile, my friends were getting new last names and fairy-tale weddings with horse-drawn carriages and profile pictures of them on their wedding days at peak hotness.

So, yeah, if you're wondering: I *did* go on the show for love, but I was also thinking that even if I didn't find love, at least I'd get to be on TV; maybe I'd even get a few thousand followers; maybe I could be an influencer or something, make some money selling Slim Tummy Gummies instead of scraping actual gum off the dressing room floors of Always 16.

So I went to the casting call, followed by three rounds of interviews, followed by a psych test and an STD test and a screen test. That's when they showed me the package about Brandon. My palms got sweaty and I knew I was in trouble.

I signed the billion-page contract, quit my job, sublet my apartment, moved in with my dad and stepmom, bought all the clothes for the packing list on my credit card. I needed tons of stuff, including five bikinis and a shit ton of gowns. The gowns were for the cocktail parties. You needed a different gown for each party. There was a party every week and a week was four days and there were seven weeks total if you made it to the end.

Pretty soon, I was dragging my luggage through this Hilton in upstate New York and my producer, Hana, was jogging across a maroon carpet to greet me.

Hana had this kind of off-camera haircut, like short and nothing, like the haircut of someone who was less looking for a husband and more married to her job. She had resting bitch-face with her lips and eyebrows in these very stern Vs. Her whole face situation made me think: chevron. But then she would sit in front of me and her face would soften, like her mouth would curve into a U, and it was like we were friends sitting across from each other in a Starbucks or wherever.

In my hotel room, Hana sorted through my luggage, separating out stuff I wasn't allowed to have, like my wallet and my keys and my romance novels and my family photos. I already knew she was going to take my phone, but there's knowing things and *knowing* them, you know? I felt seriously Sad Face when she powered it down, one-handed, without even looking at it, then set it on the bed. It looked like it was in a coma.

Hana motioned for my watch, but I clutched it to my chest. Hana was like, "We can't have clocks or noise or clutter." I was like, "Why?" She was like, "Editing, splicing, continuity." She was like, "It was all in the contract."

I held out my limp wrist and Hana unbuckled my watch, like she was uncuffing me from the digital world but also, like, metaphorically cuffing me into the analog world. For some reason, an image flashed through my mind, of a pioneer woman pounding away at butter in a wooden bucket. First through fifth grade is basically all pioneer when you live in Pennsylvania.

She held my hands in hers and looked me in the eyes. "This. Will. Be. Worth. It," she said. I pictured little clapping emojis between each word, applauding me back into the reality of this opportunity. She was like, "Your whole life is about to change. To be honest, you're *exactly* Brandon's type."

She pocketed my keycard, looped her arm around the box of my things, and stood up from the bed. "Nothing worth having ever comes easy," she said. "Love is about patience and sacrifice. If you can't start now, if you can't sacrifice a little up front, how are you ever going to make it to the end of this journey?"

It was something to think about for the next three days as I sat alone in the hotel room sacrificing a little up front. We weren't allowed to leave the room—they'd taped the door the way cops chalk tires. The TV was just sports and romance movies on a loop and dead women on CNN. There was a Bible in the nightstand, and I read the part where Eve ruins everything, and let me tell you, it's no Danielle Steel. No offense to God.

I used all the toiletries and drank Ensures from the mini fridge and jogged in place but none of my steps counted without the watch. I kept patting my pockets, thinking my phone was there. On the first night, my thumb started just kind of jerking up and down, up and down, all on its own, as if to scroll. I tried to open the hotel room windows, but they weren't the kind that opened. There wasn't even a clock radio. Or a clock. I had to guess the time based on the angle of the sun, then check the TV to see if I was right. I was never right. Mostly it was just night or day.

Whenever someone knocked it was either food or Hana. Hana was the best part of the day. She snuck me wine coolers and smoothies and even one of my romance novels. Hana saw real potential in me as a partner for Brandon. She kept saying it like that, "Real potential." Not once in my year of folding clothes at Always 16 had my manager ever said I had potential for anything. She was always just like, "Ashlee, did you even *look* at the planogram?" Which, no.

Hana taught me how to "manifest." Manifesting is when you visualize what you want in order to make it reality. She learned it from some guy at her yoga studio who'd been to India. I'd rub the edge of the bedsheet as a way to focus, and then I'd manifest Brandon at the end of a winding, cobblestone driveway, just like the driveway on the show. In my mind's eye, I'd walk up that driveway toward him thinking: *my husband, my husband, my husband.*

"Imagine more," Hana told me. So I did. I imagined the proposal, the engagement party, the bridal shower, the bachelorette party, the rehearsal dinner, the wedding, the honeymoon, the baby shower, hosted by my stepmom, for the first of many large-mouthed, tall-haired, square-jawed Irizzary children. I imagined it so hard it started to feel less like something I'd invented and more like a premonition, which was basically the point of manifesting.

By the time night one arrived, I was literally crawling up the walls. But not *literally* literally. I was *literally* literally sitting very still in my silky gown trying not to mess up my makeup or hair, waiting for Hana to blindfold me.

★ ★ ★

"Excuse me," says Gretel. "Did you say to blindfold you?"

"Yeah," says Ashlee. "Just, like, so each producer can get her girls to the mansion without them meeting each other off camera."

"There's a reason they edit that part out," says Raina.

"Honestly, they could sue me for telling you this," says Ashlee. She looks into the corners of the room, squinting. "Probably any of this."

"This is a safe space," says Will.

Ruby rubs at her neck, looks up at the ceiling. She's sitting cross-legged on the floor now, her coat splayed out behind her. "Let me get this straight," she says. She holds up a finger for each point she makes: "You were locked in a hotel room for three days, blindfolded, taken to a remote location?"

"A remote *mansion*," says Ashlee. "It's not like I was trapped in a hovel."

"You were still trapped," says Bernice.

"I had to do it. I mean, I said I'd do it. It was in the contract I signed."

"Just because you agree to something doesn't mean you aren't being taken advantage of," says Raina.

* * *

My heart was beating like crazy as Hana led me through the lobby, steering me with her warm hand on my shoulder. I got three gulps of parking lot air before I was smushed into a van, thigh to thigh with some other girl. The van was hot, like a sheet over my head, and smelled like hair spray and tanner. Nobody was speaking, but everyone was super breathy. The elastic of the blindfold pulled at my ears, making everything sound strange and funneled-in. The elastic was on your ears so as not to mess up your hair. A girl across from me—Payton, I later learned—was like, "I feel like we're walking the plank."

A voice to my left, soft and earnest: "Should we pray?" The girl's fingers were grabbing at my hand. I shook her off.

"In ancient Rome," Payton said, her voice rising, "the lions at the Colosseum were kept in a dark room for days without food or light before they were let loose on the criminals or Christians or gladiators or whoever the fuck they were supposed to eat. Know why?" She did this dramatic pause. "Made for a good show," she said.

Hana was like, "Girls, please," and then the engine roared to life and I felt this rush of cold air from a vent above me. For a second I thought we were being poisoned. But, duh, it was just the AC.

Then the van was quiet save the whoosh of AC and the silky swish of dresses and Hana's mmm-hmmming into the headset and our little *ohs* each time the van took a hard curve, which kept squashing me against the door. I felt super nauseous. I felt like Hana was my best and only friend who'd invited, like, eight other losers to sit with us at the lunch table.

In the shared van, in the darkness of my blindfold, doubt crept in and expanded, like how a little crack in your phone leads to a web of cracks, and then the touch screen doesn't work, and you're texting rando messages to people you don't even know.

What if Brandon and I were soul mates, but he didn't know it? What if he was tricked into "going in another direction"? I'd heard that one before, like once when I tried to get into modeling and they were like, "Your mouth is too big. We're going in another direction."

I could be one of *those* girls, a humiliating night-one elimination. I'd laughed at those girls, but I'd never imagined being one—tripping drunk down the steep cobblestone driveway, chased by my own rolling luggage, cheeks mascara-streaked, a white rose clenched between my teeth, tongue probably bleeding from the thorns.

Then what? Back to Park Pond, PA, with no job, no apartment, a few grand in credit card debt, and a suitcase full of gowns? I mean, where do you even wear a gown?

The van stopped, idled, turned off. Nobody said anything. It was all just breathing. We listened to the passenger door open, Hana step out. How long had we been driving? "What time is it?" I asked into the silence, and the girl next to me jumped.

"Do you think the van broke down?" someone asked.

"Who the fuck knows," said Payton. "I feel like we're about to face a fucking firing squad."

"I don't think we're supposed to swear," said the girl next to me.

When the van door finally slid open, we all gulped for air. I could hear us gulping.

Hana passed around shots. "To Brandon!" she said, and we all said, "To Brandon!" The vodka burned down my throat.

Hana's voice: "You're up, Ashlee."

As I started to stand, I felt the person next to me, the pray-er, start to stand too.

"Right," said Hana. "Two Ashlees."

"I'm Ashlee F.," I said.

"Same," squeaked the other Ashley.

I felt Hana grabbing for me. "I mean you, with all the *e*'s."

"With how many *e*'s?" said the other Ashley.

"Two," I said as I took Hana's hand. "A-s-h-l-e-e. It's a unique variation." And that's how two Ashlee F.'s became an Ashlee E and an Ashley Y.

Hana led me out as my ankles went bendy in my stilettos like a baby giraffe's.

Then I stood there, at what I assumed was the bottom of the cobblestone driveway, blindfolded, with my arms crossed over my chest.

"Do you know why I called you first?" Hana asked. I shook my head. "Because I think you could win this thing."

"Bet you say that to everyone."

Hana wrapped another shot of vodka in my hand, and I threw it back.

Hana was like, "I know it's weird for you that I have these other girls too, but, I mean, Ashley Y? She's sweet, but…What am I saying? This is my job, and I get who I get. But sometimes I get lucky. Sometimes I get a person who might actually win—like you." Her warm hands were on my bare shoulders. "Ashlee, you need these other girls. They're the show. But also, screw the other girls. If you act confident, then they don't matter, then they're just supporting characters in your journey. If you get through this, your whole life could change. You could have the happy ending you always wanted." She squeezed my shoulder. "Act like the star," she said, "you are the star."

Hana stood behind me with her fingers at my ears, prepared to unhook the elastic loops of the blindfold. She was like, "Don't look back." She was like, "I mean that literally and metaphorically. Just walk straight ahead, up the driveway, okay? And keep remembering what you've been manifesting, what you're walking toward."

She slipped the loops of the blindfold from my ears, revealing the scene. Everything I had manifested was there for real, a fairy tale come to life: the cobblestone driveway, lined in rosebushes and lanterns, winding its way up, up, up, toward the prize, the blurred man in the suit.

I was walking even before Hana whispered, "Go."

I felt so confident all of a sudden, like all the stones were exactly where my stilettos expected them to be, my heels never falling between, despite the shots of vodka. I couldn't see Brandon yet, but I pictured him tall and sturdy and in a suit. *My husband, my husband, my husband,* I thought.

Except then I started to feel weird, like I wasn't in my dream exactly but in reality—but, like, not even *regular* reality, like some weird reality, like when you walk through a funhouse at the fair, and the floors and mirrors are definitely floors and mirrors, just not in the ways you expected them to be.

In my manifestations, it was always just Brandon and me and the cobblestones, but now I was suddenly aware of everything else around me. Like, I sensed the other girls waiting in other vans like a chorus line and I saw the white tents for production set up in the grass and I noticed camera people staked out everywhere, sometimes staked out so close that the camera was, like, a foot from my head, so that it was like I was being stalked by robots or something, like I was dating in the future where some machine was constantly assessing my, like, viability as a romantic partner.

(Which is still better than dating in the past, right? When women were just objects and less free to choose?)

Climbing up that steep cobblestone driveway toward the prize was the first test, a test of endurance. My calves were burning and I was trying to look like I wasn't catching my breath. I was sort of feeling dizzy or maybe dazed, all shot through with adrenaline and alcohol and lactic acid or whatever. I heard some girls practiced, climbed up hills or super-inclined treadmills. A girl once twisted her ankle walking up this hill, yet she still limped all the way up the driveway to meet him, this grimace-smile on her face, eyes on the prize.

I was close enough to the mansion that I could make out gaunt faces staring at me from the windows, girls from other vans who had other producers and who'd already arrived. Brandon came into focus, the tall, sturdy handsomeness of him, the detailedness.

The light was bright and white. His strong jaw was thrown into just the right amount of shadow. His hair swooped over his forehead, bounced atop his head. I could already tell he was nothing like the guys I'd been with. Those guys were often hot, but they weren't, you know, *handsome*. I'd be slurping a smoothie on my dinner break in the mall parking lot while they were schlepping groceries to their cars, trying to pick me up along with the budget-brand TP. I had a dream once, that one such guy proposed to me at a Waffle House, baked the ring right into a waffle. It wasn't even a bad dream, at the time, but now I saw that it was the dream of a loser.

Hana had said I was just his type. Hana had said my confidence would shine through if I let it. *Be confident,* I told myself, and I was.

I could see the whites of his eyes. I could see the colors of the roses in the vase on the podium behind him: white, yellow, pink, red.

"Hello!" he called, smiling. He looked like a guy from a television commercial. I mean, he *was* a guy from a television commercial, a commercial for this show.

"You look so handsome," I said. I was like, "Honestly, I should've prepared something."

Brandon laughed. He took my hand and twirled me around. He was like, "You're really beautiful. Are you nervous?"

Then a dude's voice from the darkness: "Hey, can you do that again?"

I blinked out into the bright light but couldn't see, could only hear people shuffling around.

When I looked back at Brandon, he was gone. I mean, like, blotted out because I'd been looking into the bright light.

Brandon let go of my hand. He said, "You're absolutely stunning. Are you nervous?"

He took my hand and twirled—

"Actually, no," the voice from the light said again. "Can she say her thing again and then you say your thing again?"

Brandon dropped my hand, straightened his tie.

I blinked into the lights like, "What did I say?"

Brandon said, "Hey, don't be nervous, okay?"

I smiled. I was like, "Okay, okay, I think I remember." Then I proceeded to say my much-quoted line: "I guess I should have prepared something. I was not expecting you to be so actually hot."

Brandon laughed. He took my hand; he spun me around.

He said, "I wasn't expecting you to be so actually hot either." He winked, I think—I remember this or else I saw it later on TV.

My heart was racing, and not just because of walking up the hill. My skin was hot, and not just because of the production lights. I was dizzy, and not just because the alcohol had hit my brain. What I'm saying is: it was love at first sight.

I couldn't think in words, could only think in emojis: Red Rose. Smiley Face with Hearts for Eyes. Red Heart. Blue Heart. Pink

Heart. Heart with Bow. Beating Heart. Sparkle Heart. Sparkles. Also: Sun, Moon, Stars.

He reached behind him, to the vase of roses, and pulled out— thank God!—a red one.

I pulled his free hand to my stomach, set the warmth of it there. It felt so good, human contact, so good that it didn't seem like a bad trade, to give up my phone and my family and my job and time for this handsome man.

"You're making these butterflies go wild," I said, and in my mind's eye, paragraphs of Butterfly emojis flew by.

He was like, "I know what you mean." He tucked the rose behind my ear, then pulled my hand to his stomach. His abs were basically a steel plate.

I could feel him breathing. I could feel him feeling me breathing.

I was like, "Do you believe in love at first sight?"

He whispered, "We wouldn't want to ruin the ending already."

Everything was so quiet. Like, so much so that it seemed like no one was there, and that was weird, made me realize again how very many people *were* actually there, watching us, like this production guy standing in a rosebush, plus the giant camera stalking our faces, plus all the women in the mansion whose faces were plastered to the windows, and Hana, who was listening in from afar, standing next to a van full of blindfolded women who would march up this same driveway after me, who, I thought, were unlikely to feel the butterflies, or not in the same way I had, anyway.

And for a second, I did think about how adorable we were, giggling with our hands on each other's stomachs, about how great this would look on TV. I felt like the audience was with me already, cheering me on, watching my love story unfold from the very beginning.

★ ★ ★

Bernice's head hangs lower and lower until it suddenly jerks up. She looks around, startled. "I'm awake," she says.

"How do you feel about Bernice falling asleep here in the middle of your story?" asks Will.

"And *I'm* the instigator?" mumbles Ruby.

"Sorry," says Bernice. "My living situation isn't great."

"TBH," says Ashlee—she looks at Will—"TB*absolutely*H," she corrects, smiling. "I totally get it. I've lived with a bunch of girls who all dated the same guy and basically never slept, and let me tell you: super Sad Face."

★ ★ ★

The first morning was a wake-up call. Like, literally, a voice from above was like, "TIME TO WAKE UP!" It was our handler, Anthony, on the speaker system.

My head was pounding. A shade thunked and spun. Morning light poured in. We couldn't have slept more than a few hours.

The room didn't seem like a room in a mansion, not that I've spent a lot of time in mansions. It was stacked with cheap metal bunk beds like a summer camp or an orphanage. Limbs were all hanging from beds; feet dangled out with high heels attached; the strap of a silky red dress was hooked around an ankle, so the dress looked like some fancy ghost hovering in the air. Suitcases spewed gowns across the wood floor, and trails of toiletries led out the door.

Ashley Y was crawling among the debris, panicked, her gold cross necklace swinging below her as she sifted through clothes. She was still in her satiny blue gown, mascara raccooning around her eyes.

"What color did I get?" she kept saying. Even makeup-smeared Ashley Y gave off a Kewpie doll vibe: innocent and enthusiastic and easy to hate. She had this tiny body and these pink cheeks and one of those noses everyone calls a button and a mouth that was exactly the right size and shaped like a heart. She was a virgin because of Jesus or whatever, which, if you ask me, is at least as bad as being a slut.

Was my phone buzzing? Was it Brandon? I felt around for it, all around my pillow, under my pillow, between the mattress and the bed frame. But obvi I didn't even have my phone anymore. Instead, I found my rose. It was practically decapitated and missing most of the petals. *Broken Heart emoji,* I thought. *Rose emoji.* I was too hungover to generate words. I felt like a sewage plant or something. Like a Poop emoji, but not even with cute eyes, which I guess is just like shit. For some reason, my fingertips were pink.

A head popped out from the bed across from me—Payton. Her brown hair was pulled up into a tiny top bun that bounced frantically atop her head, like it was pissed off on her behalf. She was like, "A speaker system? What the fuck is this? North Korea? *Nineteen Eighty-Four?* The fucking Stanford Prison Experiment?"

From the bunk below her Bri was like, "I don't even know those shows."

Bri was still wearing the green dragon onesie she'd worn the night before. It was a whole shtick to stand out, get followers or whatever. The hood had fallen off and the front was unzipped and one giant, bare boob was hanging out, all pink and uddery. The stuffed tail with its stuffed spikes was squashed up against the wall.

Bri was like, "I was really *on fire* last night, but I'm really *dragon* this morning." Girls under blankets wiggled and groaned. "Get it?" she said.

Payton was like, "We get it. We got it last night. We got it every. Single. Fucking. Time."

"Did I totally *slay* you?" said Bri.

Payton gritted her teeth. I tried to pop the head of my rose back on the stem, as if it might magically stick back together, but it didn't. Ashley Y was sitting in a suitcase holding a giant pink acrylic earring in the shape of a heart. She was like, "Where's that girl? Angela, I think. I found her earring."

"She's gone," someone said solemnly, and Ashley Y made the sign of the cross.

Payton was like, "What is this, a fucking Agatha Christie novel? Nineteen eighties Argentina?"

And Bri was like, "Who's Argentina? Did Madonna play her in some movie?"

"You're thinking of *Evita*," said Payton.

"Which one's Evita?" said Bri, looking around.

And Payton was like, "I can't even."

The PA system was like, "It's gonna be a hot one today. Dress code: bikini tops and cutoffs."

"It's worse than I thought," said Payton. "It's a fucking Carnival cruise."

Bri was like, "I *love* cruises!"

Pointy-elbowed Saloni stood by the window, twirling a red rose between her fingers, like, "Some of us are taking this seriously, okay?" I nodded and Saloni was all dagger eyes, like, "You? *You* were totally shit-faced last night."

I shrugged. I sniffed the remains of my rose. It didn't smell like anything.

"The scent's been bred out," said Payton. "All that's left is the potent reek of symbolism." She said everything in this tone like she was narrowing her eyes, but her eyes didn't narrow. They were big and bright, like she was taking it all in, which is probably how she became a know-it-all. A pink rose was tucked neatly in the space between her mattresses and the bed frame.

I looked at the pale strip of skin on my wrist. "What time is it?" I asked.

"I don't know," said Saloni. She Vanna White–ed the window. "Morning?"

Ashley Y from among the debris: "It's red! It's red. It's red." She was cradling her rose like a baby. The petals were like velvet, and the stem was deep green and very long. I felt a pang of jealousy.

Payton with her eagle eyes was like, "Don't worry, ol' Ashleeeee, you got yours first."

I racked my brain for details from the night before. It was mostly waiting and wine and whining. A girl in a princess gown and tiara jumping into the pool. Same girl, dripping wet, white-rosed, trying to push her steamer trunk down the driveway, cameras circling. Hana pulling me, manifesting with me as I rubbed at rose petals to focus my mind, the same way I'd rubbed at the bedsheets back at the hotel. Hana asking me questions: *What do you think of Brandon? How did you feel when Angela was sent home? What do you think of Payton? What do you think of Ashley Y? What do you think of how Ashley Y and Brandon already got twenty minutes alone in the gazebo?* Production finally giving me my turn in the gazebo. The night sky obliterated by production lights, like a movie set or an alien abduction.

Brandon, tracing the line of my dress with his finger. Laughing like a dolphin, high-pitched and playful.

When we kissed, he put his hand behind my head. His lips were soft. His mouth tasted like peanut butter and whiskey.

When we stopped kissing, he just looked at me. No one had ever kissed me and then stopped and then just looked at me. Usually they were too busy trying to figure out how to unhook my bra.

"You," he said. His finger booped my nose. The other hand was still on the back of my head. "You, you, you," he said, booping.

Then production again, forcing us apart.

According to Payton, the mansion look was like an Olive Garden–Pottery Barn mash-up. I said it was like a Stone Age Sorority House—no electronics, but we did have an open bar. We were bored. We perfected the fishtail braid, sang a cappella, biceps-curled wine bottles, played Don't Touch the Floor. I made it to the top of the stairs on a pair of throw pillows. I was still standing on them when I shouted down, "How long have we been doing this?"

"We all quit, like, an hour ago," said Payton from the bottom of the stairs.

"How do you know?" I said. "Do you have a watch?"

"Jesus," said Payton. "Just come back down here. On your feet, how about?"

After a while, like a short while, the mansion seemed pretty small for a mansion. We staked out the taped-off edges, wondering what lay beyond, wondering what might happen if we crossed into forbidden territory, though we didn't dare try. There were cameras everywhere: in corners, on shelves, tucked inside cabinets. Camera people wandered around like ghosts. We measured time with mimosa pours and my red lipstick tally marks on the bathroom mirror, which counted the days.

We pooled our polishes, painted our nails, watched the soft liquid sheen slowly harden. Then we chipped off the polish, did it again. I organized the bottles by color across the mansion floor so they stretched in a rainbow from the fireplace we couldn't use to the grand piano we couldn't use either. I kicked them over one by one. With each crack of glass bottle on hard tile, Ashley Y winced. Ashley Y was getting a lot of time with Brandon, though Hana said

I shouldn't be worried. "Please," she said. *Crack.* I waited for the wince, then did it again. *Crack.* "Do you hate this?" I asked. *Crack.* The bottles rocked in semicircles.

"Idle hands are the devil's playthings," said Ashley Y, like some weirdo preacher.

Ashley Y left me there to finish the task without her. After a while, it was just me and some camera guys and, like, a hundred bottles of nail polish rolling around on the floor.

I squatted down to inspect the reds. They had names like First Sight, Heart Break, Kiss Kiss. I chose a blood-red color called True Love. I took a long sniff, sat on the floor, painted my nails, waited for them to dry. Time passed or it didn't. It was actually pretty weird. It was like time had once been a stack of cheese cubes, and now all the cubes had melted together. I didn't know if the polish was still very wet or had been dry for a long time. I thought I knew when it changed over, wet to dry, but I couldn't tell anymore. I tested my thumb with my pointer finger. Still wet. "What time is it?" I asked, but nobody was there who was allowed to tell me the time.

They don't show you this stuff on TV, obvi. What you see on TV is the stuff like the stand-up comedy-club GD—that is, *group date*— where Hana helped me come up with a few good jokes about Ashley Y, where Ashley Y cried backstage, wouldn't look at me, said, "I'm not going to say anything mean back because I'm The Nice One." And Saloni said, "Are you sure you're not The Anxious One?" And Payton was like, "What are we, fucking dwarves?" Then Bri turned toward me like, "Which one are *you* supposed to be?" And I was like, "*The One*," and I turned on my heel with all the confidence I could muster, which was a lot of confidence, considering all the things Hana was saying about what Brandon was saying about how much he liked me.

It was the same confidence I mustered on the mud-wrestling GD, which Hana said was my chance to show Brandon I was willing to fight for him by obliterating Ashley Y. "You only have so much time to make an impression," said Hana. "You have to do something bold." You should've seen me—maybe you did see me—I was bold AF, covered in mud like some bronze stucco statue, straddling Ashley Y, holding her down by the collarbone, my mouth wide as a lion's, her hand flinging up from the mud to grab at my boob until Brandon called it, proclaimed me the winner, like foreshadowing or something, and I didn't even care about the purple bruises on my boob from Ashley Y's desperate fingers. They were badges of honor in the name of love.

But mostly we were just waiting, hoping, praying for Jake Jackson or Brandon to appear, for something to happen.

One morning, I tried to DIY a sundial. I was sitting at the kitchen table, writing out the hours around the circumference of a paper plate. I was gonna jam a straw through the middle.

"What does time matter when we're just killing it?" asked Payton, taking a sip of her mimosa.

"We're not, like, supposed to have clocks," said Bri, all snotty. She was wearing a tie-dyed bikini and scrambling egg whites.

Payton turned to Bri sharply. "What is this, the fucking panopticon?"

"I never know what the fuck you're talking about," said Bri as she huffed off with her pale lump of eggs.

Payton had been sitting on the counter and hopped off to join me at the table. "Did you already find the celestial pole?" she asked.

"What?"

She tilted her head back, drained the mimosa. "Fine," she said. "I'll help." In her real life, she was a camp counselor. She put her hand over her mouth, whispered, "Meet me in the bathroom." We hatched our plan with the water running, so our voices wouldn't catch on the mikes.

The next day, I kneeled down on the pool deck near the rosebush that smelled like nothing, stretching out as far as I could to stick the straw into that perfectly manicured lawn without actually stepping into the forbidden territory.

Payton whistled. This meant she had successfully cornered Hana, who wore a watch, and that it was noon. I spun the dial so the shadow was at twelve. I put out four rocks around the edge, to keep it in place.

It was too early to read the sundial when Anthony, one of the handlers, woke me for my ID—that is, *individual date*. But I didn't care how early it was because I finally had *my* turn watching the other girls watch me get ready, their eyeballs bright in the fuzzy dark. And then it was just Brandon and me and the camera guy and the pilot in a helicopter, yellow sun spilling like a broken yolk over the Adirondacks, and then the sky was kind of awash, kind of rose-colored, and I was nestled into his warm, strong body, and we were making out because we didn't need words to communicate, we needed only our lips, which was good because you basically can't hear anything in a helicopter. After, we bungee jumped over a river.

Before we jumped, Brandon put his finger under my chin and said, "Babe, you can do this." I was so scared that I was vibrating, though that was also because it was cold and I was in a bikini, which is why my fingers had turned blue. He kissed me on the forehead as our ankles were being strapped together. "You've got to be vulnerable, you know?" he said.

Soon, suddenly, we were whooshing down headfirst toward a river, hugging each other tight, and then we were whiplashing back up and then we were settling, and my neck was aching, and the nausea was rising.

We were hanging upside down over a river, wrapped in each

other's arms, blood rushing to our heads, hearts beating wildly. His boner was pushing up against my bare thigh. We were finally alone, save the cameras on our helmets, the camera people on the shore, production leaning over the bridge above us, and all the future viewers. It seemed like Hana was right, if I was feeling butterflies and also his boner, if the other Ashley might say it soon, then I should say it, there was no time to waste, I should tell him I loved him, and I did, very nasal, yes, I know, but we *were* hanging upside down.

★ ★ ★

"Did you really love him?" Will asks.

"What kind of question is that?" says Ruby. She's lying on the floor, hands behind her head, looking up at the ceiling as if gazing at stars. "They knew each other for about five seconds."

"More like four hours," says Ashlee. "Which is four more hours than love at first sight."

"And I thought my relationship moved fast," says Bernice.

"This is some Stockholm syndrome bullshit," says Ruby.

"Which is like what?" says Ashlee.

"Which is like . . ." says Ruby. "Someone explain it."

"It means you were trapped by the producers," says Raina. "Even though they took everything away from you, they also gave you everything. It's hard to hate people who give you even just a few of the things you desperately want, even if they're the ones who took them away from you in the first place."

"So you think the producers are manipulative," says Will, nodding.

"Of course they are."

"And the editors?"

Raina looks at him. "Yes, also the editors," she says.

"I'm just wondering..." says Bernice. "I think we've all seen the promos for your season..." They all nod, even Gretel.

"I wasn't even gonna talk about that whole thing that happened," says Ashlee, picking at the knot on her shirt. "That fight wasn't even about Brandon."

"But this story isn't about Brandon," says Raina.

"Right," says Ashlee. "It's a love story, so it's about *us*."

"No," says Raina. "It's about *you*."

★ ★ ★

Everyone was on a GD except Bri, Payton, Ashley Y, and me. According to Hana, the date was a riverside picnic with rafting and swimming. The day was super sunny and the sky was super blue, and I imagined the rustling leaves and the rope-swinging into cool water. Seemed pretty chill, even if Saloni was deathly afraid of water due to her brother having drowned in it. I imagined the grass tickling the feet, grass of different lengths, grass you were allowed to stand on. I imagined Brandon comforting Saloni. I imagined the sweet smell of flowers and the fresh smell of pine trees, nothing like the stale mansion air. I imagined how Saloni would weep, spilling her super Sad Face story to Brandon, how after that Brandon and Saloni would make out, deep with feeling. I imagined her bikini top overflowing with her giant boobs. I imagined her telling him she loved him, her face streaked with tears. Hana said to be confident, but I couldn't help imagining a bright red rose tucked behind her ear, his boner pressing up against *her* thigh instead of against mine.

I sat in the living room in my ruffled, crimson bikini, painting my nails Wine Red, then went outside to check the time.

The sundial was missing.

I stalked around the patio, found Ashley Y and Bri tanning on lounge chairs, ass to sun. Bri's bikini bottom was lost somewhere in her ass crack. She was drinking a Slutty Shirley, which is a Shirley Temple with alcohol. Ashley was dozing in a red polka-dot bikini with a high-rise waist.

"Have you seen my sundial?" I said.

Bri took a calm sip of her drink and was like, "Chill."

"What sundial?" asked Ashley Y.

"How do you think I've been telling the time?" I said.

"We're not even supposed to know the time," said Bri. "Also: who even cares?"

"It's not like we have anything to do," said Ashley Y, yawning.

"Time is what separates us from the animals," I hissed.

Bri was like, "Oh, really? Because *you're* the one acting like an animal."

And I was like, "You were the one who came dressed as a dragon. You're not even in love. You're just here like it's a joke, like you're on vacation."

Payton stepped outside, threw a thumb behind her. "The kitchen is a disaster. It's like *Lord of the Fucking Flies* around..." She stopped mid-sentence, catching the vibe. "What's going on?"

Ashley Y flipped over to tan on the front. She picked her strawberry daiquiri up off the ground. On top of the massive glass, a paper plate with a straw jammed through it.

"That's why we put that thing on there," said Bri, pointing at the daiquiri. "Because of the flies."

"Where," I said. "Did. You. Get. That?"

"That's your stupid sundial?" said Bri.

"Hana gave..." started Ashley, and then her eyes went wide and she looked out at the cameras as if she had made a grave error, which she had; actually now she'd made two: calling a producer by name during filming *and* looking right at the camera guys as if they existed. They could probably sue you for that.

"You *stole* my time," I hissed.

Ashley Y must have noticed me twitch. "Let's just take a second..." she was saying, but it was too late. I was already pouncing, I was already straddling her, already yanking the glass from her hand as she tried to wriggle free, her tanning lotion slick beneath me, Payton and Bri shouting, "Stop! Stop!" as the camera guys circled up.

I thrust the daiquiri with its sundial lid high above my head, held it up like a prize, as Ashley Y, still straddled beneath me, slithered around onto her front. She tried to crawl out from under me and off the head of the lounge chair, but I grabbed her hair in my fist, my wet red polish glopping into it, her neck arching as I tugged her backward, my other hand still high in the air with the daiquiri, like I was riding a mechanical bull.

What I did next, well, it's hard to say if I did it on purpose. No matter how many times you watch the footage, or how much you slow it down, you can't quite tell if I threw the glass or if it slipped. And I can't tell you either because all I know is it fell and it shattered and shards of glass and daiquiri sprayed everywhere and Ashley Y screamed as the lounge chair tipped.

Pain cracked through me as I hit concrete, hard on my knees and palms. I felt a sharp ache followed by the sting of glass. For a second all I could hear was the blood pounding in my ears and the crunch of the cameramen trying to step quietly on shattered glass. Then suddenly Bri started screaming like she'd been shot and didn't let up. Her face was all scrunched up in horror. I turned my head to see what she saw.

Ashley Y was sitting in broken glass, looking at her outstretched hand like it was some random object. The stem of the glass was jutting through the middle of her hand, like all the way through, like in one side and out the other, like some made-up, made-for-TV, Halloween wound. She blinked, blinked, blinked. "Oh my gosh," she said.

I crawled away from her, backward out of the glass, felt it crunch beneath me.

"Jesus fucking Christ," said Payton. "Ashley Y, don't pull it out, okay? Leave it. Leave it."

Ashley Y nodded slowly. The cameramen were all around us. Security and the medics were taking their time. The sundial was just a paper plate soaked in daiquiri. Bri's scream was steady and high-pitched. Her shins were splattered in strawberry guts. Ashley Y's impaled hand was still outstretched as she tried to stand up, but she sunk immediately back down into the glass. Her lip began to tremble. Tears welled in her eyes.

I rose to kneeling on my bruised and cut-up knees. I put my hands up, bloody palms facing the camera. Like, *Not me.* Like, *I didn't do it.*

Then the sirens and the flashing lights, and the camera people and producers jogging everywhere, like it was a crisis and they loved a crisis, they lived for a crisis, this was the crisis they'd always dreamed about. I lay on the lounge chair in my bikini, covered in daiquiri and blood and bright red nail polish. The polish had smeared into the cracks of my knuckles. Below me, a medic was picking glass out of my knees with tweezers, piece by tiny piece. In the distance, Bri was wailing in the grass with the on-set psychologist, and Ashley Y was on a stretcher getting loaded into an ambulance.

When Brandon returned from his date, his disappointment was clear without a word, just a set jaw and empty eyes and a terrible yellow rose. I ran off before he could hand it to me, my knees aching. A handler chased me to the bathroom, where I locked the door, turned on all of the faucets, and put a towel over my head.

Soon, Hana was at the door going, "Come on, kid, it's not all bad. Come out here and talk to me." Very gentle. "I know it's not your fault," she said.

I sat down on the floor with the towel still over my head and leaned against the door.

"Who gave her the sundial?" I asked.

"Ash, would you turn off the water so I can hear you?"

"Who?" I said.

There was a long silence. "You have a target on your back, Ash," she said finally. "They know you're the one to beat and they'll do anything, I mean anything, to stop you."

I stopped listening to her, just curled up in the bathtub and fell asleep. When I woke up, Hana was in the bathroom with me, turning off the faucets. We caught eyes in the mirror.

Her face said nothing. It was all chevron. Her mouth said, "Jake Jackson wants to talk to you."

I shook my head.

"You can leave the show or you can talk to him," she said. "Those are your choices."

A few minutes later a handler led me into a study that I'd only actually ever seen on TV, with a giant oak desk and way too many fancy books. Two chairs sat side by side, angled slightly toward the cameras.

Jake Jackson stood by the window in a golf-casual ensemble, laughing with an assistant. In the window light, his face looked kinda hard, by which I mean like plasticky from all the Botox or whatever. He looked up at me when I walked in, flashed a smile that for a second made me feel really good because, you know, most of the women hated me and their smiles were just smirks.

"Come in, sit down," he said, gesturing to one of the chairs, as if he'd invited me over for cocktails or something. "I know it's been a tough day."

"Ready?" said someone behind the lights.

Jake Jackson sat down, tapped his hands on his thighs. "Shall we begin?" he said.

I shrugged.

"I just want us to be really honest here," he said.

"K," I said.

"First of all, I want to be absolutely clear," said Jake Jackson. "This was an accident, am I correct? Because we do not tolerate violence."

"Sure," I said.

"Great," he said. "I knew it. I knew you wouldn't do anything like that on purpose." Then we did this little game where he'd prompt me to say something and I'd just shrug. Like, "Tell me what happened today." Or, "Why don't you tell your side of the story?" Or, "How are you feeling?" Or, eventually, "You know Ashley Y is in the emergency room as we speak and Brandon is with her."

There was a lot of silence and then Jake Jackson shifted in his chair and smiled. "Listen, Ashlee, I know you've had a long day. I know you're upset. I know you're in love. I know you're confused. I know you're looking forward to the end of the interview. I understand." He tapped his fingers together, nodding. "But it's really, really important that you let out some of what you're feeling right now, okay?"

I stared at the sky in the window behind Jake Jackson's shoulder. Clouds had covered the sun.

"What time is it?" I asked.

"I can give you the time," he said. "No problem. But you have to give me something first."

"Fine," I said.

"So tell me," said Jake Jackson. "Is love making you go crazy? Are you willing to fight for Brandon? Will you do anything for love?"

"I'll do anything for love," I said. "I'll fight for love. I won't let anything get in my way." My eyes felt hot.

"But, to be clear, this was an accident? Things just got out of hand?" Jake Jackson said, nodding.

"It was an accident and things got out of hand," I said.

"And Ashley Y? How do you feel about her? Just be brutally honest here."

"Ashley Y is a bitch and I'm glad she's in the hospital," I said.

"Why don't you like her?"

"She stole my time, and now you're stealing my time, so just give me the fucking time," I said. I felt hot tears running down my cheeks. I tugged my microphone off, twisted around to get at the body pack. "Get this fucking shit off of me."

Jake Jackson squinted out at production. "What time is it?"

Someone called back, "3:34."

Jake Jackson squeezed me on the knee. "Cheer up," he said. "You'll be fine. It's all going to be worth it." He handed me a tissue. "Look at the upside: two down, four to go—am I right?"

"Two down, four to go," I said.

But anyway it wasn't true, because Ashley Y wasn't gone; she came back, came limping back with a bandaged hand and forgiveness in her heart, just in time for the sleepover fantasy dates in Italy.

That was around the time when Saloni started whispering, soft and sad, "What kind of fucked-up love story is this anyway?"

★ ★ ★

"That played differently on TV," says Ruby.

"Hana didn't have your best interests at heart," says Raina.

Ashlee looks up with a flash in her eyes. "So what? What are my best interests anyway? Isn't it in my best interest to be happy? Maybe *you* don't have my best interests at heart." She glances at her ring reflexively, her arm still folded against her chest like a broken wing.

"What does that ring mean to you?" asks Will.

"It means I got exactly what I always wanted," she hisses. "And what about you guys? You think this ring is stupid? Well," she says, pointing at Bernice, "I think your furniture is gross and dead." She points at Ruby. "And I think your coat is super-extra and totally disgusting." She points at Raina, Gretel. "And I bet you two have some messed up random things you carry around."

Everyone looks away. Silence settles around them.

"Does your arm still hurt?" asks Raina. Ashlee nods. "Can I look at it?"

Raina presses at Ashlee's forearm gingerly, asking questions in calming tones. "How does this feel?" "What about this?"

"Are you a nurse?" asks Ashlee.

"A mom," says Raina. "I'm sure it hurts, but I think it will just bruise. Of course, I'm not a professional."

"I wasn't actually trying to hurt you," says Ruby. "I mean, physically."

"Things can get out of hand during a competition," says Ashlee.

"You know," says Gretel seriously, "if you found someone you love, and who loves you back, maybe it was worth it. Who are we to say?"

"Exactly," says Ashlee. "Who are you to say? I mean, if love isn't worth fighting for…" She trails off, tries again. "It's all part of the process…" she says. "Except when does the process end, you know? When do I get to be in the Ever After stage, where nothing ever happens but happiness?"

* * *

If we'd never left Italy, if we'd never returned to real life, maybe everything would have been fine.

Real life and the show weren't synched up, like the show was airing a few weeks behind. Brandon flew back to New York for interviews, while I stayed in Italy, so as not to be a spoiler. I was alone in a hotel again—no internet, no radio, no phone. I couldn't even watch the show because *The One* didn't air in Italy.

Being at that hotel felt so much like the beginning that the middle felt like a dream. It was sort of like how sometimes I arrived to work at Always 16 and couldn't remember the drive, or how I looked down at my phone and looked up later and time was just a blur of makeup tutorials and kittens and people tripping over stuff.

But things *were* different. Like I would get dressed only in the shower in case they still had cameras on me, because I was still under contract and wasn't totally sure. Also, I had an engagement ring tucked away in my suitcase—which, yay, obviously—and little grains of glass were popping out of my knees. Plus, Hana didn't come. She was filming *Cruising for the One,* which is basically *The One* but with more people and on a cruise ship.

I arrived in New York just an hour after the finale aired, so I could go to Brandon's before we debuted together as a couple on the morning show.

In the back of the taxi, I tried to enjoy the lights of the city—I'd only ever been to New York once before. It was 2 a.m. and I was wide-awake. I didn't know if I was moving in with Brandon or just staying for a few months for the interview circuit or what. I kept picturing him as I'd manifested him, as a blurred figure in a suit. I had to conjure his face by imagining each feature separately, like a police sketch.

We pulled up to a brown brick apartment building in Brooklyn with a brown fire escape zigzagging up the front. When Brandon had said he lived in The City, I pictured him in a Manhattan penthouse with sleek black counters and a rainfall shower. But love isn't about money, obviously—it's just what I'd pictured.

I buzzed the door and it buzzed back and I buzzed it again and it buzzed back and finally a fuzzy voice was like, "You have to open the door." I waited in the cold tiled entryway, but Brandon didn't come down to meet me. I dragged my suitcase backward into the elevator.

The guy who opened the apartment door was wearing sweatpants and a wrinkled white undershirt. His face wasn't bright at all but cast in weird shadows. His hair was shiny—not glimmering like Brandon's hair, but greasy. His mouth looked annoyed. Behind him, the apartment was dim with a big black leather couch with a video game controller lying on it, shining with grease. On the coffee table, an open jar of peanut butter with a knife sticking out of it. On the TV, some animated guy in camo with a machine gun just marching in place.

I couldn't figure it out—like, who this guy was and why I was in front of him. Maybe it was a prank. Like, *The One* was doing some kind of prank. But when I looked behind me, up into the corners in the stairwell and hallway, I couldn't figure out where the cameras were.

But actually, wasn't it worse if this *wasn't* a prank? If this was just real life and I was actually just standing at a stranger's door at 2 a.m. in a strange city, with no phone and no money and a suitcase full of bikinis and gowns?

"Hey," said the guy.

"Brandon?" I said, and it was like he came into focus, like I could see that this was really Brandon, or was probably Brandon, or else was a Brandon look-alike. But without the lights or the smile or the suit, he looked less like Brandon and more like just some guy.

He stepped aside, let me in without a word, then plopped down on the couch. He poured a splash of whiskey into the jar of peanut butter, mixed it around, then licked it off the knife.

The door fell closed behind me. I had this yellow-rose feeling in the pit of my stomach. I glanced around again, checking for cameras.

"I couldn't wait to see you," I said.

"Your phone and your other stuff's over there," he said, jerking his head backward to indicate the table behind him.

A box was filled with the stuff that Hana had taken away: my family photos, my wallet, my romance novels. My phone was in there too, still in a coma. It made me want to cry. I took it in my hand, felt the familiar, comforting weight of it.

Behind me, Brandon was shooting people on the TV and blood was splattering everywhere.

I was like, "Brandon? Is something wrong?"

He was like, "I watched the fucking show. That's what's wrong."

I'd never heard him swear before. He'd never even spoken to me without looking at me. He'd never worn sweatpants in front of me. He'd never been distracted by a video game. I tried to play it cool. "I haven't seen it yet," I said.

He was like, "Yeah, but you did *live* it, though, didn't you? Like you were actually literally there."

I blinked at the back of his head. His character was dying super dramatically, and Brandon made this loud annoyed noise and tossed his controller, then turned and looked at me.

Maybe this was Brandon's evil twin. Maybe the real Brandon would jump out from a closet, take me in his arms, take me to his real apartment, and make love to me on a plush down comforter.

"Hana told me..." I started. My throat was dry.

"If Hana told you to jump off a bridge, would you do it?" he asked.

"We *did* do it," I said. "On the helicopter date."

"That's not my point," he said. "I chose you, and now I look like an asshole." He picked up the controller and started messing with the buttons. "I mean, were you *trying* to get people to hate you?"

"No," I said.

"They tried to tell me. They told me to go with the other Ashley. They said it over and over again. Said who cares if she can't have sex before marriage if you're going to get married anyway."

"What?" I felt sick. I sunk down in a chair. "They told you that? Hana was so sure you were going to pick me. The whole time, she was so sure."

"They were setting you up for a downfall," said Brandon.

"I don't understand."

"It's called plot, Ashlee," he said with a heavy sigh.

"But why would people want to see my downfall?"

"Try to keep up, babe," he said. "It's because you're the fucking *villain*."

The whole room seemed to wobble. Some sour version of my airplane pasta shot up my throat, and I had to swallow it back down.

I held the HOME button down on my phone, and it buzzed back to life. For a quiet, blissful second, my screen was just my apps hovering over my kitten background. It was like that moment in a horror movie when the door pops open and you're like, *Oh, whew, okay, everything's fine,* and then: BOOM, a giant axe cuts you in half. My phone began to convulse with messages and alerts and missed calls—they buzzed and popped and flashed. Twitter hate and YouTube links and messages from my family and friends. We're getting death threats and Is this what we taught you? and UR hilarious but also WTF?

I clicked on a YouTube link. There I was, night one, plucking petals off my rose one by one, rubbing each to smithereens between my fingers. I had been manifesting with Hana, but now there was no Hana because Hana wasn't part of the show. It was just me tearing my rose apart, my eyes closed, my mouth huge and open and red from wine and shouting, "I'm gonna be the winner! I'm gonna be the winner! I'm gonna be the winner!"

My Twitter account was trashed. I scrolled through, looking and not looking, getting the gist: Stupid bitch. Ugly slut. Kill yourself. Sew your mouth shut. I know where you live.

There was an account called @AshleeesMouth—that's with three *e*'s and 250,000 followers. It chronicles all different things that could fit in my mouth. For example, an entire pizza or a baby rabbit or a pack of birth control pills or a dozen dicks. It also pairs GIFs of me, mouth agape, with other things with gaping mouths: me next to a yodeler, me next to a roaring bear, me next to a woman getting a root canal, me next to a sex slave wearing a mouth plug, me next to The Joker, from some scene in which The Joker has cut off his own face and is wearing it as a gruesome mask with a gaping, red-lipped smile.

The tweet with the GIF of me shouting "I'm gonna be the winner!" had over 30,000 likes. The comments were like Practicing for Brandon's Huge Dong and What a bitch and How many EGGPLANT EGGPLANT EGGPLANT EGGPLANT EGGPLANT does it take to fill an Ashlee E? and Wonder how that mouth got stretched? and A good face fuck might shut her up and Terrible example for our daughters!!! and I hope this makes her feel ashamed—which, congrats, mission accomplished.

My fake Twitter account followed another fake Twitter account called @BrandonsHairTroll, which is this little troll that lives in Brandon's very tall hair. The joke is that the hair troll is, like, both a bridge troll *and* an internet troll who hates me and also hates Brandon. There's a Photoshopped pic in which the troll's very tall hair is actually almost hidden by Brandon's very tall hair, like you see just this tiny point of blue hair sticking up above Brandon's hair. Also, fun fact: the troll is yet another thing that could fit in my huge mouth, according to this Photoshopped picture where I'm smiling and just a little poof of blue hair is sticking out of my mouth.

Brandon was standing before me, freshly showered with a towel wrapped around his waist. "We have to be ready for the morning show pretty soon," he said.

"It wasn't like this," I said. My cheeks were cold and wet. "Did you see all this? They're saying I should kill myself."

"Come on, they don't mean that," he said. His face was softer, more like him. He smelled like peanut butter and whiskey, and not because he was eating pad thai and drinking a squat glass of whiskey in a suit as I'd imagined, but because he was swirling whiskey into a jar of peanut butter and eating it with a knife while playing video games, but what did it matter? "Come here," he said. I stood up and hugged him. I could feel his boner pressing up against me. I wondered how many of the other girls had felt his boner up against them, and also how many of the other girls had felt his boner inside them, like probably Saloni and who knew who else.

"Every love story has obstacles, right?" I said. "It's all part of the journey." But for some reason I felt like I was opening my mouth and Hana's words were tumbling out.

★ ★ ★

Ashlee's mouth hangs open, as if she expects to keep talking, but nothing is coming out.

"Sometimes it feels like the whole world is against you," Bernice says.

Ashlee sniffs back tears. "But, like, why wouldn't they be? Because I wasn't, like, my best self."

"I mean, no," says Ruby. "But who is their best self? You think Hana was her best self? You think Jake Jackson is his best self? Probably the criminal mastermind behind the whole enterprise and he's getting fan mail."

"Or maybe he's just another cog in the machine," says Will.

"Cogs don't have power," says Raina.

"It's all about power, isn't it?" says Bernice.

"But I have the power," says Ashlee. "Because I won."

"You 'won' Brandon like you 'won' Unmusical Chairs," says Ruby. "I mean, if you lose your dignity while winning the game, have you *really* won?"

"Sounds like something a loser would say," says Ashlee.

"Maybe don't think of it in terms of winning and losing," says Raina. "Maybe think of it this way: Brandon chose you. But what if it were the other way around? What if it were your choice? What would you choose?"

★ ★ ★

I didn't choose the vermouth bar we went to last weekend. I think martinis taste like pine trees, but he was paying because I don't have any money. I hadn't been out much since the morning show my first day in the city, where, outside the windows, girls had stood with poster boards that said, WE HEART BRANDON, DITCH THAT BITCH, and WRONG ASHLEY!

The bar looked like an Apple store, white and slick. The tables were triangles with tiny white vases with little buds in each one. The place was packed with women who wanted selfies with Brandon. One of them wanted an autograph on her stomach. Brandon laughed his trademark dolphin laugh, lifted her shirt, and signed next to her navel with a Sharpie. I looked down at the table, but nobody noticed me anyway.

After a while, the crowd thinned. This girl sidled up next to him, some sorority chick with super-shiny long hair, perfect eyebrows, and cold, confident eyes. If she wasn't under twenty-one, she definitely looked under twenty-one, except for her super-big boobs, which were even younger. Honestly, she looked like every other girl. She looked kind of like me, except her mouth, it was completely average.

She was wearing a black miniskirt with silver buttons up the front and a cropped V-neck tank so boxy it made her look extra thin. She pinned her arms to her sides so her boobs spilled out even more in her V-neck as she leaned in to whisper into Brandon's ear. *I love you.* I saw the words on the shape of her lips. I was sitting right there. I was right next to them.

The super-soft peach-fuzz hairs on her skinny arms looked electric in the white light. She opened her mouth and stuck out her tongue. On it, a tiny piece of paper folded up, damp from her mouth. Brandon, my fiancé, smiled a smile that said he was ready to play. I knew the smile. It was the smile he'd smiled at me not too many weeks ago. He plucked the paper off her tongue. He stuck it into his pocket.

The girl swiveled her head around, owl-like, scanning right over the top of me, said, "Bitch must not be here."

I was like, "Bitch right here."

It was good TV, or it would have been good TV, but it was just real life.

Her eyes started to focus in on me.

Brandon was like, "Come on," as if he was above it all.

She looked for a moment like she was sucking on something, savoring her tongue. Then she jerked her head back and from her mouth flew this wad of spit, which landed on my cheek, right below my eye.

My mouth immediately opened wide in shock. I could feel the spit sliming down my cheek. My head suddenly felt full of extra air, so full that I couldn't hear anything. My vision started to pulse. Blood pounded through my temples.

The girl was looking at me. She was like, "What are you gonna do? Impale me with a glass?"

I wanted to throw something at her, but I couldn't move. All I could seem to do was just sit there, spit sliding down my face, mouth agape. I could feel it being agape, could feel it just hanging stupidly open, and thanks to YouTube and GIFs and Twitter and the internet in general, I knew exactly what I looked like: my neck jutted out a little, my giant mouth like a black hole, this shocked, crazed, murderous look in my eyes. And even as I was making the face, I knew I was making the face, and I didn't want to be making the face, but I couldn't help but be making the face, because it was my face—it was just the face my face made.

She was already walking away by the time I managed to say, "Bitch." I wiped my cheek with my damp cocktail napkin.

Brandon was looking right at me when he leaned back in his chair and reached behind him, groping for something on the table. He couldn't seem to find it, and when he looked back he saw he was reaching too high, that these vases were much shorter and not filled with roses.

When he looked back at me his face was drained pale. He drew his arm in, set his hand on the table, tried to smile.

"What. Color?" I said between my teeth.

"What are you talking about?" he said. "Don't be crazy." He looked out into the bar, took another sip of his drink.

And I had this feeling, this heart-drop feeling that's hard to explain because I can't even think of a word for it. It's like the opposite of butterflies *and* the opposite of déjà vu. It's a feeling like: *Who am I?* and *What am I doing?* and *Who is this guy anyway?* And I guess it's the same feeling I have sometimes when I come back to the apartment after being out and Brandon's sitting on the couch in his boxers and T-shirt, licking peanut butter off a knife and hawking up loogies, not even looking up to say hi because he's so busy killing everybody.

I mean, what if Brandon really is no different from those strip-mall parking lot guys asking me out during their toilet paper runs? What if he's worse? What if makeup and reality TV and weddings are all just a trick of the light? What if love with Brandon is not even really falling away, not even unhappening, but, I don't know, what if it's more like a thing that never really happened in the first place?

The Office

Someone is watching the footage.

Wait, what? The footage?

Yes. The footage.

We see him—that is, in retrospect, we imagine him—in a study, his naked, aging body silhouetted by giant computer monitors. He rubs his hands together enthusiastically, as if anticipating an exquisite meal—the meat of a rare creature he has hunted down himself, that someone else will make edible.

He scrubs the footage forward and back, watching the women file in and out of the room, watching them open and close their purses, cross and uncross their legs, watching Will not look nervous at all.

The man pumps lotion out one-handed with his thumb as Ashlee spouts the dogma of *The One*, the perfect acolyte about to be broken. He slathers the lotion on his hands, up his arms, on his legs, on his stomach.

The man pauses the video, leaving a smudge across the space bar. He rubs the lotion in with his fingernails, so he can scratch and distribute at the same time. Bright red wheals streak across his skin. The lotion accumulates in a white film. He looks like buttered raw meat. He rubs lotion into his scalp until his hair is slicked in grease. Everything in the study is covered in grease. The cleaning woman must think he's insane.

The experiment is a huge risk. The Will suit cost a small fortune. The cameras—tiny as the head of a pin! almost impossible to see!— were no small change either, nor was the audio equipment. His arsenal of technology is incredible. All of it, as far as the man is concerned, is a miracle and worth every penny, not least because he's filthy rich.

The man believes in the power of narrative. He believes that stories change the world, and that these women deserve to tell their stories and that the world deserves to hear them. He'd love to sell it that way, really. He'd love to just say: "These women deserve to be heard!" But the industry is the industry, and he'll have to go harder than that, and besides he'd be remiss not to mention that the concept is, frankly, groundbreaking. It pushes the limits of genre. It's a reality show and a tell-all, a buddy comedy and a drama. It's true crime meets gossip column. It's *Celebrity Rehab* meets *Oprah*. It's the voyeuristic thrill of *Candid Camera* coupled with the heart-wrenching pull of tragedy.

Above all, he wants their honesty and truth and spirit to shine through. Obviously. Which isn't to say he won't have it edited. Stories will be simplified, personalities exaggerated, but that's the name of the game. It's the fee you pay for people to care. Ironically, he does know someone who is—or was, at least—a genius in the editing room. But it isn't someone he can hire. God, at this point it's barely someone he can speak to.

All in all, the cast—if he has to look at it that way—is pretty good. He had carefully curated a long list of potentials, emailing all of them, knowing not everyone would be right for the project.

With some, there were red flags from the start. He couldn't even find a direct email address for the teen girl who'd been trapped in some abandoned Bavarian castle covered in vines. To reach her, you had to go through the publicist of her boyfriend, the teenage You-Tube adventurer who had climbed the walls, discovered her passed out inside. Then there was the woman from the memory foam mattresses commercials, the one with the *Real Housewives* mother-in-law who made her son's girlfriends sleep on old spring mattresses, waiting for them to complain so she knew they came from money. She had responded *too* eagerly, referred him to her agent.

The curly haired girl who claimed she was almost devoured by a pack of bears initially emailed with interest, then emailed back saying it just didn't feel right. The socialite who had disappeared without a trace, who was found years later living as a carny, claiming she had run away because her stepmom was trying to kill her? She scheduled a screening, then didn't show.

It was a disappointment, but he didn't follow up. He had purposefully made the email sound just the teensiest bit question-able, just the tiniest dash like spam. It was a sorting method. He did not want women who were too wary or too savvy. He wanted desperate. He wanted naïve. The former would make for good TV. The latter would be more amenable to the final sales pitch. Not that they necessarily had to be on board, but it certainly would make things easier.

With the women, Will plans to frame it less as a TV show and more as a philanthropic opportunity. He'll tell them that airing their sessions is part of a broader "experiment," an attempt to bring catharsis to the masses, to show other women they aren't alone, that trials and traumas can be overcome, that lessons can be learned. Wasn't it almost selfish to stay silent when they had the opportunity to help so many other women simply by sharing more widely what they had already shared in group? He'll tell them it's their choice. If all goes well, they'll actually be grateful.

If all goes poorly, he will have to make the difficult choice to air it anyway. It's possible they will sue him. The whole enterprise is almost certainly, technically, illegal, though he has their signatures on confidentiality agreements that may or may not have been missing a few pages when they were signed. Nothing a few staples didn't cure. But mostly: what was their reputation against his? To be honest, this very footage could be used to discredit them, though he hopes it doesn't come to that.

One other fly in the ointment: Raina. He hadn't meant to include her in the email. He was so thrown off to see her reply that it had seemed, for a moment, less like an error and more like fate, though he understood his mistake when he looked back at the email list: Raina's email was similar to another he had meant to include. He must have clicked on Raina's when it auto-suggested.

He was curious, so he agreed to the screening interview, just to see what she would say, but the screening only made him more curious, and then he somehow found himself accepting her into the group even though he'd entered the conversation planning not to. If necessary, he is sure he can have her edited out.

Bernice will be a big draw, especially given her refusal to do public interviews. Gretel and Ruby may be tabloid has-beens, but the cult of mystery surrounding them has never entirely waned. Sure, Gretel's a little dull, but Ruby certainly makes up for it. My God, she passed out! There were paramedics! He couldn't have planned it better himself.

Ashlee is the real win, the true wonder, a gift to him and to the television-viewing public. It's unclear how *The One* will survive a tell-all like this, a potential by-product that, to be honest, he would relish.

Then there's Will, the future celebrity, the consummate host. Will nods, smiles, frowns, purses his lips with concern. He is attuned so perfectly to them, even when he isn't. All he has to do is keep asking questions, pushing buttons. To be pleasant and unspecific, that's exactly how you become the face of a franchise.

He pumps even more lotion into his hands, rubs it into the depths of his behind. For a moment, the man's eyes cannot focus on the monitor. Instead, they fix on his reflection hovering inside it. That face is wan, ugly, and, somehow, it is his. Somehow he never expected this, never really imagined the one inevitable: that he would age.

He has to stop second-guessing himself. He has to remember his successes: they're talking, they're coming back, they're revealing their deepest, strangest secrets. And Will, young and attractive, has his whole career ahead of him.

The man presses the space bar again, unpausing the video, and Ashlee's astounding, miraculous mouth opens, black as a jump cut hurling them into the next hit show.

Week Four

Gretel

Gretel sits hunched, her back curved in a crescent, like a curl of her own hair. A cup of black coffee is nestled between her thighs. She won't drink it hot—lukewarm is best—but often she doesn't drink it at all. Mostly it's a prop, something to hold on to, to look into, her reflection a dark, rippling shadow.

Her earbuds are a prop too. She isn't listening to anything, just the occasional crackle from the headphone jack. She can't comprehend why anyone would want a second voice in her head—isn't one's own enough? She doesn't even like the feel of the earbuds in her ears, but she likes it better than small talk.

She's arrived first, as usual. Every Friday, she comes straight from work, taking the 4/5/6 downtown from 86th. Gretel knows every detail of this room, knows the contours of the ceiling with its excessive fluorescent lighting, knows the way the late-afternoon sun bounces off the bricks outside in a warm golden red, knows the linoleum tiling with its beige flecks, knows the textured ripple of the high-end disposable paper coffee cups.

Soon, Will arrives carrying those cups, among other things. He smiles at her, as he usually does, like a store clerk angling for an upsell, then gets to work while whistling, a high-pitched sound that grates on her, seems presumptuous of her taste and his talent. He sets up the other chairs and then the snack table, which he retrieves from the storage closet filled with bright rubber balls, jump ropes with red handles, those floor scooters she remembers from elementary school, seats in primary colors. Excess storage for the activity areas upstairs. There is a basketball court above them, though she has never heard anyone on it.

He's making a round of coffee when Raina enters in a mock-turtleneck sleeveless sweater that shows off her delicately toned arms. Will looks up right away and smiles. He is charmed, Gretel thinks. It is not the same smile that Will gives her.

When Ashlee arrives—white sneakers, a pastel-pink-and-white bodycon dress so tight it's like a second skin, a bruise on her fore-arm from the previous week—Raina and Will are already deep in conversation.

"My daughter's going off to college next week," Raina tells Will. "School's always been difficult for her."

"How so?"

"It's not the classes or anything," says Raina. "She's very bright. It's socially. She's..."—Raina searches for the right words—"beautiful in a way that people have a hard time seeing, and in a way she can't see at all."

"And you're helping her through that," says Will.

"I try," says Raina. "I wish I could do a better job of it."

"What about her father?" asks Will.

"I think he would help if he were around."

"He works a lot?"

"It's a longer story," she says.

"Perhaps we'll hear it today?"

Raina shakes her head, then looks at Gretel. "I mean, if you're willing?"

Gretel pulls at the cable to remove an earbud, and Raina repeats the question Gretel has already heard.

"You should just get it over with," says Ashlee from the snack table, where she fills a coffee cup right to the top.

Gretel feels herself nod at the same time as she feels the hard lump in her throat. She knew her turn would come eventually, but that doesn't mean she has any idea what she's going to say.

Ruby arrives on time, catching her breath in the doorway, sweaty as usual. "Check it," she says, pointing at Ashlee's watch. "I want everyone to remember this moment." She bows, and Gretel can see the greasy crown of her head.

Gretel knows a lot about these women, and not just because of the stories they've told or what she's heard about them in the news. She knows, for example, that Ashlee and Raina always wear lip color—Ashlee's is a gentle pink gloss that disappears by the end of group; Raina's is a pink-beige matte lipstick that lasts the whole way through. She knows that Raina uses lotion with sunscreen in it (a contrast to Will's, which features great quantities of cocoa butter) and that Bernice is partial to a men's-brand deodorant—she can smell it on them. She can smell all their soaps and lotions, shampoos and deodorants. She knows that Ashlee is right-handed but tries to lead with her left to show off her ring, though this week she appears to have abandoned the ruse, even if she's still wearing the ring.

Gretel knows about Ruby most of all, because Ruby is always shifting, moving, picking, smelling, doing, because Ruby just won't sit still. She knows where each drop of sweat on Ruby's face is dripping, knows where the crumbs of her cookies have fallen, knows Ruby's scent so thoroughly that she's sure she could sniff Ruby out of a lineup.

It's amazing, to Gretel, what Ruby is willing to do in public—what she doesn't even notice she's doing. She gobbles down cookies, mouth open, crumbs everywhere. She spits up sugar, gags up cum, drags her sweat across surfaces, bleeds her way across the city. Everywhere Ruby goes, it seems, Ruby leaves a trail: *This is me, I am here, I was here.*

Bernice arrives last and late, exhausted eyes punctuated by dark bags. She's wearing loungewear—knit drawstring shorts, a pink T-shirt with a stretched neck, old sneakers with ankle socks.

Most notable, however: the step stool looped under one arm. The stool is a single step, China blue with an inlaid mosaic of bright white-petaled flowers with leafy stems and big centers, wide as shocked eyes.

She walks across the room, plops into her chair, then carelessly thrusts the stool onto the floor. She pushes it as far into the center of the circle as she can with her foot, leaves her leg outstretched, the tip of the sneaker still in contact with the stool. She looks around with a set jaw. "The furniture is beside itself," she says.

The women throw glances at one another. "What's wrong?" ventures Raina.

"They're dead," says Bernice.

"So, same?" says Ashlee.

"I'm awake, they talk. I try to nap, they talk. I leave, they just keep talking." She taps the stool with the toe of her sneaker. "But not Astrid. Astrid's quiet as a mouse. Quieter. She hasn't said a single word." Bernice stares the stool down. "Right?" she says, then louder: "Right?"

The stool is a stool. It doesn't move. Bernice removes her foot with a jerk.

"When's the last time you slept, Bernice?" Will asks.

"For more than a few minutes?" asks Bernice. She starts pushing down a cuticle. "I sleep between the screaming, you know. The crying. The wailing."

"If you want them to shut up, then that stool is basically a model citizen," says Ruby as she inspects a package of cookies at the snack table. "What the hell is this? Sugar-free?" Raina offers her a granola bar instead.

"Why is it so important that this stool speak?" Will asks.

Bernice drags the fingertips of her thumb and forefinger down her nose, then slides the fingers across the purple bags under her eyes. "We have to hear her story," she says.

"Do we?" asks Gretel.

"How else can we help her?" says Bernice. "And if talking doesn't help, then what are *we* doing here?"

"Isn't it, like, maybe different with the furniture?" says Ashlee. "Because they're dead?"

Raina nods in agreement. "The furniture isn't really capable of change the way we are."

"But are we really capable of change?" asks Gretel. Will nods his *Say more* nod. "Bernice still has the furniture," she says. "Ruby still wears the coat, Ashlee the ring."

"You don't have to throw us all under the bus just because you're afraid to take your turn," says Ruby through chewed granola bar.

"I'm just saying that the past is over, the damage done."

"This isn't about changing the past," says Will. "It's about changing the future by learning from the past. You don't think there's a benefit to sharing stories?"

"I do," says Bernice, looking pointedly at the stool.

"I believe stories have a cumulative cultural effect," says Gretel. "But even that isn't always positive. It depends on who's telling the story." She picks up her coffee cup, as if to sip from it, but simply holds it instead.

"But in this case, that someone is you," says Raina. "You get to tell your own story."

"What story exactly?" says Gretel, more harshly than she means. "What story do I have to tell?"

"How would we know?" says Ruby. "You've said, like, ten sentences this whole time."

"The premise of the group presumes a relatively coherent narrative," says Gretel.

"Yet you're here," says Will. "You wanted something out of this."

"I try not to waste too much energy wanting things," says Gretel.

"What was your reason for coming?" asks Will.

"I lost someone important to me," Gretel says.

"And you think this relates to your past?" asks Will.

"I don't know."

"Will it hurt to find out?"

"Of course it will," says Raina.

★ ★ ★

My memories come in flashes of feelings, not words: a hard ache in the stomach, the tickle of a fingernail rising up a neck, the hot acid scrape of sour candy on the tongue, of bile in the throat. Details strewn like crumbs down a dark alley, leading me nowhere.

Hans and I rarely talked about those three months we were missing, not least because we didn't agree on what happened. When we did talk, we talked about work, his as a bartender at a bougie Manhattan hotel, mine at The Met, where I am a conservationist. He asked me about which items I was working on, which exhibits were closing and which were forthcoming. He had a collection of the colorful tin-plate museum admission buttons corralled in a tray on his entry table where he set his keys. I don't know where he got them, because the button system was replaced with paper tickets long ago. Still, I knew he was proud of me.

About a year ago, he was married at the City Clerk's Office. He had been dating the woman for years, but somehow I imagined it wasn't serious. I stood by his side in a plain gray dress with a handful of other attendees: two couples, the bride's sister, the bride's parents, ours being dead.

After, we all went out for dessert in a pricey, clean-lined bakery with a checkerboard floor and battalions of bright cupcakes lining lit display cases. Somehow I hadn't realized this was the plan, a little reception at a bakery. Everyone else seemed to know, had dressed for it. They were wearing bright pastel ensembles that matched the frosting.

The air inside the bakery was nauseatingly thick with butter and sugar. A cupcake appeared on my plate. Hans's bride had set it there. She was smiling before me, her face excessively heart-shaped, like a box of valentine chocolates. I didn't want to know what was inside.

I quartered the cupcake, halved the quarters, scraped a thick glob of baby-blue buttercream frosting onto my spoon, scraped it back onto the plate. Eventually, I took a small bite. As soon as the sugar hit my tongue, I felt a nerve in my jaw contract so thoroughly it was as if liquid were drawing through it.

"Eat, eat, eat!" said Hans's wife. She loved to offer me things I didn't want. She often offered to set me up on a date with a woman from her office. "Thank you," I always answered, shifting my mouth into a smile. "I'll think about it."

Eventually, she changed tack, suggested I try online dating.

At this, Hans had offered a slight, knowing glance, the kind of glance our childhood was built on. I didn't even use social media. We both knew I would never try online dating. It was all allure, like browsing shop windows. As if it mattered what you looked like. As if you could tell from a picture or even a person what was hidden beneath. As if everyone weren't impossible once you got to know them. As if people were possible to get to know.

But then, here was Hans, married now, proving different. Here he was in the bakery, face flecked with frosting, reading his vows to love and protect.

He laughed, his fillings shining silver in the afternoon sun. His laugh was full-throated, openmouthed, extravagant, the laugh of a traitor.

I felt far away, as if I were watching him through a crack in a door or the bars of a cage, as if I were outside looking in.

Love and protect? I kept thinking. I already did that. I already did that.

* * *

Gretel hardly knows what she has said and doesn't know what to say next. Her earbud cord, she realizes, is still coiled around her index and middle fingers, splinting them together. She slips the cord off, slides it into her pocket, stretches her fingers apart.

Is she really planning to tell near-strangers secrets she hasn't dared tell anyone else? And how is she supposed to concentrate? Ruby is tearing the granola bar wrapper into tinier and tinier shreds. Ashlee keeps adjusting in her seat, simultaneously and constantly pulling her dress both up and down, to cover her boobs and butt respectively, but it just keeps snapping back to size. Raina's legs are crossed and the foot hanging in the air is turning in circles from the ankle. Bernice has decided to use the stool as a footrest, though she doesn't look comfortable with the choice and keeps shifting.

"Do you often feel on the outside looking in, Gretel?" asks Will.

"Yes."

"Do you put yourself on the outside?" asks Will.

"Yes."

"You're impossible," says Ruby.

"And aren't you?" says Gretel, but there is no malice in her voice.

"Not to change the subject," says Ashlee. "But didn't your sister-in-law have, like, color guidelines for the bridal party?"

"I think it was meant to be a more casual affair," says Raina.

"But, like, why choose *gray*?" says Ashlee.

"Gretel's cultivating a downer, rain-cloud aesthetic," says Ruby.

Bernice repositions her feet on the stool, crossing her ankles, reconsidering, recrossing them in the opposite direction.

"Maybe you wanted to blend in," says Will. "Or maybe you were sad that your brother moved on and you couldn't."

"I don't blame him," says Gretel.

"No?" says Will.

"I want him to be happy."

"But, like, do *you* want to be happy?" asks Ashlee.

"After the wedding, I made the mistake of hoping."

★ ★ ★

I met Jade at a bookstore. I treat bookstores like Saks Fifth Avenue: perusing but rarely buying. I am a connoisseur of bargain bins, libraries, used bookstores. But still, guiltily, I'll slink into a new bookstore from time to time, let my fingers glide across the spines, sleek and shining as if glazed.

I saw a woman in the Nonfiction aisle with a book in her hand. She was flipping it over, back to front, front to back, her lips set between her teeth. Her short, dark hair was collected into a tiny bun. Frizzy hairs ran up the nape. Her black skinny jeans pulled against her thighs; her blouse was salmon colored with pin tucks and lace. I was wearing my standard ensemble: jeans and a button-down.

When she looked up at me, I saw the delicate mole on her chin. I was embarrassed she had caught me looking, but she just smiled. Her teeth were a testament to a lifetime of dental insurance.

"I can't decide if I should get this," she said, holding up the book so that I could see the cover, black and white with art deco type.

I'm not one to accept advances, especially in the sober light of day, but I took a step toward her. "It's good," I said. Abruptly, I turned ninety degrees and scanned the shelves, as if I had just been browsing there.

She was undeterred. "You've read it?" she asked, impressed. "It looks sort of depressing." She slipped it back onto the shelf, pulled out another. "What about this?" she asked.

Soon, we were sitting in the bookstore's tiny café. She was downing an iced coffee so fast it made my teeth hurt. She'd also bought a powdered Linzer cookie and two books—including the depressing one, on my recommendation. The books sat dangerously close to a pool of condensation, though she didn't seem to notice.

"I'm Jade, by the way," she said. She took a bite of the cookie.

I was so busy watching the white powder transfer to her upper lip that I simply said, "Gretel." As soon as I'd said it, I felt frantic, like I'd dropped something priceless down a sewer grate. I usually introduce myself as G, though mostly I try not to introduce myself at all. It's the name, of course, that gives me away. Have you ever met another Gretel?

I braced myself for the expression of recognition, the one I had seen on the faces of doctors, dentists, social workers, detectives, teachers, school principals, admissions officers, bosses, receptionists. The wary looks were one thing, but the pitying looks were worse—the cocked head, the big, sorrowful eyes, the pursed lips—

always under the guise of helping. But even they wanted to know the sordid details, wanted to decide for themselves if I had told the truth.

But no look crossed Jade's face.

I smiled, but I felt uneasy. Was it possible she didn't know?

It was possible. Jade, it turned out, was six years my junior. She was too young to have paid attention when the story broke: a brother and sister went missing, reappeared three months later miles from home.

It was possible she had never seen the award-winning photo that made us famous, had never heard the motherly warnings, the wild versions passed down on the playground. It was possible she had never fallen down that particular internet rabbit hole, had never read the great Reddit debates about what really happened. Had the kids run away or gotten lost? Had they been kidnapped off the street or had someone taken them in? Who was the mysterious woman? Why was she never found? Had one of the children killed her? What to make of the different conditions in which the siblings returned? Had they invented outlandish details as a ploy for attention? Were they covering for someone? Was it possible that their "disappearance" was an elaborate scheme by the parents for media attention? And what about what the little girl kept insisting, had never stopped insisting: that the woman's house was made of candy?

Jade broke off a piece of cookie, stretching her hand toward me. "Want some?" she asked.

I reached toward it, then caught myself and drew away.

To want is to be bewitched, I've long thought. If it's beautiful or sweet, it will ruin you.

★ ★ ★

187

"I heard all about you in middle school," Ashlee announces. "And I'm even younger than Jade."

"What did you hear?" asks Will.

"It was all, like: candy house, evil witch," she says, clawing her hands and making a face, as if to make an impression of a witch.

"I fell into the rabbit hole," admits Bernice. She has slid down in her seat, her feet still on the stool, knees bent, T-shirt bunched behind her. "I was so intrigued, which horrifies me now. To be fascinated by tragedies. I was into all that stuff, the crime mysteries. Why are you so curious until it happens to you?"

"So it was wrong to listen to these fucked-up stories when you *wanted* to hear them," says Ruby, "but now that you *don't* want to hear them, it's wrong not to?"

"You're supposed to bear witness, not enjoy it," says Bernice. "It's not supposed to be entertainment."

"You expect people to care about this depressing shit without a hook?" asks Ruby. The silver shreds of granola wrapper are littered around her like confetti.

"Drawing people into a story is a way of ensuring they'll bear witness," notes Will.

"People should listen because they want to understand," says Bernice, "not because they're voyeurs or amateur sleuths."

Ruby gestures to the stool. "You think *forcing* someone to share so you can 'bear witness' is better than being a true-crime junkie?"

"I'm trying to help her," says Bernice.

"Like I said before, you've got some fucked-up masochistic martyr thing going on."

"Masochistic? Me?" says Bernice, laughing a little too maniacally. "Me?"

"Tell you what: you get rid of your furniture, I'll get rid of my coat," says Ruby.

"I can't just throw them away," hisses Bernice. "Your coat isn't *talking* to you."

"Do they even like hanging out with you?" says Ruby. "How would you like being an ottoman in the house of your ex's only surviving ex?"

Bernice removes her feet from the stool and squirms up in her seat, looking embarrassed.

Raina fills the ensuing silence. "You know, Gretel," she says. "I was a teenager when your story broke. I wasn't paying particular attention to the news at the time, but I've never forgotten that photo of you and your brother reuniting with your father. It's stuck with me all these years. I thought the picture was about love, about the bonds between a father and his children. It tugged at my heartstrings—tugged at everyone's heartstrings." She tucks her hair out of habit, though it's already behind her ears. "It's ridiculous, but I always thought of that photo as the end of your story. It never actually occurred to me that you'd grow up."

* * *

In the famous photo, my brother and I are running toward our father in a hospital hallway so blindingly white it looks like a passage into heaven. My father is a blurry figure in the foreground. He's crouching, arms wide, back to the camera. I am in focus, out front, skinny as a twig. My brother is slightly behind, chubby but cute. My curly hair stretches out behind me. We are cleaner than we've ever been, thanks to a hospital wash and polish. We look like children from a detergent ad. We are dressed in brand-new, coordinated green gingham ensembles, stiff and bright, perfectly sized, like no hand-me-down I'd ever received before. My eyes glisten with tears. We are so small, so much younger than in my memory.

The photographer just happened to be in the hospital with her son, a coincidence that changed my life. The reunion picture was too perfect, the kids too cute, the mystery too intriguing for this not to make national news.

But where was the news when we were poor and dirty and missing? And what story did that picture tell?

The click and flash of the camera, and then the scene keeps going. I don't run into my father's arms. I stop in the middle of the hall as my brother rushes past. My father groans as he scoops Hansel off the floor. My father is skinny and gray, and his eyes are inscrutable. I look around the hospital hallway, searching for our mother. Where is she hiding? I can't picture her face. When I try, all I can see is that terrible woman. "Where've you been?" my father asks, as if we had decided to walk away. And then he descends into thick, heaving sobs, which could be guilt or sadness or relief.

For a long time after, what struck me most about that day was not being found, not being reunited with my father, not the news of my mother's death, but the new gingham dress. I remember touching it before putting it on, rubbing the puckered cotton between my fingers. A cardboard hangtag with elegant cursive hung at the back, along with a tiny plastic bag of pearly, emerald buttons that matched those sewn on the front. I left it all attached. I liked the feeling of the cardboard riding stiffly against my back, the tiny bump of the buttons reminding me that the clothes were brand-new. I could be a girl who wore a dress like this, I thought. It seemed, for a moment, so simple to strip away the past, to start anew.

Afterward, I wore that dress to school every day. I won't forget my teacher laughing, holding scissors with bright orange handles: "Have you been wearing it like that this whole time?" she asked. "The tag is supposed to be cut out, sweetie."

My face burned—not just from embarrassment but anger too.

I knew instantly that my dress meant nothing. My brother and I, we still lived in a shitty part of town, in a tiny apartment where cigarette smells clung to the carpets. I had been missing, homeless, kidnapped, stuffed with sugar only to be starved. I had done the unimaginable.

There was nothing sweet about me.

"I'm not a child," I hissed, and she stepped backward, as if I might hurt her, though she was the one with the scissors.

In the hospital, we were clean and adorable. We were alabaster white and wearing J. Crew. For a few weeks, we were heroes, survivors. No one appeared concerned about the more fantastical details of our stories. A psychologist noted that "inventive confabulation" was "an ingenious defense mechanism in response to trauma."

But soon we were back in our old, stained, ill-fitting clothes, our trashy Section 8 housing, and the frame shifted. People began to question our stories, our motivations, our parents' motivations. Perhaps we weren't heroes so much as victims—it was possible, even, that we were victims of ourselves, of our own circumstances, of our own baser instincts. Rich kids are inventive. Poor kids just lie.

It's true, of course: our stories didn't add up.

Also true: the fucking story will never add up.

★ ★ ★

Bernice is standing at the snack table with the step stool, working a napkin into a crevice between mosaic-tiled bones, trying to clean off the dirt that came from her sneakers.

"There'll always be a bunch of assholes who think you're lying," says Ruby.

"It's different when you have proof," says Gretel.

"What is your deal with proof?" says Ruby. "Why don't you just believe what you remember?"

"I get it," says Bernice. The napkin is tearing to shreds. "You want proof for yourself. For example, it wouldn't exactly hurt if someone else heard my furniture speak."

"Perhaps that's why you brought the stool," says Will. "Because you wanted us to hear her speak, because you wanted corroboration."

"If I wanted you to hear someone speak, I would've brought a Tiffany," says Bernice. "Maybe I should've brought a Tiffany."

"Maybe you were afraid of what would happen if you brought her and we didn't hear her," says Gretel. "Maybe it was safer to bring Astrid."

"Sort of like how I wish I had all of the footage from the show, to prove I wasn't a total bitch the whole time?" says Ashlee. "But also, like, I sort of don't want it? Because what if I *was* a bitch the whole time?"

Bernice looks at the mangled napkin as if it has wronged her, then throws it into the trash.

"Do you need wet wipes?" asks Raina.

"If I needed a screwdriver, would you have one in there too?" snaps Bernice.

"A tiny one for your glasses, yes," says Raina.

"Why do you keep taking Bernice's shit?" Ruby asks.

"Sorry," says Bernice sheepishly, accepting the wet wipes.

Ashlee turns to Gretel. "Quick quesh," she says. "I'm wondering if maybe we can get back to the romance part of your story?"

Ruby smacks her palm to her forehead. "Not every story is a love story, Ashlee. *Your* story wasn't even a love story."

"I don't know," says Gretel. "Maybe this one is a love story after all."

* * *

More surprising than Jade's original appearance were her subsequent ones. There she was in my apartment, frequently with food in tow, entire meals, frozen pizzas and premade salads, rotisserie chicken and mashed potatoes, pork tenderloin and carrots for roasting, because it turns out I had often forgotten to eat.

"How do you forget to eat?" she'd ask with a giggle, drawing the items from her tote like a magician or a witch. I'm wary of gifts. Nothing is free. You always pay for it later.

There she was, plié-ing down to assess a shelf, her face bright in the light of the buzzing fridge, her Lycra jeans taut against her thick quads. There she was, tossing the spoiled milk, the sweating green deli meats, the brown peaches soft with rot, making room for the sourdough bread, the bags of apples, the fat wheels of cheese.

There she was, extracting the enormous bottle of extra-strength Excedrin from the spice drawer, relegating it to the medicine cabinet instead. There she was, trying new recipes in my narrow kitchen with the sticky faux linoleum floor, the beige square of countertop too small for food production. My apartment, I realized, had only one chair. The bed was a twin. There was no art on the walls.

I would hear her clinking, clattering, sighing in the kitchen, and even so, when I looked up from my book, I was surprised to see her there. I liked the way her tongue broke between her teeth when she was concentrating, the way she bent down level with the meniscus to make sure the measurement was exactly right. I liked the way she set a timer, then sunk into my desk chair and asked what I was reading.

And so I took bites of food I didn't want to eat, butter and grease slick on my tongue.

"Thank you," I said automatically.

When she pressed her hand into the small of my back, my throat tightened and my chest swelled, a feeling like nostalgia, like she was someone I had already lost.

At night, Jade looked sleepy and satisfied. She would give me a gentle kiss on the forehead, a flourish, then extend her arm out below my pillow, so I could curl up into the nook of her arm. She would fight off sleep a little for my sake, her tired, brown eyes glistening like wet lollipops. She was so kind, Jade, and yet whenever her thick eyelashes came together, I thought of a Venus flytrap snapping shut, sucking the protein out of some insect that was probably still alive.

She slept so peacefully, until she met me.

One night, I awoke sweating and terrified. I could still see the afterimage of an old woman's face, her eyes strange—too wide and rarely blinking. Jade was beside me, rubbing her jaw, her own eyes shining in the dark. "You got me," she said.

"Shit," I said. "I'm sorry." My tongue felt like sandpaper; my jaw was clenched tight as a fist; the veins running from my temples pulsed. A dentist once told me that I grind my teeth so hard, I've worn through the enamel. I'm down to the dentin. Next is the pulp, raw nerve.

"No, no," said Jade. "It's okay. It wasn't that hard, just surprised me."

She lay back down, stacked herself into me, her hair sweeping over my face. I tried not to smell her tropical shampoo. I let my fingers glide against her jaw.

"You have a lot of nightmares," she said. "What are they about?"

How could I answer? What could I say without giving myself away?

In some dreams, I didn't tell her, I'm a piece of dark, hollow chocolate living on a grocery store shelf in an airtight box with a clear plastic front. I have giant eyes, but I can't close them. I have a mouth, but it doesn't open. I feel like I'm slowly suffocating. Some grocery store shoppers pick me up, shake me around. Others don't notice me at all. They walk by carrying sharp knives that glisten under the lemony fluorescent lights, they carry assault rifles as dark as licorice, they carry scythes slung over their shoulders, the crescent blades curved like a witch's beckoning finger.

In other dreams, I struggle to stay afloat in a rich sea of butterscotch with a consistency between molasses and mud. When I thrust my hand from the muck, butterscotch pulls from my fingers in strings, like spit that drags at the corner of a mouth. On a distant shore, translucent blue and red bricks are stacked to form cabins that shimmer and wink in the orange sun. But I don't dare swim to them. I would, it turns out, rather drown. Something flicks past me—a fish, bright red and rubbery.

Even in the dream, I think, *What the hell is the moral of this fucking story?*

There's a dream in which I am reclined in a dentist's chair. My mouth is open wide and a light shines on me from above. The dentist is an older woman with big eyes, a thin face, a dark mole on her chin. As she smiles, her lips curve, and her teeth, sharp as candy corn, seem to rise above the line of her lips. "They are all cavities," she cackles. One by one she begins to tear out my teeth, which are square and matte like Chiclets. Beneath my teeth, hiding in my gums, are strings of candy necklaces. The dentist pulls them out like gauze. I feel them drag against the raw interior of my gums. On the little steel tray beside the dentist's chair, candy is piled high and bloody.

"G, what are they about?" Jade asked again.

Outside the gray bedroom, a siren wailed like a pained animal, faded away. "Car accidents," I said. "Police cruelty," I said. "Zombie apocalypse," I said.

"Your nightmares," said Jade, "sound like what someone would make up about nightmares." She yawned in little sucked-in breaths.

"I guess I'm not that deep," I answered.

"Oh, I don't think that's true," she said. "I wouldn't love someone basic."

My jaw contracted, as if my mouth were full of sugar.

In the streetlight angling through the blinds, Jade's skin seemed to shimmer like some bright thing dropped on a dim street. But where did that get me?

It made me uneasy, to be in public with her, as if the relationship might disintegrate when exposed to fresh air. Since I lacked haunts, we went to hers—dimly lit gastropubs, clean imitations of farmhouse grit, rough-hewn wood tables and exposed brick walls, poverty made sleek and expensive. I was both appalled and drawn to the uncomplicated pleasure with which she ordered and ate food: lobster mac and cheese served in a greasy skillet, bright orange cauliflower disguised as buffalo wings, flourless chocolate tortes, dark as a blackout.

She shared everything with me. Not just her food but also her passwords, all of them: Netflix and the *New York Times,* Comcast and Capital One. Her toothbrush appeared in my medicine cabinet, an immersion blender in a kitchen drawer. She spoke in soft, nostalgic tones about her parents, how her father coached her softball team, how her mother made potato bread on snow days, setting dough in a silver bowl by the window so that it could rise in the warm winter sun. Her childhood was made up of cartwheels and lemonade stands, stuffed animals and ski trips. Her parents owned a sprawling summerhouse upstate, not far from the vacation estate of a certain reality TV host.

"What about you?" she asked, her arms curling around me. "Tell me more about you."

I told her about my job as a conservationist, explained that art is not always received in its original condition, and that's where I came in. I was not a restorationist, I clarified. A restorationist restores a piece to its original form, whereas a conservationist simply preserves a piece so it won't change any further. As the conservationists like to say: a restorationist would have put arms back on the *Venus de Milo*. A conservationist ensures no more limbs fall off. She seeks to be invisible, to neither reimagine nor reinvent, to keep what is broken exactly as it is, to never replace what is missing.

"That's kind of sad," Jade said, frowning, caressing my forehead.

To improve her mood, I told her about the Japanese art of kintsugi, in which broken ceramics are rejoined with gold lacquer. The narrative draw of such a piece is the damage itself, the breakage and its healing.

"That's so beautiful," said Jade. "I like that." She drew her finger down the middle of my chest. "Where have you broken?" she whispered. Then she zipped it back up. "Where have you healed?"

I didn't tell her about the years I had spent searching for evidence from my own life, sifting through the theories and clues of amateur sleuths, analyzing old newspaper articles on microfiche, combing through satellite footage. Even if the house was gone, I reasoned, some remnants might remain: crystallized foundation of sugar, stain of red dye #3. But I found nothing.

Instead, I told her that I was the first in my family to finish college, never mind go to grad school, that I had worked like a dog to pay my way through.

"You must be very proud," she said. But she wanted more.

What could I say? There are parts of my real life that feel like a nightmare, and not just the parts you are thinking of. There are years that I can only recall as a series of free dental clinics, of long lines in the cold dark, a Black Friday of healthcare. The gymnasiums, lined with padded lounge chairs, echoed with groans and screams. My teeth throbbed. After, I would find myself shaking, unsure of how much time had passed, of which teeth had been fixed and which had been pulled. The pain waited patiently beneath the Novocain, my face so numb that I could not possibly arrange my mouth into a smile, though I tried. "Thank you," I managed, my tongue fat. The dentist would smile that furrowed-browed, pursed-lipped, cocked-headed smile that I hated so much.

My brother and I, we paid for our childhood with these smiles. We were raised on the pity of strangers: EBT cards and blue lunch tickets, hand-me-downs pulled from black garbage bags in a musty church basement, shelf-stable goods for Thanksgiving each November, and, at Christmas, gifts presented by old women in a YMCA rec room that smelled much like this room, like gym socks and basketball rubber.

Cans of creamed corn and of cranberry sauce, a Candyland game missing the pieces essential for playing it, enormous T-shirts, extra-small snowsuits, and, once, a hot-pink chiffon dress with giant bows running down the back, as if I had an occasion for wearing it, or wanted to.

"Thank you, thank you, thank you," my brother and I said, turning our mouths into smiles.

"Don't take candy from strangers," the warning goes, and I am the poster child. As if we hadn't been taking everything, all along, from strangers.

I didn't want to tell her these things, so I told her a handful of cleaned-up childhood tales, the drama-less highlight reel, as if poverty had brought us together. I told her I spent summer days throwing pebbles off the overpass, fall days chucking acorns at the prep school kids, kids not unlike Jade herself. I told her we broke all the right rules. That my mother took us to the playgrounds in richer neighborhoods, then swung us higher than any of the other kids. I told her that my father snuck us toys from work, stuff from the loading dock that had been damaged during shipment. I told her we siphoned TV from neighbors, that I stole books from school, then stayed up late reading them in bed. I told her about the cold winter night the power went out—didn't say *was cut off*—and the whole family slept in the den under a pile of blankets.

As if life could be packaged up like this, contained, delivered in a few anecdotes, bright and glistening, easy to swallow: all insight, all joke, all moral. As if real life offered any consistent essential truths. As if it were possible for me to explain myself. As if I wasn't always leaving out the most important parts.

I didn't describe the essence of poverty, how tragedy begets trag-edy: my father's job gave him a hernia, the hernia lost him his job, the lost job lost him his health insurance, the lost health insurance meant bills for the hernia and my mother self-medicating again, which eventually would prove fatal. I didn't tell her how each night I went to sleep listening to my parents' voices rising into the night. I didn't tell her about the mice running through the walls, about the black mold creeping from the corner of my ceiling, until one day it was over me and my mother's voice through the wall shifted from hysterical to coldly practical. "What choice do we have? There's no food, there's no fucking money. Tell me, what are the fucking choices? At least someone else will be able to take care of them."

And these are the *believable* parts.

One night, half asleep, I said to Jade, "Imagine this. Imagine a smell: thick, warm, and sweet. Butterscotch and chocolate, cinna-mon and yeast." I smiled, but my stomach was tied in knots.

I peeked through my eyelids to see Jade's face: soft and grateful, as if I had just given her a fragile gift. Her thumb caressed the middle of my palm so lightly yet repetitively that the skin started to feel numb. "Your mom must have been quite the baker," she whispered.

"Do you have pictures of when you were little?" she asked.

If she had typed my name into any browser, she would have had a picture in an instant.

* * *

"Why didn't you tell her anything?" asks Ashlee in a near whine, wringing her hands. "On *The One* you really get a leg up with a traumatic story."

Gretel stares out the window. Her eyes feel heavy, hard, excessively round. The brick wall is bright red in the late afternoon light. Some bricks are darker than others, and each week she finds herself searching for a pattern, as if what is obviously random might have some secret structure. "Tragedy isn't capital," says Gretel. "It doesn't buy you anything. It doesn't automatically make you a better person. And it certainly doesn't make people fall in love with you."

"Buys you time," says Ashlee. "On the show. You get to stay longer. Shows your strength of character."

"Trauma, in and of itself, bestows nothing," says Gretel.

"It gives you power," says Ruby. "People are fascinated by us."

"You're mistaking pity for interest," says Gretel.

"I'm not mistaking anything for anything," snaps Ruby. "People are drawn to us."

"Like a horror movie," says Bernice. The stool is now sitting on her lap. "Like a car accident. The thrill is that they aren't us."

"We're specimens," says Gretel. "Zoo animals."

"Okay, whatever," says Ruby.

"Stay with this, Ruby," says Will.

"Are you a fucking Magic 8-Ball, Will?" says Ruby. "Are there only eight different things you can say?"

"You're angry," says Will.

"To be honest, I thought Gretel, of all people, would get it," says Ruby. "We both escaped being eaten for lunch, just to have the media eat us for dinner." She pauses to pick at skin on her lip. "We're a rare breed, you know. Child stars of tragedy."

"I'm not a star," says Gretel stiffly.

"So humble," mutters Ruby.

"I don't want to be known for being a victim," says Gretel.

"When did what we want matter?" says Ruby. "You're fighting reality. I'm leaning in." She tears off a piece of skin, flicks it to the floor, sucks the blood off her lip.

"You're stewing in it," says Gretel.

"I'm not stewing," says Ruby.

"You're literally sweating in a coat made from the skin of your abuser."

"At least I'm actually *living* my life," says Ruby.

"You cultivate misery," says Gretel.

"Oh, and you don't?"

"My life isn't defined by what happened to me."

"Are you kidding? That's like saying a shadow isn't defined by the sun."

Bernice puts her fingers in her ears, starts quietly humming.

"Guys, you're making Bernice go crazy," says Ashlee. "She gets enough of women arguing at home."

"Bernice is making herself go crazy," snaps Ruby.

Raina, concerned, looks to Will, but he's too enthralled with the scene to notice.

Gretel throws a hand in Bernice's direction. "Is this *better*? This public drama?"

"You don't think your smallness, your quietness, takes up space?" says Ruby. Ruby turns to Bernice, who is still humming. "But also: Stop it! Fuck. You're freaking me out."

Ashlee taps Bernice on the shoulder. Bernice stops humming, opens her eyes with a dazed look. Ashlee pats her hands in the air as if asking a museum visitor to bring down the noise level. Then she turns to the group, narrowing her eyes. "Calm down," she hisses, putting her finger to her lips, her bright pink nail so long it's almost in her nostril.

"Thank you, Ashlee," says Will. He thinks for a moment. "Gretel and Ruby, maybe there's a way to explore this tension." He pats his thighs, stands up. "Let's pull two chairs—"

"No," says Gretel, shaking her head. "I'm not doing it."

"Well, there's something we can agree on," says Ruby.

"There's been some ground—" says Will.

"I really don't give a shit about how fucking groundbreaking the research is, Will," says Ruby.

Will sits back down, presses his lips between his teeth, exudes disappointment. "I know it can seem silly," says Will. "But there's value in reaching beyond our comfort zones."

"I think a lot of us are already far outside of our comfort zones," says Raina.

Will picks a piece of phantom fuzz off his pants.

Ashlee, in an apparent effort to comfort Bernice, has taken the step stool off Bernice's lap and is squatting on the floor, patting it like a good dog with one hand as she pulls at the hem of her dress with the other. "She seems sweet," says Ashlee.

"Well, we wouldn't know, would we?" says Bernice, her voice cracking.

"This is a fucking shitshow," says Ruby. "Bernice, look at me," she says. "You have to find a way to sleep this week."

"I'm not getting rid of them," says Bernice.

"Then buy a white-noise machine. Take a nap at your sister's. Something. Okay?"

"Okay," says Bernice. "The earplugs aren't working."

"No shit," says Ruby.

They all sit quietly for a minute. Ashlee traces the bone flower on the stool, which looks even brighter blue against Ashlee's pink nails. "Why didn't you just tell Jade?" she asks Gretel. "Were you afraid she wouldn't believe you?"

"Even if she did believe me, she wouldn't have understood," says Gretel.

"So you were afraid she would believe you?" says Raina.

"I'm afraid that I don't believe me," says Gretel. "I'm afraid that I don't know what to believe. My own brother doesn't even believe me. He was *there*."

Bernice looks down at the stool, follows Ashlee's finger as it traces bone. "Maybe it's better to spend our energy being okay with what we don't know than obsessing about trying to know what we can't," she says.

"I'm just tired of convincing people, over and over again, of the same thing I have to keep convincing myself of," says Gretel, "that the worst things that happened to me might actually be true."

★ ★ ★

Here are the facts, insofar as they are written in the police report: two children, ages six and nine, are discovered by a woman on her way back from picking up ramen at a corner store. The girl is severely malnourished; the boy is not. They are both dehydrated.

They are both dirty. The kids seem a little spaced out. The girl twirls around on the sidewalk. The girl refuses to eat. The woman takes the children to the hospital. The girl crawls under the nurses' station, extends a pencil out to nobody. She closes her eyes, grabs the pencil with her other hand, clutching it. "Too skinny!" she cries in a haunting, high-pitched tone that is not how a little girl should sound.

I remember the police interview, the two detectives: a woman with short brown hair and a face like a moon; a man, all muscles, with a pinched face and a long forehead. I remember a tiny room with a big mirror. I remember sitting in a blue chair at a high table. I remember concentrating very hard on drawing black loops with a broken crayon, terrified that I was in trouble.

What are you drawing? they asked.

Scribbles. Licorice.

How did you get lost?

My parents left us.

You mean you got lost?

Yeah.

What did the house look like?

Covered in candy.

You mean it was brightly colored?

Yeah, because it was made of candy.

Who was she?

An old woman.

How old?

Like my grandma's age. Like old as a witch.

And was she nice or was she not so nice?

Not nice. First I could eat only candy, and then nothing at all.

But your brother could eat?

She was fattening him up.

How did you get out?

We escaped.

By the end of the interview, my paper was full of black loops, rising, rising. Already I was learning the art of tailoring the story, adding and subtracting so I wouldn't get in trouble. My brother was somewhere in another room, telling his own version.

Why didn't you call home? they asked him.

Because we wanted to stay.

Then why did you leave?

She was dead. The house smelled terrible.

My brother backtracked on only two details. The first was that the house was made of candy. The second was that the woman was dead, though he could not explain why we had left.

When I read the police report many years ago, much of what I remembered about that day matched up with what was written in the report. However, the interview was not conducted by two detectives. It was conducted by one woman. I suddenly realized that my memory had overwritten her with two detectives from a famous, long-running cop show. If a detail like that could shift so easily, what else might have shifted?

Could I be wrong about the house?

But I remember it.

But houses aren't made of candy.

But then where the fuck were we?

I was alone slicing cucumber in my tiny kitchen when the phone rang. As soon as my brother's number popped up, my heart clenched. He never called.

"Hello?" It was a woman, not my brother. "Hello? Gretel?" the voice said.

"Yes?" I managed. My knife was poised mid-slice.

"Gretel?" it said again. "You're dating someone?"

"What?" It was my brother's wife.

"My sister told me you were dating someone," she said.

"What?"

"My sister said your"—I heard the split-second pause, the word-choice grope— "partner posted a picture on Instagram or Facebook or something. They went to the same high school."

"What did your sister say?" I asked. Eight million people in this city, but of course. If Jade had posted my picture, it was only a matter of time before someone identified me. Or maybe they already had. Maybe Jade already knew. How long did it take, I wondered, how close did you have to be to someone, for a secret to become a lie?

"That you were dating someone," she said. "She figured I knew. Apparently it's been, like, six months."

She waited for me to say something, maybe explain or apologize, but I didn't.

"Well, okay," she said finally. "I don't know why you didn't tell us. We'd like to meet her. Anyway, here's your brother."

In the background, the muffled handoff revealed my brother hadn't expected to be given the phone.

"Uh, hey," Hans said. "You're dating someone."

"Yeah," I said. An awkward silence. I leaned into the knife, finally finished cutting through the slice of cucumber. "Can I ask you a question?" I said.

"Sure."

"What did you tell your wife about the whole thing that happened?"

"Which whole thing?" he asked. I heard him shuffling to another room, closing a door.

"Come on," I said.

"I don't know," he said. "I told her the situation generally. I mean, she'd read about it."

"Did you tell her about the house?" I asked.

"What could I even say about the house?"

"Do you remember it?"

"I remember what we thought," he said.

I can still see it exactly, at the end of a dead-end alley, a row house without a row. I can still see the brown walls, the gloppy mortar, the coal-black cornices, the red-and-white-striped trim, the cloudy stained-glass windows, the bell-shaped lawn ornaments in every color, glittering in the evening sun. Even then, I had been sure my mind was playing tricks on me. We were lost, we were hungry, the rats had ruined our plan, were scampering across the city high on the Adderall we had planned to follow home. I'd read stories about men lost in the desert who walked toward water glistening on the horizon, but the water just kept getting farther away. But when Hans and I sprinted toward the house, it stayed right where it was.

"We were kids," he said.

I can still see Hans—still baby-faced at nine, with all of that hyper energy, those swirls of greasy blond curls—clawing at the mortar, scooping palmfuls into his mouth, his eyes glistening with frantic energy. I can still taste the gingerbread on my tongue, can feel the rawness of my elbow from cracking the wall.

"Who was that woman?" I asked. Her face was narrow, her eyes were wild and wide, her teeth were yellow and too white and missing and filled with gold and silver, like they had endured generations of haphazard, free-clinic dental work. She had the deep, hoarse voice of a former smoker.

"Why do you keep calling her 'that woman'?" Hans asked. "Sure, she was a little strange, a little lonely. But, Gretel, she took us in when we had nobody."

"Took us in?" I hissed.

"If it was so bad, why did we stay?" asked Hans.

"She was holding us captive!" I said, thwacking off another slice of cucumber, then another. "If she was so fucking nice, why didn't she call our parents?"

"What did we have to go home to? Come on," said Hans.

"She kept us apart," I said.

"She gave us our own rooms," he said.

"I hardly saw you," I said.

"There was a PlayStation in my room," he said.

"My room was empty," I said, thwacking. "She was *starving* me. I was only allowed candy. Then it was nothing. Then I was licking the windows for lack of real food." I had been sticky from it. My teeth ached with sugar. My tongue stung. There was a raw emptiness inside me, hunger beyond hunger, my stomach like a bag I kept flipping to the seams: still empty. I grew used to the hunger, came to think of it as power instead of weakness. I needed nothing. I could live off nothing. I could exist on willpower and air.

"You refused to eat any actual food, Gretel," he said. "She was *trying* to feed you."

Beef stew and quiche, spaghetti and chicken parm. Hans ate it all, but I didn't dare sneak a bite. Somehow that woman could sniff out any trace of food on my breath, could smell my secrets. I can still feel the tingle of her fingernail rising up my throat, clavicle-divot to chin-point. "Open," she'd wheeze, already knowing what I had snuck inside.

"You didn't see it," I said. "She was different with me."

"I just don't understand why she would feed me and starve you, treat me like a prince and you like trash," said Hans.

"She had plans for you," I said with a hiss. "She was fattening you up."

The words had just fallen from my mouth. There was a long silence in which I wondered if he'd hung up, but then his voice came through in a whisper: "You must have thought so," he said softly. "I remember what you did."

My jaw loosened. It seemed I'd been clenching it for years.

"Does it haunt you?" he asked.

"No," I said. "I would do it again in a second."

What I wanted to say, what I didn't say, was that of all the memories that haunt me now, of all the memories that might haunt me forever, it won't be the house that was or wasn't made of candy and it won't be that woman. It won't be her greasy gray hair, not the way it seemed to crawl on her head like thousands of centipedes, not her wide strange eyes, not her fat brown mole, not her rotting yellow teeth, not what I imagined was behind those teeth—the black pit of a stomach that had digested children before. Not her laugh, not the cackles that pierced the air like breaking dishes, not her screams as she burned, like the wails of an infant, not the sickening smell of burning flesh mixed with the sweetness of candy, not the mess we saw in the oven after, slivers of yellow bone sticking out of a sizzling, tarred lump of blackened flesh.

What will haunt me is what came before that, before the woman. It is my parents leading us along the sidewalks at dawn, through a part of the city we didn't know, my stomach so empty it felt full, my head seeming to drift above me like a balloon, and my brother holding up the rear, dropping Adderall in a trail behind us: just in case, just in case.

★ ★ ★

Ashlee's mouth hangs open.

"Don't dislocate your jaw," says Ruby.

"What?" whines Ashlee. "What kind of parents ditch their kids in the middle of a city?" She is sitting on the stool in front of Bernice, and Bernice is braiding her hair.

"Interesting," says Ruby. "I assumed you were shocked by the murder."

"Sounds like the psycho lady deserved it."

"We can't know for sure," says Will.

Raina shakes her head. "You're missing the point," she says. "Gretel was abandoned by the people who were supposed to love her." She turns to Gretel, says in a soft, motherly tone, "It makes sense that it's hard for you to trust people, to trust Jade."

"If you don't trust someone, can you, like, really be totally *with* them?" Ashlee asks. She seems startled by her own question. "Like, can you love someone fully if you don't trust them?"

"Do you think you're capable of fully trusting?" Will asks Gretel.

"She's trusted us," says Bernice, tying off Ashlee's braid. "She's told us all of this."

"I've conceded to the premise of the group," says Gretel.

"Do you think you're capable of love, Gretel?" asks Will.

"Of course she is," Raina responds, fast and firm. For a moment, Will looks taken aback, and then, almost, impressed.

Raina turns to Gretel again. "What you did to that woman you did for your brother, which shows your great love for him, and also how capable you are of loving."

"You've said that with conviction," says Will. "And I think you're right. I think there's wisdom to pull from the wreckage." He purses his lips, taps his fingers together, thinking. "I wonder what other lessons we can take from your stories."

"What do you mean by 'lessons'?" says Ruby. "Like, *Don't take candy from strangers*? Like after-school-special shit?"

"You don't think we can learn from the past?" asks Will. "Do better in the future?"

"Of course," says Raina. "But maybe we shouldn't parse these stories for morals."

"Aisha says morals create a labyrinth of rules geared toward blaming the victim," says Bernice.

"Gotta agree with the lamp," says Ruby. She sits up, wags her pointer finger, takes on an air of mocking authority. "Be patient, be kind, be good, say please, say thank you, don't speak unless spoken to"—her voice is rising, quickening—"don't forget to smile, don't give it all away, don't disobey your teachers..." She stops suddenly, looks round at the group to see if they are with her.

"Your boyfriend," Bernice adds.

"Your husband," says Raina.

"Your producers," says Ashlee.

Ruby glances at Gretel, offers her a beat to contribute. Gretel looks in her lap.

"But don't, you know, follow them blindly either," Ruby says.

"Hold this key, but don't go in there," says Bernice, shaking her head. "Don't you dare open that door."

"Don't cross the street without looking both ways," adds Ashlee.

"But don't dawdle," says Raina.

"Yeah, don't get distracted on your way," Bernice says, wagging her finger at Ruby.

"Or, actually, you know what?" says Ruby. "Maybe don't even be out there, on the street, not if it's dark, not if you're alone, not if you're a kid, not if you're a woman, not without a rape whistle around your neck, not without pepper spray clutched in your hand, not, anyway, if you're wearing that outfit."

"But, I mean, don't be a prude either," says Ashlee, pulling at the hem of her dress.

Ruby nods at Ashlee, and then all of the women, save Gretel, smile at one another with a kind of surprised delight, like band members who finally got the song just right.

Gretel watches Will. He is trying to smile, trying to join into the moment, but the look on his face is awkward, disoriented, like he is the captain of a ship—startled by the direction the wind is taking him and searching for a way to course-correct.

"Maybe just don't leave the house at all," Gretel pipes in. "Maybe stay home."

"But isn't that where accidents happen?" says Ashlee.

"So lock all of the doors," says Ruby.

"Doesn't always help," says Bernice.

"Don't let anyone in," says Gretel.

"Unless you trust them," says Ashlee.

Gretel feels a shiver run through her. Her bones feel cold. Her teeth. She is overcome by the strange sensation that they are, in fact, the wind, and not as tractable as the so-called captain might think. Because here they are, going somewhere without him.

"Especially not if you trust them," says Gretel.

★ ★ ★

Jade and I were at the convenience store picking up beer. A little TV hung from the ceiling showing news of women no one cared about until they were charred remains. It was not a story, at the time, that I was paying attention to, but the volume was so loud and the details so gruesome it seemed impossible to ignore, though the cashier had managed. He was laughing at something on his phone as Jade and I waited for him to ring up the six-pack.

When the cashier finally looked at my card, he did a double take. He raised his eyebrows. He smirked. "Gretel, eh?" he said. "Want to buy some candy?"

The TV blared death. My smile was a melon rind, a meat hook. For some reason—to buy time, perhaps—I glanced at the candy rack, as if contemplating his suggestion: Warheads, Atomic Fireballs, jawbreakers, Cry Babies.

I turned back to him. "The name's German," I hissed, as if I were some other Gretel.

Jade waited until I was sliding the six-pack into the fridge to ask, "What was that about?" Her voice was too high to be nonchalant.

"How would I know?" I said. I couldn't tell if she really didn't know or if she was bluffing and she already knew, was giving me one more chance to tell her first.

I lay down on the bed and fell asleep almost instantly, though it was the middle of the afternoon.

I woke a few hours later sweating, suffocating in a daze of smells. I couldn't parse reality from dream, dream from memory: pancakes and syrup, garlic and butter, lemon and sugar, roast chicken and honey. My stomach heaved; bile rose in my throat, then retreated. My apartment was full of smoke. Meat sizzled in the kitchen. Garlic invaded my nostrils. A cloying sweetness hung in the air, seemed to stuff up my lungs.

In the kitchen, beyond the humid haze, I found Jade humming, leaning over the hot pan, tea towel tucked like an apron into the rolled waist of her bright pink pj pants. She stopped humming to taste-test from a black plastic spoon.

My T-shirt clung to my chest. My pj's were pasted to my thighs. The stove made my apartment into a hotbox, yet Jade hadn't opened any windows. Behind her, in the window that she hadn't opened, the fluorescent-orange, post-sunset clouds were stretched across the sky like pulled taffy.

The kitchen was a disaster. Blue flames licked stainless-steel pans. Food simmered on every burner: jasmine rice, chicken covered in orange sludge, glazed carrot rounds bright as peach rings. On the counter, two half-used sticks of butter, half melted.

"I can't eat all that," I said.

Very slowly, she stirred the orange chicken. "Maybe you can eat some of it," she said in a tone with a tone beneath it, like a board that had finally begun to creak under my weight.

How had I believed that it was possible to date someone?

"My teeth," I said.

"I know," she said, sighing.

"The dentist is expensive," I said.

"You work at one of the best museums *in the world*," she said. "You can afford to go to the dentist."

A thick silence descended.

We ate in our usual configuration: Jade on the bed, pillows stacked behind her, me at the desk-table. I could feel the negative energy radiating off her like heat. I'd opened a window, but no breeze blew in. I took a bite of rice for show. "This is nice," I said, trying to fill the silence, though only managing to highlight it. I made my lips smile, a rope of licorice held slack. I pushed the chicken around on my plate, watched the orange oil slick it left behind.

Instead of eating, I drank, and the more I drank, the stranger Jade's face became, narrower, a moon shaved down in phases, until it was just a sliver of itself, in danger of disappearing. But her teeth, they didn't shrink. Instead, they seemed to grow: longer, whiter, white as Necco wafers, teeth that might consume anything, foie gras or human flesh. She was still on her parents' plan.

Soon, Jade's plate was empty, her lips stained orange, her teeth licked clean. She set her beer on the bedside table and walked into the kitchen without a word, pulled a lemon meringue pie from the fridge that I hadn't even realized she'd made. She cut a single slice, for once not bothering to serve me something I wasn't going to eat.

Back on the bed, she began consuming the pie by puncturing it, licking the fork, puncturing it, licking the fork.

I felt a dark nastiness rising within me.

"Let's just watch something," Jade said.

We scrolled the endless scroll of streaming shows, thumbnails beckoning with fat fonts and bright colors. I am picky, but Jade liked everything, every strain of prestige and trash TV, drama and comedy, true crime and reality.

Maybe one day there would be a true crime series about me and my brother, I thought. It would be called *Little Liars*. Jade would watch it. She'd accuse me of never telling her something everyone insists I lied about anyway. Or maybe there would be a reality show called *Little Sister*. It would be about a couple of poor kids whose parents have too many jobs and not enough money. The older brother makes the little sister SpaghettiOs for dinner. The twist: it isn't even a TV show. There aren't any cameras. No one's watching at all.

Jade's mouse had landed on a thumbnail of *The One*, and the preview for the season automatically played. Bright music and laughter, lush green landscapes, deep red roses, a turquoise sea, a massive sparkling engagement ring.

"Let's watch something light," said Jade, talking over the preview, "like a superhero movie." Couldn't she move the mouse a centimeter so it would stop playing?

In the preview, an abrupt shift in tone: a woman I did not yet know was shouting, "I'm gonna be the winner! I'm gonna be the winner! I'm gonna be the winner!" Then her mouth hung wide-open, lips ringed with red wine.

I couldn't focus. I seesawed the tab on my empty beer can. My lip curled. I wanted to pick a fight. "Light?" I said. "What about the collateral damage? The superhero swoops in, takes out a few bodegas? What about all the traumatized bystanders? The small business owners? What about, at the end, when the hero refuses to

215

kill the mass-murdering psychopath? Even when the hero's got him right there, in a choke hold?"

On the screen the woman's eyes were stony, mascara smeared. She said, "I'll do anything for love. I'll fight for love. I won't let anything get in my way." She hissed, "You *stole* my time." Then she pounced.

"You think each person should just be their own judge and jury?" Jade asked, as the girls on the screen wrestled and screamed. "That people should get to define justice on their own terms?" She wouldn't look at me. Did she know what I had done? "It's about not stooping to their level," she said. "It's about not reacting to one's baser instincts."

Jade's pie was abandoned, the plate lopsided on the beige comforter. The mole on her chin seemed like a crumb that had been dropped there.

Jade's morals were all theoretical. Whereas, I would kill for love—I had already proven this—I would do it without blinking an eye.

The woman on the screen held her bloodied hands in the air, as if in surrender.

I dragged my tongue across the caps of my teeth, some of them flat-filled and dimensionless, the texture of concrete, and then that one smooth spot—no tooth, just a space, all gum. I set my tongue in the gap, a snake lurking between the rocks. Then I let it loose. "Do you recognize my name?" I asked.

"Should I?" she said.

"I knew a woman once," I said. "She had a mole on her chin, just like you." I pointed to Jade's mole.

"Okay," said Jade. Cautious. "Who was she?"

"Either a saint or a cannibal." Why would I start like this, angry and in the least believable way?

The ad was looping around, the same scenes playing over again.

"You *stole* my time," the woman hissed. But no matter how many times you say it, you don't get stolen time back.

"I don't understand what's happening," Jade said.

"You asked about when I was little," I said. "Unless you already know?"

She blinked at me. "Know *what*? How would I know anything about you, Gretel? What have you given me? What of yours do I have? You won't take anything of mine," she said, gesturing toward my full plate of food. "And you won't give me anything. *Anything*."

When we broke up, there would be nothing of mine to extract. I had no items at her house, no passwords to change, no accounts to unfollow, no pictures to take down. I still had a single bed. I still had only one chair. This time, I hadn't even left a trail.

The Office

The man scrubs the footage back, replaying Raina's entrance, watching the muscles of her arms shift, ever so slightly, as she walks. Have her arms been that toned all along? Has she always looked like this? Raina, these past few weeks, has seemed so bright and fresh, so confident, so independent, so beautiful it almost feels like a slap in the face.

He scrubs the footage back again, plays it forward in slow motion. On the monitor, Will smiles slowly. His eyes are practically twinkling. Raina, slowly, smiles back, just a glance with the corners of the lips turning up, but it's a genuine smile. He pauses the video. The man feels strangely, inexplicably jealous.

Having distributed the first layer of lotion, the man is on to the second, massaging it top to bottom into his skin. He works it into his scalp, making his hair greasy. He rubs it into his face and his neck and his chest and his arms and his belly, and all the while he watches the footage, scrubbing backward, watching again.

"It's a longer story," she keeps saying, as if insisting, as if taunting him, though she only keeps saying it because he keeps playing it back.

What the hell is she hiding?

He scrubs back further, has Raina enter the room again and again.

He's not making it up, is he? About the way they're looking at each other? Will and she would be fairly close in age.

The footage plays, but the man at the desk can't pay attention to Gretel's story. "Love and protect?" she says, and it's like the words have drifted in from a dream.

The man, already naked, already covered in lotion, already rubbing it in, watches Raina, and does the one thing that Will, for lack of parts, can only dream of doing.

Week Five

Raina

Raina sits alone in the basement rec room watching the window-panes weep as she waits for the others to arrive. The rain has escalated to a downpour, sounds like a crowd running toward her, chasing her down.

That morning, Raina had sent her daughter off to college with homemade snacks, a mini fridge, a new computer, and a whole new wardrobe. "Ma," she kept saying, "this is too much! This is enough! I'll be fine."

After, Raina had stood at the floor-to-ceiling window, watched the storm over the city; Manhattan sprawled out forty stories below her like a diorama. She could hear her husband pacing in the office above, invisible yet present, like a mouse in the wall. The view made her lonely, as if she were a queen standing on a stone balustrade balcony, everything and nothing within reach. She couldn't stand to be in the house anymore, so she left for group early, making her way on foot in the rain, Upper East Side to Lower, fueled by low-fat lattes poured in and out of her travel mug.

Raina pulls at the skirt of her dress. It's a floral dress from another era of her life, a little shorter than she'd typically wear now and tighter than it used to be, though cheaply enough made that the elastane has mercifully loosened. Her hair has grown a little since the first week of group, and she doesn't bother to tuck it behind her ears.

She wonders if the cheap dress looks strange paired with her chic leather tote and her double-breasted gabardine trench, which she's unbuttoned but hasn't taken off. Does she look like one confused person or two different people, put together? She has an interest in halves, in how people divide, how one part of yourself can separate from the other so completely, so definitively, that the division is impossible to repair.

She discovered the dresses among her father's personal effects, which had been shipped directly to a storage unit in Brooklyn many years ago. She'd never even been to the storage unit until the week before.

The boxes smelled like mold and cheap whiskey, mostly contained useless knickknacks—a golden saltshaker shaped like a foot, a hedgehog toothpick dispenser, scraps of paper of all sizes and types, notes written by her father on Post-its and legal pads and the torn pages of books, contextless names and numbers. It was a little note like one of these—a cocktail napkin with ten numbers written on it—that had changed her life.

Will and the women trickle in with dripping umbrellas and an array of rainwear: Gretel an old, oversized anorak, Will a tan trench, Bernice a black shell, Ashlee baby-blue Chelsea boots and a coordinated anorak that looks like an updated, spunkier version of Gretel's. It gives Raina the sense that time has circled back, as if we, as a culture, just keep reusing and readjusting the same basic templates crafted long ago.

Gretel listens to whatever she listens to, her hair frizzy from the rain, while Bernice and Ashlee talk about a TV series, Bernice patiently explaining subtext that Ashlee missed. Ashlee yawns an extravagant yawn. The two women are from different worlds, different lunch tables at least, though they look equally exhausted. Bernice, less so than the week before. Ashlee, more so. Raina assumes Bernice has found some sort of briefly manageable sleep schedule—maybe sleeping at her sister's as Ruby suggested. As for Ashlee, Raina imagines there have been fights, that it's only a matter of time before a breakup. Though you never know. Some people stay together forever whether they should be together or not. Some people stay together for reasons more practical than love.

Raina and Will make small talk about the weather. His smile is like a sliver of light shining through the slats of a blind. That very first week, when he had made his way around the circle, looking at each of them, she had waited for him with a taut, courteous smile, preparing to make eye contact so that he not only would register her presence but also would know that she was registering his. It was a look practiced from years of attending Parents' Night solo at her daughter's schools. But when Will looked at Raina, she had been disarmed. He was not searching over her features. He was not trying to place her in relation to someone else. He was, in fact, looking *at* her.

Ruby arrives late and last and drenched, furry hood up, pink-stained fur slicked down from the rain. She bundles the bottom corner of her coat in her hands and wrings rainwater out onto the tiled floor.

"Ugh," says Ashlee. "Why are you always dripping? You look like a used tampon."

"I'd like to think I've had something to do with the improvement of your disses," says Ruby proudly. "Had a decent interview today. If you end up in the right part of Brooklyn, this coat is basically cool."

Ruby looks at Raina's floral dress. "Midlife crisis?"

"Possibly," says Raina.

Once they're all settled, they talk as a group about the previous weeks, about this week, in particular about how this is their last week, their final meeting. "I wonder what it would be like if the world heard your real stories," says Will. "The unfiltered versions, I mean. The versions you've told here."

"And in what universe do people just believe us this time?" asks Ruby as the others nod.

The downpour suddenly lets up. The lack of sound startles Raina. She sits straight in her seat. It's as if the imaginary crowd that's been chasing her down has not retreated but rather caught up, is waiting to pounce.

"So," she says.

"Last but not least," says Will.

From her purse, Raina draws out a stack of papers torn carefully from a legal pad. Her hands are shaking. "I hope you don't mind, but I've written some things down," she says. She smooths the papers on her lap, shuffles through them. The handwriting varies: some sentences are small and precise, others rush in slanting loops of black and blue and red, cut through with cross-outs, annotated with arrows and stars.

Each evening since group began, she has stayed up late, writing and rethinking and adjusting these pages. She imagined that eventually she'd pin it all down, record some definitive version, as if a story were a fact you could just get right. But the story kept drifting, ebbing and flowing, some details gaining importance, others receding, memories floating to the surface like seaweed.

Raina picks up the first piece of yellow paper. It rustles like a leaf in her trembling hands. She places the paper back on her lap, presses a clawed hand onto it, as if the paper itself were making the noise. She tries again, picks up the entire stack in two fists.

"It's okay, Raina," says Will. "It's okay. Just begin." He is leaning forward, hands clasped together, already on the edge of his seat.

★ ★ ★

"Hey," said my father to Jake—yes, *that* Jake—whom he'd met by chance at a bar and recognized from TV, "you should hire my daughter. She can do anything. Footage? Editing? She can do it all. She has the magic touch. She's in the film business, she's on the market, she can spin a yarn, she can spin a piece of motherfucking straw into gold." It was my father, of course, who could spin the yarn. When I was little, he'd whisper stories into my ear at night, his breath warm and sweet: a beautiful woman with hair like a rope, a beast with hunger in his stomach, another with hunger in his loins.

"She's a looker too, and young, but not *too* young. Plenty young enough. Anyone will tell you, she's the most gorgeous girl in the whole town." Perhaps the men in the bar all turned and nodded; perhaps no one said a thing. Perhaps they were all impressed that my father was talking to this man, the difference between them clear by their skin alone: my father's cheeks ruddy, wine-colored, tiny branching veins visible like faulty wiring; Jake's skin smoothed over, almost blurred, a retouched photo. They were nearly the same age, their hands both empty of rings. My father had given up on women even before my mother died, but Jake was newly bachelored and, rumor had it, ready for a wife.

Perhaps my father pulled out the picture of me from his wallet, the one from prom where I'm wearing a powder-pink princess dress and a sparkling tiara. "Could be yours," my father said—perhaps my father said.

I wasn't there, of course. I was in my room, asleep, and I stayed mostly asleep even after my father came home, his hard steps echoing through the tiny house. Then a thin strip of light below the door, my father's drunken whisper floating in: "Hey, I found you a real job in the city. Can you hear me? A real job!"

The next morning, I discovered a clean white cocktail napkin on the kitchen counter, set at the cleared epicenter of dirty dishes. *JAKE JOB IN CITY,* it read in all caps, a phone number written below it. My father's handwriting was precise, and I thought of the immense concentration it must have taken him to write that information down and get the napkin home in such good condition after his usual night of drinking. I slid it into my back pocket and went off to work.

I'd worked at the Centerville Queen Diner part-time through high school, full-time ever since I'd graduated almost two years before. I was taking night classes at the community college, fewer and fewer by the semester. Financially, I was barely keeping my head above water. Just when I'd saved a little, something would go wrong—car battery dead, boiler broken, that kind of thing.

The Centerville Queen was dated, with dark wood paneling, orange vinyl booths, and stained-glass pendant lights that ran up the aisles, scalloped with an awkward fruit motif, so the lamps dripped with bunches of purple glass grapes, the stilted shapes of apples and pears.

There, the months were short, but the days were long. *A watched clock never boils,* I often found myself thinking, as if at the end of the shift there would be some sound like a kettle whistle or a school alarm heralding my achievement, setting me free. Yet the months ran together, so alike they were inseparable into days.

I marched in and out of the swinging kitchen doors carrying

platters of watery eggs and corned beef hash, spinach pie and boiled pork chops, seas of marinara and melted mozzarella, eggplant or chicken lurking beneath, stainless-steel vats of gritty coffee, crowds of red plastic cups, ice clinking inside.

I smiled all day, smiled until my cheeks were sore, and then I smiled some more. I smiled like it was my job to smile, and because of the tips, it *was* my job to smile. I apologized for things that were not my fault, like the sulfur smell of the tap water and the look of the food, which was even less attractive than it appeared in the generic menu photos. Near the register, a display fridge whirred with slowly revolving tiers of Styrofoam cakes and real pies. *Going nowhere,* I often thought, *and not even fast.*

Our main clientele were high schoolers and old men. The former, not much younger than I. I recognized some from school. They split bills into impossible configurations. They left coins as tips, spread out across the table among crumbled napkins and wet straw wrappers. I collected them like a bird pecking at seeds.

Then there was the rotating array of greasy-haired, yellow-toothed men who, when not at the Queen, sat out on the peeling porches or broken lawn chairs around town, drinking forties and smoking cigarettes. It was rare that my father didn't owe one of them money, and sometimes, as I walked to work, any one of these men would shout after me, "Hey, come back here, good lookin'!" I refused to turn around. "I know who you are!" he'd shout after me, a threat. "You're Mr. Miller's daughter!"

I already knew who I was.

At the diner, these men and I engaged in a silent barter. I let them caress and wink and pat and I pretended to like it. Then I got what I wanted: a good tip.

By the end of my shift, I felt dirty all over, the grease and sweat clinging to my clothes.

The morning I arrived at the Queen with the napkin in my pocket was unusual. I saw a string of nearly identical women drifting down our dingy two-block main street, wearing frayed denim so short that the pockets hung below the hemlines. The women appeared to be about my age, with long legs and tanned skin that betrayed no tan lines. A TV crew scuttled about them—walking backward, making quick leaps to get out of the way. I was vaguely aware of *The One*, a brand-new reality TV show that would feature an eligible bachelor from our little town, though I hadn't imagined they'd want to film anything here.

Main Street was just one dilapidated block with a few junk shops, a hairdresser, a pizza parlor, two bars, and the greasy spoon where I worked. By mere contrast to their presence, the town seemed flimsy and ridiculous, like a ghost town from a western, as if posts might be back there propping up the dirty facades.

By direction, the women all stood outside of Jo's Junk and tinkered with the items displayed outside, playing to the cameras. One leaned over an old electric typewriter, bent at the waist so her behind stuck out toward the camera, the fleshy curve of each cheek peeking out from under her shorts.

Another—impossibly thin, with sharp shoulder blades like sprouting wings—closed her eyes and made a show of randomly selecting an object out of the dollar-only basket. She swirled her hand over the top, her shoulder blade surging under her skin. Then she dove her arm in and pulled out a naked, plastic, pink-skinned baby doll with matted hair and one blinking eye. The other eye was stuck. The woman, her eyes still closed, waved the doll above her head like a prize. The doll winked from across the street, like she and I were in on a secret. When the woman finally opened her eyes, she looked horrified to discover what she'd selected, as if she'd found a real baby living in such conditions, in such a town, with such terrible hair.

Only the doll had noticed me. I was standing beside a scummy plastic sign with the diner's name in bright orange capital letters over a tan background, a silhouette of a crown floating above the Q. A corner of the sign was punched through, so you could see the interior lightbulbs, an abandoned bird's nest in the bottom. I was wearing my waitressing ensemble: beige khakis, white polo, orange apron. My hair was looped arbitrarily into something that was not a hairstyle. We were so different, these women and me.

The Queen was buzzing with gossip about the film crew, the show, the famed host—Jake, who had previously been a staple of the game-show circuit. He was in town, refusing to stay at the Motel 6 and sleeping in his trailer instead. It occurred to me that the phone number on the napkin might actually have some kind of job at the other end of it.

When I arrived home from work late that afternoon, my father was asleep in the old brown recliner, the threadbare arms scratched through by our ancient cat. The silver boom box—nabbed by my father from the junkyard, though you weren't supposed to take the electronics—was tuned to the only station that came in. It was playing a terrible rendition of an already terrible song I'd already heard at least three times that day. I switched it off.

"I saw you took the napkin," said my father, suddenly awake. "What's my finder's fee?" Save his eyes, which pulsed sleepily in their sockets, he didn't move at all. He had a waterlogged look. All the skin on his face was puffy, a palette of veiny reds and shrimpy pinks.

"I don't want to be on that show," I said.

"On that show?" he repeated. "Why would you think I'd try to get you on that show? To marry some shit from this asshole town? What kind of prize is that? With a little charm, you could reel that in at the fucking diner." He paused for dramatic effect. "He said they needed an editor."

231

"He who?"

"That pretty guy from TV."

"Jake Jackson?" I said. Had he really spoken with Jake Jackson? "I don't have those skills," I said.

"Sure you do," said my father. "Didn't you take something like that at the college?"

"Copyediting," I said. "That's books. I don't even have a degree."

"Well, fine. Who cares? You think people get jobs because of talent? I showed him your picture." He moved his hand to feel his chest pocket for his cigarette pack, as if someone might have stolen it while he napped. "Did you see those women in town today? They were attractive, sure, but you're a real person and you don't look stupid. If I had your face, I'd be a king by now." With my father, compliments were cheap and buried deep, like pennies in the sand. "Anyway, I bet him two grand you'd be as good as I said."

"Bet?" I said. "Good at what?" I asked. "Editing?"

"Editing," he said, "whatever you can do to stick around."

* * *

Ashlee is sitting perfectly still, neck jutted forward, eyes bulging as if she might explode. "Jake Jackson?" she blurts out, unable to contain herself any longer.

Raina nods solemnly.

"You worked on *The One*?" asks Ashlee.

"More or less. More like less, I guess," says Raina. "It was a long time ago. Twenty years or so."

"Why didn't you mention it?" asks Will.

"I wanted...I wanted to be me without the context," says Raina.

"Without the baggage," says Gretel.

"Exactly," says Raina.

"Still," says Bernice.

"You know, Bernice," says Raina, "you said something early on that I can't stop thinking about. You said you've spent your life overshadowed—by your sister, by Ashton, by the dead women. You said you were always a reference point for someone else."

"And you remember that?" says Bernice.

"Yes," says Raina. "You put into words what I have always felt. My reputation has never been about me. I've always been a supporting character: a beautiful daughter, a brainless trophy wife, a dutiful mother. So what now?" she says, picking up her papers to begin again. "What now?"

*   *   *

The job—if you could call it that—was issued for a three-month trial period during which I might prove myself. I didn't have the skills, I didn't really want to work in reality TV, and I had no idea if they planned to pay me. To take it was stupid, like jumping off a cliff for the breeze. But, as my father noted, I didn't have much to lose.

I leaned against the bus window on the two-hour commute into the city, watching the sun rise in a purple sky. I had washed and washed the night before, but I was afraid that the diner smells had leached into my skin, that I'd be sniffed out instantly. By the time I crawled out of the subway, my stomach was in knots. I stood in the cold shadow of my destination: a towering, gilded art deco building.

I made use of my best skill: smiling. I smiled at everyone: the suited doormen with earphones curled over their ears like symbiotic worms, the lobby receptionist whose black heels clicked across the marble floors as she led me to the elevator, the administrative assistant who welcomed me with a curt nod, the interns—was I one of them?—who glared at me as I passed, the man with the cue-ball bald head—Dave, my apparent boss—who grumbled about the audacity of a celebrity who hired women based on bar conversations and him suffering the consequences.

Dave gave me a quick tour of the office, which was generic and sparse compared to the grand exterior and lobby. The show was new, and there was a feeling of impermanence about the place, like they weren't sure if it would really get off the ground. Jake Jackson, host of many hats, had an office elsewhere. In a dark room, a dozen TV screens featured footage of the women I'd just seen across the street from the Queen. In front of those screens, headphoned men and women my age were hunched over keyboards, furiously transcribing. One of the women looked up at us with a scowl, her eyes glowing like a possum's.

I thought perhaps I was meant to join them, but instead Dave led me down one long empty hallway, then another, to a tiny, windowless office far away from everyone else, which had almost nothing in it save two office chairs and a desk topped with two large computer monitors. I would be assigned a series of editing tasks, to test my skill level. He outlined the first assignment as quickly as possible, using adjectives I knew as nouns I did not. "Of course, in Avid," I agreed, nodding avidly. He smirked, then let out a heavy nostril-sigh, dumped some binders on my desk, and left, closing the door behind him. I had a strange feeling that he had locked me in, that I was trapped in this windowless office to complete the work or die trying.

But when I put my hand on the knob, the door opened easily. I went to the bathroom, which turned out to be the chicest part of the office, with a black marble floor and individual mirrors over a trough-like steel sink. I stared at my reflection. My floral

A-line—my favorite of three floral dresses—had nothing to do with the black-and-white office ensembles everyone else was wearing. However, I did look pretty; I did not look stupid. Did it matter? I wasn't talented or well trained or well connected or well bred. I wasn't even crafty like my father. I had no idea how to get out of this one.

When I returned to my office, someone was sitting at my desk. His head was blocked by the computer monitors, but I could see his thin arm at the mouse, brushed with brown hairs, and, from under the desk, giant feet dangling a foot off the floor. A warm, rich smell emanated from him. It reminded me a little of the diner, but richer, friendlier, or maybe it was just a nice contrast to the sterile office scent.

"Hello?" I said.

The little man scooted out from behind the computer screens, rolling himself back by pushing on the desk. When his face came into view I willed myself not to look away.

His features were incongruous not just with each other but with the usual geometry of faces: severe and angular here, bulbous there—huge bumpy nose; giant ears; little, smirking mouth, crooked yellow teeth behind. His sharp, jutting chin made his entire face look like a fingernail clipping. His massive glassy eyes were almost endearing, childlike, a contrast with the rest of his ancient-looking head, which was so huge and heavy it seemed to have hunched his back. His skin had a glowing golden hue, as if he were wearing bronzer.

His clothes were something between North Pole and Renaissance fair: rust-red leggings, booties tied up with leathery string, a green felt hat and a matching cropped jacket, as if he'd stepped out of a different time, or a different world, one inhabited by different creatures set at a different scale.

He leaned back in the chair as if to prove how at home he was in it, but the chair didn't lean with him, he was too light, so he just slid limply down, cupped in the chair's gently curved ergonometry.

"Good morning," he said, squirming upward.

"Hi," I said, holding out my hand to shake his, leaning down a little—I hoped not impolitely—so he could reach. "What's your name?"

He looked annoyed, and I dropped my hand to my side. "My name," he said, "is for me to know."

"And me to find out," I finished automatically.

"No," he said sharply. "No."

"What department are you in?" I asked.

"I don't work here," he said. "I've appeared, to help you out of your little jam."

"Excuse me?"

"This stuff is easy for me," he said, waving his hand over the computer screen. "It's nothing. You're just grouping and organizing, flagging audio problems. Frankly, it's a little boring, considering my skill set. I can make a story out of anything. I can spin B-roll into TV gold."

"I'm sorry to be stupid," I said. "But I don't understand."

"What don't you understand? Editing? Or what I do?"

"Well, both," I admitted.

"It's frustrating, that people can't comprehend what I do," he said. "I'm an imp."

"I think it's 'little person,'" I said.

"Oh my God," he said, rolling his big eyes so extravagantly that I thought those giant brown irises might get lost in the back of his head. "Let me guess: you're offended by my ensemble too."

"No," I said.

"Well, you should be," he said. "I had a gig. It's humiliating." He scanned me with his eyes, but not in the way of men I was used to. "Anyway, it's not like you're a paragon of appropriate dressing."

My face flushed, and he looked sorry, so I moved on, back to the more pressing matter. "Why are you here exactly?"

"I help people," he said. "And I can help you right now."

"What do you want in return?"

"Nothing," he said. He put his elbow on the desk, rested his giant head on his hand, his tiny biceps bulging from the weight.

"There must be a catch," I said.

"I'm sure you'll get me back later somehow," he said with a shrug.

"But how?"

"Do you want my help or not?"

"I do," I said.

Without another word, he put on a massive pair of over-ear headphones, which he'd apparently brought with him, went back to the computer, and started, I guess, to work.

I sat in the office chair across from him, a little bewildered, a little hopeful. I could see his face in the gap between the two screens, which cast a blue-green glare on Little Man's severe features. Even with the office chair cranked to its highest level, Little Man had to look up. His mouse movements were almost imperceptible, just the index finger gliding over a tiny ball. His eyes were huge and wet, the pupils giant and wanting. His facial expression suggested a creature contemplating an evil plan. "Resting imp-face," he said when he caught me staring. "Can't you find something to do?" So I snuck out to the lobby and grabbed some gossip magazines, read about serial killers and celebrity crushes, examined a paparazzi shot of Jake Jackson's ex-wife carrying a Big Gulp and looking haggard. Apparently, the two had been living separately for years, but their divorce only recently had gained traction as a story, had done some damage, I gathered, to his reputation as the new host of a show about love and marriage.

Late in the afternoon, a knuckle-tap on the door, and Little Man bolted into the corner behind the desk, huddling into a ball. I threw my cardigan over him just as the door opened.

I was shocked to find Jake Jackson standing before me. I'd never seen a celebrity in real life. It was like seeing a famous site when all you've ever had were the postcards: the Eiffel Tower rising into a blue sky, Easter Island's giant heads listing out of the green hills. "Bigger than I thought," say some. "Smaller," say others. "I felt an oceanic oneness with the earth and all living creatures." Or, "Just a giant bell with a crack in it."

Jake was both shorter and more attractive than I'd expected. He had smooth, bright skin, perfect teeth, and wavy brown hair that matched his eyes. He looked at least a decade younger than he was. "Ah," he said, leaning against the doorframe, "there she is, Mr. Miller's daughter, live and in person. You look just like your picture."

I smiled.

"How's it going?" he asked.

"Great," I said. "I'm so grateful for this opportunity."

"To be honest, after meeting your father...I wasn't sure..." He laughed. "I wasn't sure what I would get. He's an excellent salesman."

"He is," I agreed.

"Dave being nice to you? Not giving you impossible tasks?"

"It's a cinch," I said.

"Really?" said Jake, raising an eyebrow. He glanced around the office. "They really didn't skimp on the glamour, huh?"

"I'm thrilled to be here," I said. "The bathroom is very glamorous."

Out of the side of my eye, I saw the cardigan heave.

After Jake left, Little Man rose from the corner, ghost-like, the cardigan still draped over his head. "'The bathroom is very glamorous'!" he said from under the cardigan. He smacked his knee, and as he bent over with laughter, the cardigan fell to the floor, revealing his strange, open face—his wet eyes slick with joy, wrinkles radiating from his tiny mouth like water rippling after a tossed stone.

★ ★ ★

Raina's voice cracks. Her chin trembles. She doesn't want to cry.

She pats the stack against the lap of her floral dress, as if it's important to make the pages flush, but she's just buying time to collect herself.

She's been sliding the finished pages to the back of the pile, though it gives her an unsatisfying feeling, like the story will never be over, never get shorter or smaller or lighter. Like she'll just keep coming up on that horrible ending, that wall of an ending that split her life in two.

The rain tinks against the window. Ruby's coat is still soaked, looks like the fur of a pink sea otter, but the other women's outerwear hangs drying on the backs of their chairs. Raina's still wearing her trench, and the coat suddenly feels very heavy. She clutches a hand to the collar, looks around for where she might put it if she takes it off.

"I'll take it," says Will, standing up.

She slips out of the coat shoulder by shoulder, Will taking it from her as she does. It happens so smoothly and elegantly that they almost look like a couple arriving at a party. He drapes it over his arm, looks around the room, decides to hang it on the corner of the storage closet door for lack of hooks.

"Thank you," she says, taking her seat again.

"Telling this story is making you emotional," says Will.

"He was important to me," says Raina.

"Jake," says Will, nodding.

"Little Man," says Raina.

"Ah," says Will.

Raina feels different without the coat, lighter, like she has shed a skin—no, peeled off a scab—like what was beneath before is reappearing, raw.

"Who was Little Man, really?" asks Ruby. "Why was he there?"

"I didn't really know," says Raina, "but I also didn't really know why I was there. If I had questioned Little Man, I would have had to question everything. And I didn't want to think about it."

"Also, gotta ask," says Ashlee. "Jake Jackson's been divorced? Like, when? I never heard that or else maybe I forgot it. I thought he was married to his wife for, like, twenty..." She gasps. "Oh my God." She puts her hand over her mouth. For a moment, she can't get out any words. "I know who you are," she manages finally. "I've *seen* you before."

"Jesus, Ashlee," says Ruby. She squints at Raina through her rain-smudged glasses. "Who are you?"

A strange smile slides across Will's face.

"Yes," says Raina. "I'm Jake Jackson's wife."

★ ★ ★

I arrived at the office the next day to find a shimmering rose-gold office supply set on my desk, with a note from Jake Jackson: *To add to the glamour,* it said.

I sat down, chopped the scissors through the air, then realized that Little Man was asleep under my desk, curled up like a cat.

I leaned down. "Excuse me?" I said.

He rubbed his eyes. "It's all done," he said. "Plus some extra stuff, to show off your chops." He crawled out from under the desk, jumped on top of it, took a moment to yawn and adjust his leggings, and then hopped like a spring toy directly into the heating duct in the ceiling.

"Hey!" I called upward. "Wait! Are you coming back? What's your number?"

"I'll be back in the afternoon," he called as he disappeared with echoing clangs.

Dave was impressed to the point of suspicion. "This is beyond grouping and filing," he said, eyeing me. He spun a pen in his hand a few times, then stopped it abruptly. "Community college?" he asked. I was offended by the implication but only nodded.

When Little Man returned—this time in child-size jeans and a tee—I asked him to show me what he'd done to impress my boss. Little Man grew excited, asked me to flip off the lights and pull up a chair.

With the lights off, the glowing monitor made Little Man's features appear even harsher, his eyes brighter and wider, his skin more golden. The editing program looked like the dashboard of an aircraft, but Little Man navigated through it as if it was nothing, using keyboard shortcuts to show off various tools: an audio window with a dozen slider controls, a color-correction window with bright gradient dials. "You can manipulate almost anything for the sake of narrative," he said, his enthusiasm palpable.

Little Man played an unedited and uneventful three-minute clip of Jake Jackson announcing that Tammy had been chosen for a coveted individual date. The date was princess themed, as evidenced by the dress that Jake Jackson had rolled out behind him on a garment rack. When her name was called, Tammy balled her hands over her face and squealed as a few women politely clapped.

Little Man paused the video. "Boring," he said. He opened his mouth and pretended to yawn. "The real magic," he continued, brightening, "is in the timeline."

He showed me a timeline featuring a series of rectangular segments placed side by side, each rectangle representing a separate clip. "Think of it as a collage," said Little Man. "Tammy is the natural choice for a villain."

"Why?"

"Because her neutral expression is smug. Because she's a messy drunk. Because the lead likes her, so the producers can prime her to be overconfident and everyone else to be jealous."

He hit PLAY. Now Jake Jackson's date announcement was accompanied by a musical crescendo, then a long pause in which the women waited with bated breath. "Tammy," Jake Jackson said, and the women seethed—jaws dropped, eyes widened, one woman gasped. The scattered claps seemed icy, mean. Someone walked out of the room. In individual interviews, the women railed against Tammy. "What a total bitch," said one, her words set over a close-up shot of Tammy looking smug.

When Little Man stopped the clip, he looked up at me with needy eyes and a toothy smile, awaiting praise.

I didn't know whether to be amazed or horrified.

He swept his hand past the monitor. "Reality TV 101," he said. He explained that the twentysomethings I'd seen sitting in the dark room had been doing the editorial grunt work, tagging and logging raw footage, of which there were hundreds of hours per day of filming, including long, individual interviews with each contestant, conducted by relentless producers.

The producers knew which role each woman would play before she even stepped onto the cobblestone driveway, knew who would be the villain, the hero, the sob story. The producers acted like confidants—found traumas and blind spots and sensitivities—then used their secret knowledge to create rivalries, elicit tears. Like inquiring into someone's allergies just so you could sprinkle the allergen into the meal. The producers deposited earworms, started rumors, asked leading questions. They woke the women in the middle of the night for interviews, had them stand for hours in high heels waiting for Jake Jackson to appear, took shots with them, though the producers usually just shot water.

The women were pawns in service of the story, Little Man told me. The key to editing was turning what actually happened into what you wanted to have happened. With good producers it was a cinch, but even without, there was always a way to make a story. Reactions to anything could be cut to look like reactions to anything else. Even non-reactions could be reactions. Resting bitch-face was a gold mine. Someone blinking blankly or staring into space could look like sass—or worse—if positioned right. You could imply nudity by adding a black box or a blur over a bikini. Frankenbiting was a last resort, an ethically ambiguous trick of cutting and pasting audio together, placing it over some neutral video footage. Using this method, you could get a girl to say just about anything about anyone in any tense. Little Man showed me examples as he talked, opening and closing windows so quickly I could hardly keep up. The "What a total bitch" line was not about Tammy at all but a complaint about waking up early.

"Do you feel bad about doing this to people?" I asked.

"Do *I* feel bad? This is *your* work," he said. "Besides, these women aren't heroes. You know how much capital beautiful people hold in the narrative economy? This hardly rectifies the imbalance. Anyway," he said, his eyes narrowing, "whatever happens on this show, these women will be fine. They'll get married. They'll have children. They'll have everything they ever wanted. What's more, they'll think they deserve it."

★ ★ ★

Raina looks up from her papers, right at Ashlee. "I'm sorry," she says. "What editing does, what production does, it isn't right."

Ashlee shrugs, examines her dried boot print on the tiled floor. "Not really your fault," she says.

"I could have spent more time thinking about how the show treats people," says Raina.

Will strokes his chin in thought. "It's interesting," he says. "Many people are made famous by these shows, make careers out of having been on them. Maybe it's more of a two-way street than we like to imagine."

"More like a dead-end street," says Ruby. "More like, embrace it or you're fucked."

"People are ruined by those shows, Will," says Raina.

"Ashlee," says Will, "if you could go back, would you decide not to be on the show? Would you rather still be working at a clothing store, unknown?"

"But, like, are we even 'known' anyway?" says Ashlee. "It's like the 'us' we see online or on TV or whatever isn't even us."

Gretel nods. "That's why we're here, isn't it? We've been reduced to a photo or a sound bite or a moral."

"Or, like, five hundred different memes," says Ashlee.

Will turns to Raina. "What about you? If you could go back, would you still call that number?"

"I can't say that I wouldn't," says Raina.

"What's even the point of asking that?" says Ruby. "We *can't* go back."

"Yeah," agrees Bernice. "Maybe it's not a thought we should entertain if we're trying to accept what happened and move forward. What if, for some of us, moving on involves finding good in the bad? Or being thankful for how we changed? That doesn't mean we wished it to happen."

★ ★ ★

Days turned into weeks. My office was tucked in an empty hall far away from everyone else, as if I were a princess hidden in a remote tower. When I did leave it, to go to the bathroom or the employee kitchen, no one spoke to me, though sometimes the interns or the loggers from the dark room would make a point to glare.

The assignments, which had no bearing on the actual show, were an increasingly difficult series of tests. Make Lindsay seem petty, make Tammy look peppy, imply that Georgia sleeps around, imply that Marissa is talking to a squirrel. Each time Dave gave me a new task, I had the sense that he wanted me to fail. But Little Man loved the challenge. Little Man nailed them all.

For me, the show itself was an afterthought. I spent half my day on public transit, and the other half sitting across from Little Man in the office, reading books and reveling in not being at the diner. I checked the clock often, just to think about the meal I wasn't serving, how sore my feet weren't, knowing full well I could be back to waitressing in three months. I enjoyed the reprieve and my time with Little Man. He was fond of office pranks—zip-tying my scissors, crawling under my chair just to press the release, leaping down from the heating duct before I knew he was there.

I had few expectations and no end game. The opportunity felt mysterious and fragile, a Jenga tower that would topple if I poked at the wrong block. Maybe Jake Jackson had some rich-guy savior complex. Maybe he made a habit of popping into junky towns, giving the prettiest girl a job, and waiting to see how she fared. Or how he fared—it had crossed my mind. As for Little Man, maybe he wanted a friend. Maybe he really did like the work—he talked about TV all the time, claimed the golden age of television was coming.

"Reality TV isn't exactly high art," I noted one day over lunch.

Little Man was sitting with his feet propped on the edge of the desk, but he'd had to slide way down in his chair to make it happen. His paper plate took up most of his lap. "I love *Starry Night* as much as the next guy, but you can only stare at it for so long," he said. "I *change reality*. I change what people think."

"Okay, Van Gogh," I said.

"Too much?" he asked.

I shrugged. "It must be nice to have a talent, though."

"You have talents," said Little Man.

"Like what?"

"Reaching high shelves," he joked.

"Flirting for tips," I said.

"Talent doesn't mean as much as people pretend it does," said Little Man.

I tore the crust off a triangle of sandwich. "Why are you doing this for me?" I asked. "You could get hired in an instant with your skills. You could get a job just like this. Maybe *this* job, in fact."

"Maybe," he said.

"Don't you have to pay rent?" I asked. "Health insurance?" He shrugged his tiny shoulders. "Is there something you want me to do for you?" I asked.

He squirmed up in his chair, wiped the crumbs off his lap. "Don't worry about it," he said.

He reveled in his own mystery. I knew almost nothing about him.

*

One afternoon, Little Man hopped down from the duct with a look of pure joy on his face, like he'd just won a big prize. He pulled something small out of his pocket, held it out in cupped hands—inside, a tiny furless creature that looked like a swollen thumb. A baby rat, he told me. He'd found it huddled all alone in a subway station.

I must have made a face.

"He's just a baby," Little Man scolded, pulling his hands away from me.

"Right," I said. "Sorry."

"Such a cute wittle baby," he said, petting it with a finger, looking at it with sparkling eyes.

He hardly touched the computer that day, was too busy ripping up printer paper for a nest, figuring out how to feed it, singing it songs. Before I left him that evening, I watched from the door as he leaned over the cardboard box in which he'd made the rat a bed. His eyes were big and bright. "Go to sleep, Tiny," he whispered to it. "Don't worry, I'll take care of you." My heart swelled.

Much to my continued surprise, Jake Jackson visited the office often, coming and going by way of the back stairs. Day by day he got closer and closer to my desk, until he was sitting on it, one leg crossed over the other. From my spot in the office chair, I was often eye level with his knee, and Little Man was hiding in a lidded trash can, which I'd scrounged from a supply closet and lined with a sheet from home.

Jake told me about his fitness regimen, laughed about the young and sometimes vacuous women who paraded past him each day—laughed, even, about a certain vacuousness that he himself embodied on TV, and even in his real life, in order to be fit for TV. "It's all in good fun," he said. "Honestly, we *do* help people find love."

One day he suggested I take a break from burgers and grab lunch with him, his treat.

"Burgers?" I said.

"Yeah, it always smells like burgers in here," he said. Was *that* Little Man's scent?

Over crab crostini and endive salads, over salmon filets and blackened fluke, Jake Jackson and I talked. He asked me about my life, about the town I grew up in, about my father's gambling, about my mother, who'd died in an accident when I was young. We didn't discuss my work, though we discussed his. He explained that hosting was just a stepping-stone to bigger and better things. He was grateful for the job, of course—he had, in fact, won the part over an older host who, sadly, was aging out of the business. Jake Jackson told me that the most important thing in his life was that he believed in love, that love was hope and that he hoped to be married again. It was the greatest tragedy of his life that it hadn't worked out the first time.

★ ★ ★

"What a tool," says Ruby.

"You think so?" asks Will.

"Yes," says everyone.

"He 'believes in love'?" says Ruby, rolling her eyes. "Who even says that? I'm pretty sure he just believes in rehabbing his image. Kind of a try-hard if you ask me." She looks at Raina. "I mean, sorry, but right?"

"But he's also kind of charming somehow?" says Ashlee. "He sort of nods at you like you're important? And then when he stops nodding you wonder what you've done wrong and you really want to be important again?"

"Sounds healthy," says Ruby.

"He's being replaced, you know," says Raina.

"WHAT?" says Ashlee. "No. Way. As host of *The One?*"

Raina nods. "Traded in for a younger model. He hasn't taken it well. I guess we're both having crises right now. My life was my daughter, his life was that show."

"Maybe you can trade *him* in for a younger model," suggests Ruby.

"I never understood why Jake Jackson got such great media coverage," says Bernice.

"Jake was different at the beginning—energetic and hopeful," says Raina. "Or maybe it was me—maybe I was different." She pauses. "I think there's another reason why people like him. An incident occurred"—Will leans in closer—"one that the media never fully understood, one that Jake didn't even understand. Ultimately, Jake's publicist used it to portray him in a positive light. Most people don't even remember the incident, but I don't think that light ever faded."

"Ohhhh," says Ashlee. "What happened? Was it something with...? I feel like I heard something. Like, was he some kind of hero?"

"We'll get there," Raina says.

★ ★ ★

I always relayed news from my lunches with Jake to Little Man. One afternoon, I relayed, perhaps a little dreamily, that Jake Jackson "really does believe in love." Little Man had come in moody that morning, in his Renaissance fair apparel. I couldn't see his face behind the monitor, just that little finger scrolling on the ball of the mouse with such ferocity that I was sure he couldn't actually be working.

"Little Man," I said. "It's possible that he, you know, *likes me.*"

"Of course he likes you," said Little Man sharply.

"I mean, when a guy like that likes a girl like me..."

"A girl like you?" he repeated. By the time I understood my mistake, it was too late, his fist was already hitting the desk with such force that the wood splintered with a thunderous crack. It seemed impossible that such a little body could wield such power. I cowered in my chair.

His hand was bright pink where it had hit the desk. I was worried he might have broken a bone.

"I'm sorry," I said.

The room was quiet. He leaned out from behind the monitor. His face was splotchy and pink, his giant eyes wet and welling. "No, I'm sorry," he said. "I guess you're so beautiful that you have to weed people out." He tried to smile. "And I'm so ugly that I have to weed myself in."

"Little Man," I said. "I'm a dime a dozen. But there's no one else like you."

"You know what people call me?" he said. "Uggo. Fuggly. Freak Show. Funnel Ears. Circus Act. Special Ed."

"Tell people your real name," I said. "Then they can call you that."

"They won't use it," he said. He pulled at his green jacket. "I demean myself. You know what I've done for fast cash? I've played goblins and trolls, mythical dwarves and Christmas elves. I've done stuff you wouldn't imagine." He was quiet for a minute. "My kind," he said, "in books we're always a certain way. Sneaky. I use it to my advantage. I play into it."

"You follow the template you're given," I said. "You become who you're told you are."

"Yeah, but now I have this problem," he said. "Sometimes I

don't know how to separate who I'm supposed to be from who I really am."

"Well, I know who you really are," I said. "You're talented, persistent, spry, a magician in the editing room, an exceptional keeper of secrets. You can jump so high it's ridiculous. That's practically a dating profile," I said. "All we need is your name."

He sniffed his massive nose, smiled sadly. "Yeah, and a picture," he said. "But thanks."

I started sleeping at the office during the week because it had become clear that I wasn't going to get paid—no one had even asked for a W-2. I was running down my meager savings on expensive commutes into the city. What's more, the timing belt on the Mazda had broken. I had to bike nine miles to the bus, on a rusty bike with a loose chain. My father kept saying, "Patience pays off," which was a little unlike him, though he had skin in the game. His favorite aphorism, which perhaps he invented: "Nothing's free and everything's sellable."

One rainy night, I was huddled up in a sleeping bag next to my desk when Little Man popped through the duct.

"What are you doing here?" I shouted.

"What are *you* doing here?" he shouted back.

Little Man leapt down from the duct and onto the desk, then the floor. "I was just going to catch up on some work," he said, pressing the release and then crawling up into the chair.

"You really don't get paid enough to work nights," I said.

"Neither do you."

I watched rainwater drip off his dangling booties as he worked. After a while, I tugged on a wet toe. He took off his headphones. "Yes?" he said.

"Do you like editing this much?" I asked.

"Yes," he said.

"I don't like anything that much," I said.

"Jake?" said Little Man with a frown.

I tried to deny it, though I couldn't help but smile.

"Raina and Jake, sitting in a tree," he tried. "Doesn't sound right," he said. "It sounds dumb, actually."

"I like hanging out with you," I said. I patted a spot on the floor next to me. Little Man looked unsure. "What's the point of working all night?" I said. "Take a break."

He crawled down from the chair and squatted at my side. I leaned toward him, sniffed, took in his hamburger aroma. "Where do you go all the time that you smell like this?" I asked.

"It's my natural musk," he said, yawning.

I tapped next to me again and Little Man curled up in the nook of my arm. He was so small. His knees only reached my waist.

I pulled the sleeping bag out from under me, stretching it across us both. We slept that way that night, and for many more after.

Jake Jackson was away filming in the Maldives when Dave called me into his office. "Sit down, sit down," he said. He tapped his pen on the desk and glanced out the window. "Need anything? Espresso?" I shook my head. "Listen," he said, "I never imagined you'd be able to complete all of these assignments. No one can ever do them all. To be honest, I'm not sure what to do about it, given the situation at hand." He adjusted his glasses, glanced at me, then glanced away, embarrassed. "You understand that I don't really have the power to hire for your, uh, position? That it is unlikely that you will be here long-term in, um, an employment capacity?"

"Oh?" I said.

He bit his bottom lip, looked at me. "Your situation," he said, "is entirely between you and the host."

That Friday, I came home, and my father wasn't there. Instead, a Post-it from the police lay in a curl between the screen and the front door: my father was in the hospital. I biked back out to Route 23, up the road I'd just biked down in the half-mooned dark. The air was windy and crisp, and my ears burned from the cold. Though there were no men out on the porches, I imagined their voices echoing behind me: "Hey, good lookin'! I know who you are! You're Miller's daughter."

My father was slumped in a plastic chair in the emergency room, his chin resting on his chest. But then he turned to me slowly, as if just coming to life. He had a black eye and a dark, bloody mouth. I knew he was drunk. "You're wondering how we're going to pay for this," he slurred. Then he winked. He held a cupped hand out to me. In it, a bloody tooth. "The tooth of Thomas Jefferson," he said. "Knocked out of his head by a rival."

"Which rival?" I asked.

His head lolled back on his chest and I thought he had fallen asleep or passed out.

"Adams?" I suggested.

"I'll sell it on eBay," he said without lifting his head.

"I want everything to be on the up and up," Jake said. His hands were on the arms of my chair and he was pulling me toward him. "What do you want?" He smiled. His teeth glowed like a magic portal into another world.

"The same things as you," I said. "I want those things."

Then I was perched on him on the big office chair, in a squat over his thighs, unable to get a handle on the rhythm.

The chair groaned beneath us. My skirt surrounded us in bloated floral hills.

"That's good, that's good," Jake kept saying.

I couldn't focus. My legs burned. He smelled like protein powder and mouthwash. I thought of Little Man, who at that very moment was crammed in the trash can, trying to make himself even smaller than he already was. I leaned into Jake to get a look at the trash. No movement.

I pictured Little Man in the darkness, crunched up tight as a rock, his giant head craned down, knees squashed to his forehead, his big feet thrust against the plastic side of the bin. An image flashed in my mind of that baby doll hovering in the air with her awful hair, her bright nakedness, her wild eye winking at me. It seemed as if that naked doll had been held in the air eons ago, a lifetime ago. The doll, Little Man, they were nothing like Jake, they were more than imperfect, they were grotesque.

But lovely, in a way, too. I know what you're thinking about Little Man, about his features, the more bulbous and severe of them. But there were certain unexplainable qualities about him, qualities of light and spirit, uncapturable by mere proportional fact. He was harsh and specific, like a pungent cheese or a piece of kitsch, a golden saltshaker shaped like a foot, a bile-green sweater you can't help but love. You don't love these things *despite;* you love them *because.*

I shuddered and then Jake shuddered, gripping my shoulders tight as if to save me from rocketing off.

My thighs twitched as I rose off him. I felt like I was dismounting a ride at the mall because my quarters had run out. Had I given something away stupidly, for free? Was it more like a trial offer, or like throwing away your only bargaining chip? "Why buy the cow..." my father always said. Why was my father always saying things? Why was I listening?

When we parted ways, Jake kissed me on the forehead and handed me an envelope. "This is for your father," he said. I furrowed my brow, but I knew. "Gratitude, my dear," he said with a smile. "He led me to you."

You could say my father sold me off, like an ancient bride. You could say that. You could say he cheated me into a new life. You could say that I had been his accomplice.

A few days earlier, I had spied a rose-gold stapler on an intern's desk, same as the one Jake had given me. She scowled when she caught me looking. "You know someone else used to have your little lair back there," she snapped, the first words she had ever deigned to speak to me. "The rose-gold office supplies are standard issue for Jake's attractive and unqualified new hires. Last one left hers behind."

"What happened to her?" I asked.

"Who cares?" she said with a shrug. "She gets to put a prestigious internship on her résumé." She looked back at her screen. "I guess it's one way to get a job, but the rest of us have to work for things."

To be blunt, she was not an attractive person. She had a pinched nose and tiny eyes. But she had her advantages: rich parents, which afforded her a degree from NYU, an apartment in SoHo, the money she needed to ride out an unpaid internship worry-free, a financial safety net that would allow her to try and try and try until she succeeded, until she could say she had worked hard and it had finally paid off, that success was a matter of pluck, not luck of the draw. She had never waitressed—I was sure of it—she had never smiled at lecherous diners for an extra buck. She was born into money, and I was born into my body. Why was it so different, to use one advantage or the other? "Believe me, you can bargain with anything," my father always said. "Sell what you have to give," my father always said.

★ ★ ★

Raina catches movement in the corner of her eye and glances up from her papers. Bernice is pressing and depressing the toggle button of the elastic cinch cord on her jacket, which is hanging off the back of her chair. "Sorry," Bernice says, dropping the toggle. She adjusts in her seat. "I should say something," she says. "I was acting just like this stapler woman, acting like your life was just handed to you because you're attractive and, I don't know, put together."

"It's okay," says Raina.

"No, it's not," says Bernice. "One, I was envious, and I didn't actually know anything about you. Two, I was acting as if using one's femininity is somehow the worst offense. Isn't that what the media did to the Tiffanies? And to so many dead women? And to Ruby, for that matter? Didn't Ashton do it to me? It's not like *we* made up the rules of the game."

"Society defines the terms of payment," says Ruby, "then gets pissed at you for how you pay. Meanwhile, Jake Jackson gets off scot-free with his envelope move? Super fucked up."

"How so?" asks Will.

"What the fuck do you mean 'how so'?" says Ruby.

"It's like her father sort of gambled her away to Jake Jackson?" Ashlee explains to Will.

"The money appears to have been a gift of gratitude, not a fee," says Will.

"Call it what you want," says Ruby. "Doesn't change the situation."

"No," says Gretel. "Don't call it what you want. The words are important."

"Raina was a consenting adult," says Will.

"It's true," says Raina.

"I'm not saying Jake Jackson committed a crime," says Ruby. "Just that he's an asshole."

Will scratches at his forearm. "She had a choice," he says flatly. "She wasn't forced into anything."

"Well, we all had *choices*," says Ruby. She scrapes at a piece of skin on her bottom lip, tears it off with a jerk. "Gretel chose to go into a stranger's house, and Ashlee chose to go on the show, and Bernice chose to date Ashton, and I chose to flirt with a wolf. Maybe the more important thing is that that bitch shouldn't have been holding kids captive and the producers shouldn't have been running a reality TV show prison camp, and Ashton shouldn't have murdered all of his girlfriends, and a wolf shouldn't have been chatting up a kid in the first place. And maybe Jake fucking Jackson shouldn't have made a fake job offer to a broke waitress twenty years younger than him by way of her father."

"You're bleeding," says Will calmly, pointing at where on his own mouth.

Ruby licks her lower lip, glaring.

Raina twists at the rings on her finger, as if they are suddenly too tight.

Will leans toward Ruby. "I can see you're upset," he says. "I wasn't attacking you. I wonder why you saw it that way."

"Fuck that," says Ruby.

The room grows quiet. Outside, the muted rumble of a broken muffler, the hiss of exhaust.

Bernice considers her fingernails, starts pushing cuticles back with a thumbnail, then abandons the task and looks up at Will. "You're doing exactly what Ruby is talking about, Will," she says. "You're reframing this conversation the same way people reframe our stories. They shift the focus onto one little detail—like what choices we made—and miss the bigger picture."

"That's called Victim Blaming," says Ashlee.

"That happens to be correct," says Ruby.

"The point is, you're shifting this whole conversation, Will," says Bernice, "making it about some issue with Ruby instead of what it's really about."

"Which is?" asks Will.

"To be honest," says Gretel, "I think it's about an issue with you. Can't you respond to what she said?"

"I'm responding here to the nonverbal content," Will explains, bringing flat hands together as if to highlight the importance of the point, "to the dialogue happening beyond language."

"But, like, maybe we want you to respond to the dialogue happening *within* language," says Ashlee.

"Something's hit a nerve," says Will, nodding. "Let's all take a deep breath, reset."

"Or we could just *stay with this,*" says Ruby.

"We could," says Will. "But this isn't about me. It's about all of you, and this week it's specifically about Raina." He turns to her. "Now, where were you?"

Raina glances at Ruby.

"Go ahead," says Ruby. "We're not getting anywhere here."

"Okay," Raina says. "We were talking about choices. In the end, I had two."

★ ★ ★

My three months were almost up, and everyone was still keeping up pretenses. I was keeping up quite a few of them myself.

It was late. Little Man was sitting on the floor of the office, his legs stretched out in front of him, gawky feet splayed to the sides. I'd been trying to tell him something all day.

"Listen," I said to Little Man, but I couldn't seem to finish the sentence.

His eyes darted to my belly.

"Ah," I said. "You know. How?"

He sniffed the air, as if to say he could smell it on me.

"You don't have to do it," he said.

"I'm keeping it," I replied. A week prior, I wouldn't have imagined saying those words. But something changed as I sat waiting for an answer in the bathroom of my father's house where a jar of saline solution with a tooth in it sat on the toilet's tank. My future crystallized along with those two lines, those Rorschach lines. They looked like a path, a purpose, a direction, a magic road that would lead me out of that bathroom, that house, that town.

Little Man shook his head. "I didn't mean that. I meant that you don't have to marry Jake Jackson."

I knew as well as Little Man that Jake Jackson would propose, that he had chosen me from a parade of office girls, that even if he wanted to change his mind, he couldn't now—a baby with someone as young as me was not a good look without a love story attached. I could already picture the proposal: rose petals strewn across a white bed, an ice bucket of virgin champagne, a black velvet box with a sparkling ring.

"What if it's what I want?" I replied.

"Is it?" Little Man asked. He traced his craggy fingers up and down the stiff carpeting. "I could help you," he said. He could find a job in editing. There were new reality TV shows every day. He'd make more than enough money to support the baby, and maybe I could even finish college.

"Little Man," I said. "I don't know anything about you. I don't know where you live. I don't know how old you are. I don't even know your real name."

"Do you know Jake Jackson's real name?" Little Man asked, crossing his tiny arms over his chest. "Do you know his age? Do you know where he lives?"

I didn't actually know any of those things. Jake Jackson, I would later learn, was a stage name—his real name was Jacob, pronounced with a *Y*. I'd assumed he was in his thirties, but he was actually in his forties. And I'd never been to his apartment.

"I don't even know why you're here, Little Man," I said. "Why did you do this for me?"

"It wasn't for you," he said stiffly. He picked a staple out of the rug, inspected it, then flicked it across the room. "I'm not a brownie. I'm not a cupid. I didn't come here to set you up with a celebrity." He wouldn't look at me. He rooted around for another staple. Then I saw his shoulders start shaking. He covered his face as giant tears splashed dark circles on the carpet. When he looked at me finally, his cheeks were pink and streaked.

"Come here, come here," I whispered, tapping next to me. "I still want you in my life, Little Man. I do. I do."

I woke up in the middle of the night to Little Man's nubby fingers twisting at my hair, his eyes shining like glass in the dark. "I'm giving you three days," he said.

"To do what?"

"To decide. Him or me."

"Little Man," I said.

"Think about it. If you say no, I'll be gone for good."

"I don't know who you are," I said.

"Then find out."

When I woke up in the morning, he was gone.

Little Man didn't show up the next day or the day after. I spent the time alone in my office, doing nothing, playing B-roll from the show for background noise, watching the girls sitting in the back of a pickup truck in a wheat field in my hometown, the dilapidated church with its old cemetery of listing gravestones cropped out of view. The women were wearing cowboy hats and denim, chewing on straw, trying to sell the backwater suburbs-of-the-suburbs as sexy.

Little Man's words echoed in my head: "Find out." But how? With what information? It was the flip-phone era. The internet was useless for tracking people down. I checked the garbage can for clues. I found a nest of things: paper clips, crumbs, a half-eaten package of orange peanut butter crackers, a dry-cleaning ticket, a bent MetroCard, and then, there it was: an LIRR ticket to Flushing–Main Street.

I don't know what possessed me to think I could find him there, except that I had nothing else to go on. I escaped from the office at six o'clock sharp, realizing as I clacked across the marble lobby that there had been no reason for me to wait. It wasn't a punch-in, punch-out kind of job, and I wasn't getting paid, and no one cared what kind of work I did, and I wasn't doing any work anyway.

An hour and a half later, I stepped off the 7 train and into the dark, brisk fall night of Flushing–Main Street. I had never been to Queens before—it felt like a different city. The sky was a bright foggy wash of purple; the streets were packed, people walking past four- and five-story buildings stacked with storefront signs in Mandarin.

I followed my impulses; I asked around. "Yay high," I kept saying, holding my hand horizontal at his height. I smelled Little Man here, a scent more complex than burgers, but it didn't surprise me when I found out that he lived over a burger joint.

I climbed on top of a dumpster in an alley with a crate to look in his window, making use of my place in the narrative economy, knowing full well I wouldn't be mistaken for a criminal, though maybe I was one, more or less.

It was a messy, one-room apartment: dirty dishes in the sink, pile of laundry on the floor, movie posters tacked to the walls, the living space you'd imagine for a bachelor in his twenties, save for the size of the furniture—a little wooden table with tiny chairs, a squat desk, a child's bed shaped like a car. The pull switch on the light in the middle of the room had been extended with a long green ribbon.

Little Man was standing on a tall stool in the kitchen wearing a boy's T-shirt and tighty-whities, which revealed the outline of his thin, sinewy legs, the slight bulge of his crotch. He pulled something from the freezer—potato peels, it seemed—then climbed down and brought them to a cage that was as tall as Little Man himself. Inside, bright toys—a hammock and a transparent tunnel, a ladder and a wheel. A gray rat scurried to the edge of the cage, sniffing at Little Man for his treat.

After, Little Man flipped off the lights and watched TV from bed. It flickered in the dark room, his shadow flashing on the wall, impossibly tall and narrow, the silhouette of his face a crescent. He crawled across the bed, turned up the volume, and—much to my surprise—began to sing and dance. He flung his tiny body round and round, jumped in the air with such bounce that his knees rose higher than his waist.

The TV was playing a song about a name from a famous musical, but Little Man wasn't singing the name. Instead, he was squeezing in something else, something so long and ill-fitting that I thought, at first, it was nonsense. He sang it over and over again until it finally coalesced in my ears.

He was singing his own name.

I felt like a thief. Even so, I didn't move, couldn't seem to, was riveted as I listened to his shouts fade into a gentle lullaby as he sunk into the bed, arms crossed over his chest, rocking himself back and forth to the lull of his own name.

Exhaustion overwhelmed me. It would take me hours to get home. I dragged myself back to the train, whispering his strange name over and over. My tongue seemed to move around it, like it was a real object in my mouth. Maybe it was the length of it, the silliness and sibilance, all those hard consonants, the splittable *p*. Was it the name his parents had given him? Or was it a name he had given himself, perhaps when he was very young?

My whole life, I'd been my father's daughter. "Hey, I know who you are. You're Miller's daughter," the men always shouted as I passed. They wanted to remind me where I came from, wanted to remind me that I was trash. I already knew. I lived in a tiny shithole town. I waitressed in a diner of dark wood and orange vinyl, where these same men slipped tips into my pockets as if I were a stripper, which is something else I could have become.

"Hey," my father said once, to a man in a bar, a man he recognized from TV. "You should hire my daughter. Do you know what she can do? She can do anything. She has the magic touch. She can turn a goddamn piece of straw into gold. You should date her. You should marry her, for Christ's sake. Have you seen her? She's gorgeous. The whole fucking town wants her. Prime real estate. Could be yours."

What would people call me after I married Jake Jackson? I wondered. When I returned home for a visit, what would the men shout as I passed? Would they say, "Hey, you! You Jake Jackson's wife?" And when I didn't respond, "What? You too good for us now?"

I envied R——————— his secret name, a name no one could sully, no one could change, a name of his very own.

The next day, I was playing footage again, randomly, just for noise, the girls posing in a golden wheat field, when I smelled him. I looked up, and his bright face peered down at me from the duct. He hopped down, crouched on the floor, looking at me. I will always remember him this way: dazzling in the monitor's golden light, sun-kissed and radiant, gleaming like an iridescent beetle. His skin was luminous; the hair on his arms took on an ethereal glow; his face flickered like a randomly faceted gem.

"R——————," I said. His head cocked, as if he had just heard a wrong note in a song. "I can't," I said.

His face seemed to change color, gold to red. I can still feel the heat rising off him. I wanted to touch him. What I would give, now, to reach out and touch him again.

At first, inexplicably, I thought he was going to laugh. Even as his face contorted, bloomed scarlet, I thought the warmth radiating off of him had something to do with the reflection of the monitor's light. Even as he flung his right knee high into the air, I was sure he was going to smack his thigh and break out into laughter, and even as he didn't, even as he plunged his leg down instead, hard and fast, even as his heel hit the floor with such incredible force, even then I didn't realize he was angry. For a millisecond, the floor seemed, simply, to *bend*.

Then, it broke with a crack like thunder, floorboards splintering up from beneath the carpet. The heel, the ankle, the calf, the knee, all crashed through. Now he was in a one-legged crouch, the other leg submerged in the fractured floor. He yanked at the stuck leg with both hands, but it wouldn't come loose.

Only then did I realize he was angry.

What he did next, I cannot unremember, I cannot unsee. Time chugs forward, but my mind thrusts me back like a scratched record, back, back, back to this. I feel pulled, always, in two directions, stretched like taffy, one end forward, the other back. There are so many ways to be torn in half.

His foot does not come loose. In a fit of wild inspiration, he grabs his left foot with his right hand and pulls, tearing himself in half like a piece of paper.

Except that it's not like paper at all. At first, he looks like a costume unzipping itself from the bottom up, the noises insane: breaking bones, strange pops like cracking knuckles, a goop-sucking sound like boots in mud. I can't comprehend it even as it's happening. He's dividing, I think. Divide and conquer, I think. He's dividing like a cell; it's a kind of reproduction.

Time is slow. The room is vivid with color. His face is a brilliant red.

Neither of us screams.

I want to take it all back. I want to unsay his name. I want to just know it, a secret between us. The way he knows my name, the way he is the only one who ever calls me by it, just sometimes, in a whisper, a little cry.

His brown eyes are wide-open. Those eyes say that I have betrayed him, that he pities me, that I am doing this to him, tearing him apart. They say all this. They just keep talking. They say, *Wrong choice.*

I feel as if something inside of me is being ripped apart too. I feel it as a sting in my chest, as if I am being torn in half along with him, red muscle wrenched from red muscle, tattered edges, guilt surging like blood flowing out, evacuation from the wound.

The skin on his neck pulls apart like string cheese. Right before his face splits in half, he looks at me squarely, and he seems to understand that I am hurting because he is hurting, because I have hurt him. It is awful, how in this final moment—*his* final moment, his strange final moment—he should think of me and offer this kindness, a smile, a smile that says: *Hey, it's okay. I'll be all right.*

But even as he smiles, the chin breaks in two with a bony snap, and then the mouth, the very smile begins to split, blood running up the center of each lip; they could just be dry-cracked winter lips, but now they are apart, they are two half-mouths, they are still smiling, each of them, like a canoe that's broken in two, stern and bow flicked up even while sinking, and the tear is rising, rising up the bridge of his nose, a red line running through his forehead marking the trail of unzipping, and the skin pulls apart like rubber, and the skull ruptures with a final crack, and there are two of him now, completely, and he is not a cell dividing, and there is nothing to conquer, and it is only this: the self divided against itself.

The stuck half hits the floor. The freed half manages a strange half-turn, blood flinging across the room in glimmering strands, as if flying from the skirt of a twirling ballerina. Time is so slow that it seems we'll be frozen forever like this, the body hovering, the blood mid-fling, my mouth open. I think of one of those photographs taken at high speed, where a bullet floats nonchalantly, a playing card or piece of fruit torn in its wake.

It seems as if the body will never touch ground, but it will, it does; the blood splatters and the body lands, one half rocking back and forth like a cradle before it settles into stillness, and then there is quiet and quiet and quiet.

This is the end, I think. Maybe everything is over. Maybe time has stopped. Maybe nothing happens next. Maybe the entire plot has already occurred. What of any consequence could happen now? But, of course, time always ticks forward, no matter the perceived rate; it can't be stopped; *next* always happens; it's happening now; it's the only thing you can count on.

★ ★ ★

Outside, it has grown dark. Raina takes a breath, trying not to cry. "I was cruel." On her lap, a page where capital *R*'s sit beside long dashes.

"I don't think so," says Bernice gently.

"I've seen cruel," says Gretel. "You weren't cruel."

"I betrayed him," says Raina in a near-whisper.

"He, like, asked you to make a choice," says Ashlee.

"It must have been so terrible to watch him come apart," says Bernice. "But you can't blame yourself for what happened. *You* didn't split him in two."

"He is dead because I was selfish, because I was unkind," says Raina. "He is dead, and I get to go on, get to live this entire, privileged life."

"A life you don't even like, do you?" says Ruby, who has rubbed all of the damp fur on her coat so it's sticking straight up.

"My life is fine," says Raina. "My life is good. What's more, it's the life I chose."

"You don't have to like it just because you chose it," says Bernice.

"It was kind of a stacked deck, choice-wise," says Ruby.

Raina brushes her thumb across the edges of her papers. She looks around at them. "Your mistakes, if you can even call them that, were about hope. Ashlee, you wanted to believe you were in a love story. Ruby, you wanted to be seen the way any kid wants to be seen. Bernice, you wanted to feel special, to be seen for who you were. Gretel, you were protecting your brother. And what did I do? I hurt someone"—her voice shakes—"I *hurt* someone I loved and for what?"

"For the life you have now," says Will.

"For the baby," says Ashlee.

"Those weren't good reasons," says Raina. "Those were very bad reasons."

* * *

How long had I been staring at the two halves of his body before the door flung open and Jake Jackson appeared, the color draining from his face? For a second, I thought he would vomit. "What the fuck?" he said.

This is After, I thought. *Here I am. I have arrived. I will live the rest of my life over here.*

I couldn't look away from R——————. One half of his body had landed gruesome-side up, revealing a cross-section of anatomy: slimy pink flesh, soft organs, tiny-holed bones. The organs were mostly whole, having each chosen a side, so to speak, but the slick gray brain was split precisely down the middle, still tucked in his head like a walnut half in its shell. Parts of his intestines were hanging over his stomach and onto the floor. The lanky leg was bent at the knobby knee. The rest of the leg was twisted into the splintered floorboards. The arm was partially pinned under him, but the hand was free—palm up, finger-splayed, thrust forward, beseeching.

Blood had darkened the carpet, soaked into the cracked floorboards where he had stomped his foot, pooled into spots and congealed. A musky, animal stench filled the air: fresh meat and manure, iron and salt.

I tried not to look at his nether regions (there must be some dignity left, some scrap of dignity to be maintained?), but I couldn't help it. They were right there, cut in half. A spongy, pink nub, a smooth tube at the center. I wished I could cover it up. I did not want Jake to see it. I did not want him to make a joke, or even think a joke, though he did not look in a joking mood.

When Little Man was whole, it was difficult to imagine how his body worked. How did he carry the weight of such a huge head on such a narrow neck? How did he manage such agility with those clumsy feet? The construction had always seemed impossible, but now I could see the mechanics: the curving spine hooked under a thick muscle of hunched back—tight and strong from bearing such a weight.

Ultimately, it was not the gruesome side that was most disconcerting, it was the other half, the half that was faceup, that looked like a creature who could still be alive, whose mirror side could be, somehow, hovering beneath the floorboards. I stared at his half-face and it stared back at me: half-nose; half half-smile; bright, unblinking eye, like an antique milk-glass marble swirled through with brown.

"Are you okay?" asked Jake. His hand was on me somewhere, my shoulder. My brain was on a different plane than my body.

I looked down at my floral dress where blood was spattered in an energetic burst of crimson. My brain wasn't working right, was playing tricks, was inventing its own timeline, and for a moment I thought the blood on my skirt was somehow in transit, was still in the process of splattering, in which case Little Man was still spinning in midair, already split in two but perhaps still sentient, the way they say a decapitated head can still think and see, and if he were still alive, if that were the case, then there would still be time to take it back, to unsay it, to apologize.

But no. Everything in the room was still.

"What the fuck happened?" Jake asked.

"He just...fell out of the heating duct," I said. "He was angry about something. He split in two."

"What the fuck," said Jake, trying not to become hysterical. "That is not a thing. That is not a thing that happens."

He had a point. Many of us were torn apart by anger, but never so literally.

He started pacing in the tiniest circle, his boat shoes squeaking.

"Look at his little..." Jake said, shaking his head.

"Body," I said quickly. "His whole body is little. He's a little person."

"That is not a person," said Jake. "That's a troll, a creature of some kind." This coming from a man who would one day have so much plastic surgery that he'd be half bovine and botulism.

Dave appeared. Jake seemed to have called him. "Holy shit," said Dave. "What the fuck..." He walked closer. "Oh my God. I know this guy."

My head snapped toward him. "What?" I said.

"It's Little Rumpy," said Dave.

"*That's* Rumpy?" said Jake Jackson.

"I mean, come on, nobody else looks like that guy," said Dave.

"Who?" I asked.

Apparently, everyone in reality TV production knew of "Little Rumpy," "the teeny tiny rising star with the great big fall," as Dave put it. Rumor had it that while working on *Celebrity Losers* several years before, Little Rumpy had refused to edit a man in a mechanical wheelchair to look like a villain, claiming the trope was tired, overdone. It was a sticking point that got him fired. In a fit of anger, he destroyed the office. "I mean, really fucking destroyed it," said Dave. "Karate chopped some desks in half. Threw some monitors out of some windows. Lot of fucking damage for a little guy. Heard he begged for a job at every network. But, I mean, who would hire someone after a blowup like that?"

I couldn't think.

Jake looked at the body. "Maybe he was here seeking revenge on the industry."

"Or maybe he was seeking a comeback," suggested Dave. "Maybe he wanted to prove himself again, just needed a front." He looked at me carefully. "Never seen him before?"

"No," I lied. "He just…" I pointed at the heating duct. My throat seemed to close.

"Fell from the sky," said Dave.

"The media's going to have a field day with this," said Jake.

Jake called his publicist from my office phone as I sat in the chair, too stunned to move. I was so overcome with grief that it was as if the wind had been knocked out of me. Grief not just over R——————'s death but also over—what?—a future that it was now too late to choose. The only creature who had ever helped me, who had ever called me by my real name, and I had treated him like a sideshow attraction.

I didn't hear any of that phone call, but later I would understand how the publicist spun the story. She would imply that Jake Jackson had saved my life from a disgruntled former industry employee. Out of tragedy, she would say, our love had blossomed. When asked about it later, Jake would only say that he wasn't a hero, he just did what he had to do. So few details of the incident actually escaped that the story itself more or less evaporated. All that remained was the sentiment that Jake Jackson was a good guy.

Jake was still on the phone, nodding enthusiastically, when, from the corner of my eye, I swore I saw something move. Between R——————'s two halves was his heart, alone, flung from his body, lying several inches from his half-face. I hadn't seen it until now. His big, brown eye seemed trained on it. The heart was pulsing. Was it pulsing? Or was it a trick of the eye or of the light or of the brain? The heart glistened and winked in the office light. Jake's head swiveled toward it too.

The heart, laid bare, is disgusting: a red-brown fist of muscle and slime, whitish at the edges like fat on a piece of meat. If it was moving at all, it was not so much beating as clenching weakly. Was that even possible? Did it matter? Hadn't what's "possible" burst wide-open already? Wasn't there a heart, flung there, on the office floor? This heart, in particular, appeared to be relentless, to have hope beyond what seemed prudent, seemed possible, to hope for. For a moment, I understood what such a grotesque organ had to do with love.

My hands trembled.

His outstretched fingers, his pulsing heart, his wide eye? They ached with longing.

I thought about the phrase "better half," as if it took another person to make you whole, but both of my halves were inside of me. One followed the path of least resistance; the other rebelled.

I bent down toward the small, upturned half-body. I was so close to him that if he were still alive—he couldn't still be alive, could he?—my breath would have forced him to blink.

He didn't blink.

Jake put his hand over the receiver. "Honey," he said. "Don't touch him." His tone implied I was crazy. But I was perfectly calm. Day after day after day, I'm calm. A lifetime of reasons to tear myself in half, and I never do.

I stared directly into Little Man's one wide, brown eye.

And then, with two gentle fingers, I closed it.

★ ★ ★

Raina starts to cry in earnest, hands over her face, shoulders shaking, tears dripping on the lap of her floral dress. Will sits slouched, scratching at his wrist, mouth slightly open, staring at Raina. He hardly seems to notice the rest of them are there.

Bernice offers Raina a pile of napkins. "Sorry," she says as she hands them over, "but the only actual tissues we have around here are in your purse."

Raina wipes her eyes, blows her nose. She looks out the windows. The rain has stopped, but the brick wall is wet, glazed, sparkling in the light coming from a streetlamp at the end of the alley, where a car honks, a bus groans.

"I still can't seem to admit what is true," she says. "I can't seem to say it and I need to say it; each moment I don't I betray him further. I've avoided the truth for all of these pages," she says, flipping through, her pitch rising. "I've avoided it for all of these hours, all of these years. If I don't tell you this, the whole story is as good as a lie." She shuffles through her papers, selects one black with edits, and reads from it, the paper shaking.

★ ★ ★

His knobby, calloused hands were always so light and shy on my skin. I had placed them there. The scent that rose off of him was strong and dark, a warm meal. He seemed to feel he was owed nothing. His tongue, once I coaxed it from him, more adept than I'd expected, and longer: a pink velvet ribbon that could curl and curl. Small but mighty, all of him, compact and nimble. The usual positions employed, then the usual positions a moot point, new positions created. Just once I looked through squinted eyes to see him, gargoyle-like, on his haunches between my open thighs, pumping that little hand in and out fiercely, a raffish, wild expression on his impossible face, the little mouth whispering my name, my real name. A hot shiver ran through me, and I saw his skin change— was it a trick of light, a trick of memory? Or was he really gilded, briefly? And I mean this truly: more than sun-kissed, but leafed in gold, glimmering in the almost-dark, so that he looked sleek as a statuette, weighted and worthy, something I was embarrassed and thankful for at the same time, a prize I never deserved to win.

★ ★ ★

"Wait, so is she saying...?" Ashlee whispers.

"Jesus," says Ruby. "Yes. Just give her a minute."

Raina blinks, and a single fresh tear runs down her damp cheek. She clutches the page, but doesn't read from it, just speaks as she stares out the window.

★ ★ ★

The night of R————————'s death the moon was out, but not golden at all. It was pure white, like bone, like Jake's teeth, and all the rats in the garbage cans sounded desperate as I slowly managed my way to the 7 train like I was dragging a body.

Six months from that very day, I would be married. I would have a famous husband, a new name, a beautiful apartment in Manhattan, a sprawling summerhouse upstate, and a pet rat named Tiny. Soon after, my daughter, Oribel, would arrive with her strange little face, her golden skin, her pointed chin and remarkable ears, her giant wet eyes I love so much, like chestnuts slicked with rain.

The End

What? What the fuck? Will feels so dizzy that he clutches both sides of his chair. Perhaps he misheard. Misinterpreted. Perhaps it's not true.

He watches Raina wipe the tear away with a knuckle.

Why is she sad? he thinks, gripping the chair tighter. *Why does she get to be sad?*

He can't help but notice the way her arm bends as she wipes the tear, the way the fabric pulls a little, revealing the gentle curve of biceps under a scatter of flowers.

Part of him wants to punish her, really punish her, another to comfort. That's the problem with being two people, isn't it? You hardly understand which version of yourself you are.

Raina turns from the window, smiles at Will sadly. He matches her sadness and smiles back. He thinks about that bare office, about that ugly little body, so strange and mysterious—skin ripped in two, such a clean line. He would never allow himself to be that ugly.

"Jake must know?" says Bernice.

"I really don't know what Jake knows," says Raina. "He has never taken a lot of interest in her."

"Isn't it, like, kind of obvious by looking?" says Ashlee.

"Probably too up his own ass to notice," says Ruby.

Will can hardly hear them. Raina seems like someone else. He has been this close to her a million times, and closer, and yet it's the first time he has noticed that arm, really noticed it, how it's at once strong and delicate.

He imagines bringing her flowers, red roses, a dozen, tucked in a cone of white paper. Which him would give them to her? Which him would she accept them from? Would she take the flowers with her smooth hands and then kiss him with her soft pink lips? Is it possible that this group, all along, this whole enterprise, was simply *his* love story, disguised as something else? He wants her so much it's painful. To be turned on by the thought of a kiss makes him feel young, so incredibly young, and to feel that young excites him even more.

It happens in an instant. A draft of cool air rushes up his back like a tickle, and by the time he understands what's happening, it's already happening, it can't be undone: his own desire has blown the seam. His skin pinches and snaps around him. It's as if his skin is being sucked off with a vacuum. His hands ripple as if melting. The skin of his face puckers in, the brown head of hair encroaching on dark holes where his eyes and mouth had been.

Bernice jumps from her chair, knocking it over behind her. Ashlee tries to say "No," but her mouth is so agape that the word is merely aspiration. Gretel stands up slowly, backs away to the wall nearest the door. Ruby leans closer, pushes her glasses up her nose, squints through them. Raina covers her mouth with both hands as papers flutter off her lap. *Is he imploding?* she wonders. *Is this what I do to people? Make their bodies impossible?*

"Shit," says a voice beneath the soft shell of face, just a moment before it falls onto his chest, revealing the face beneath: a face with dry, flaky skin stretched taut, the hair tucked in a net.

"What the actual fuck?" says Ruby.

"Oh. Em. Gee," says Ashlee.

"Jake?" says Raina, blinking in disbelief.

Jake's real face is so masklike that Raina has the uncanny feeling that this could just keep happening, that faces could just keep falling off, that there might be no end to the subterfuge. Perhaps there would be no skeleton beneath at all, just skin and skin and skin, and finally, after all of the faces are stripped away, just those glimmering, perfect teeth, searching for another face to invade.

"It's not what you think," he says, shaking his real head while the other head, the one that has landed on his chest, jiggles, the hair swaying.

Ashlee's eyes dart frantically into the corners of the room. "I knew it," she says. "I *knew* we were being filmed."

"We're not being..." starts Ruby. "Fuck."

"I can explain," he says.

"Is there a contract?" Ashlee squeals. "Did I sign another contract?"

"Forget the contract," he says.

"Really, Jake?" says Raina, looking at him. "Really?"

"You cheated on me with an imp," spits Jake. "I've been raising a child... Jesus, Raina. An imp?"

"If you wanted to know my secrets, you didn't have to punish everyone else."

"This wasn't about you," he hisses, scratching at his face. "This is much bigger than you. You weren't even supposed to be in the cast."

"The *cast?*" says Bernice.

"You're really just trying to make a fucking reality TV show?" says Ruby.

Jake forces himself to take a deep breath. He has literally blown his cover, but he can still pitch it to them, can't he? He has to try. He has to stay calm.

"Don't you see?" he says. "This is an *opportunity*. You've all been so misunderstood. Here's your chance to show the world who you really are."

"Please," says Gretel from the doorway.

"Talk about missing the point," says Bernice.

"Wrong reasons," squeals Ashlee. "You are here for the wrong reasons."

"This is about more than me and it's about more than you," he says. The head of hair on his chest bounces. The hair on his actual head bristles through the hair net. "It's about the greater good. Do you understand how many other women can learn from your stories?"

"You were such a fucking bullshitter from day one," says Ruby.

"You all need to think very carefully about what you want," Jake says. "I'm happy to have you all on my side. Even you, Raina," he adds, "despite what you've done."

"Come on," says Ruby, rolling her eyes.

"You're crazy if you think we're going to be part of this," says Raina.

Jake laughs. He's had so much Botox that his skin barely moves. Flakes of dry skin just fall from his face. "I'm crazy?" he says. "Have you listened to yourselves?"

"You're the one hiding in a human skin suit," says Bernice.

"It doesn't matter," says Jake. "This isn't about who I am—it's about who people think I am." He smiles. His teeth gleam from his dry, awful face. "Do what you want, but I have the footage. It's your word against mine. The public is already on my side."

The Epilogue

Bernice

In the silence, new noises emerge: the old spring mattress moans, the toilet takes a noisy five minutes to refill post-flush. I drop a quarter on the floor, and it whirrs in a vibrating circle, then stops with a plunk that echoes through the empty apartment. I dump forty laundry quarters on the floor, straight out of the coin roll, and they spin and rattle and finish with a thunk.

And then it is quiet. Extra quiet.

It shouldn't be so easy to clean up spilled quarters, but there is no furniture for them to hide under.

I take out the AC unit, open the windows wide, let the outside tumble in: crisp air, rumbling cars, screeching children, and a man yelling, "Bitch!" over and over at the sky.

I feel free and lonely. I buy different furniture, secondhand—no leather, no bone. A wood armchair with a seventies-striped cushion, mustard and olive, a cheap black futon with a steel frame. I hang thrift-store prints randomly on the pre-nailed walls, corporate-bland shades of orange and green, add a few beach views with pink sunsets and cracked skies, painted by my sister.

A moan, and I am on it, looking under the cushions, interrogating the chairs, and then I realize it's coming through the wall. Are there dead women over there too?

No, I'm mistaken. It's just the living, making living noises, the disembodied sex sounds of the neighbor and her girlfriend.

Ah, ah, ah! is how the louder one comes, like a revelation every time.

The cashier at the bodega, always the same guy, rings up a bag of M&M's, then nods over toward the tabloids, where I don't see my face anywhere, only rumors of reality TV breakups—one of a show's star, another of its host.

"You're old news, eh?" says the cashier.

"For now," I say. The host is embroiled in a vicious legal battle with his own vindictive soon-to-be ex-wife and four other women, yet to be officially named.

"You sued that Bluebeard bastard's estate?" the cashier says. "That's what I heard. I heard you're about to be very rich."

I shrug. I smile.

"You single?" he jokes.

I will probably be single forever.

I take the M&M's and then I take the 7 to the 6 to The Met, where Gretel is waiting in the museum café. The café is a beautiful enclosed courtyard with statues dotted across a marble floor and a wall of windows facing Central Park. The sky is oppressively cloudless and crystal blue. I turn away from it, toward Gretel, who carefully peels the lid off of a creamer, pours a few drops into her coffee.

"Can I ask..." I say sheepishly. "Did you hear the jars speak?"

"Does it matter?" she says instead of saying no.

"I don't know, maybe it doesn't."

"Someone once gave me good advice about making peace with not knowing what you can't know," says Gretel.

"Ironic, isn't it?" I say. "The group was a total scam, but we did learn some things after all."

"Yeah, I know," says Gretel. She looks out the window behind me, stirs her coffee. "Do you think the show will air?"

"I'm not sure," I say. I have already imagined the promo. Ashlee screaming at the top of her lungs. Raina sobbing. Gretel confessing to murder. Me in loungewear talking to a stool. Ruby passed out on the floor, fur coat drenched and face streaked red, sirens whirring in the background, and Will, the hero, by her side. Wouldn't you watch?

"We have an excellent legal team," I say. "Though there's always the possibility that he'll leak the footage regardless."

"Have you finished all the interviews?" she asks.

I nod. I catch her up on the other women, tell her that Ruby is working at a bookstore café in Brooklyn, that she kept up her end of the bargain and is no longer wearing the coat. Raina, who is living upstate, sent Ruby a new one—cropped, faux fur—along with a box of cookies. Raina is considering going back to college, finally finishing her degree.

"And the new roommate?" Gretel asks.

"A mess, but she'll recover." She came with a giant suitcase half full of gowns. She spent a lot of time, at first, talking to me through the bathroom door, tap water running. I'd sink down in the hall, listen to her. It felt like the old days with the Tiffanies.

Gretel and I make small talk as we finish our coffees, then I make my way alone to the ancient Egypt wing to see the new acquisition: four canopic jars.

The wing is just as I remember it from childhood trips, lined with bright, painted coffins, inscribed sarcophagi, bandage-wrapped mummies of all sizes. There are smaller objects too: glazed scarabs, an intricate ivory comb, jewels of glass and gold and lapis lazuli. You can't take it with you, the saying goes. It's the living who keep the spoils.

The jars stand in a glass case under bright white lights. "Hey," I say, leaning in close, barely moving my lips.

I'm not used to all this fucking attention! says Human-God Tiffany proudly. *There's a dead cat around here somewhere. And a monkey, and a dog that barks all night.*

Don't you think that coffin over there looks like me? says Falcon Tiffany. In the corner, a small wood coffin with the stoic face of a bird.

"Do you want it to look like you?" I ask.

Guess what? squawks Falcon Tiffany. *Nobody's in there! That thing is just filled with random shit like sand!*

I'm highly likely to learn ancient Egyptian in here, says Baboon Tiffany in a tone that makes it unclear if she is excited or annoyed. *Bi-fucking-lingual.*

Money, money, money, says Human-God Tiffany. *They're making money off of me, and what do I get? It's worse than the fucking strip club.*

"What would you do if you had money?" I ask.

Electric scooter, says Human-God Tiffany, and Jackal Tiffany snickers.

I'd sit around just like this, says Baboon Tiffany. *I feel like a fucking model in here. I think the mummies are jealous.*

A museumgoer with an angular bob approaches.

"Listen," I say to her, nodding toward the Tiffanies.

"What?" the woman asks, leaning in, eyes bright. She fumbles with her phone, where she appears to be activating another stop on her audio tour.

Idiot, says Human-God Tiffany. *I'm not even on the audio tour yet.*

There is very little information about the jars. The placard reads: CANOPIC JARS WITH LIDS, CIRCA 900–800 BCE. Gretel said we would probably never know whose organs were first inside, and the craftsman who made them was likely anonymous from the start. We might never know how many hands these jars had passed through, how many people had owned them or sold them or stolen them. I had wanted Gretel to confirm that Tiffany was inside, but apparently opening the jars would risk oxidation and contamination of the remains.

Even if the museum did discover her in there one day, I doubted the audio tour would highlight her, a Hooters waitress whose disappearance nobody noticed. Perhaps she would be a footnote in a story about a certain serial-killing billionaire mastermind.

I follow the ebb of tourists to The Met's most iconic room, which houses an ancient Egyptian temple. The temple stands in a beautiful room designed specifically to showcase it. It's surrounded by a reflecting pool like a moat, set against a massive, angled window, stacked with blue sky. For a moment, I imagine the windows are keeping the blue out, but the color leaks in everywhere: it's reflected in the water, it's in people's eyes, it's on their clothes, it surrounds me in every conceivable shade. The color is inside of me too, in my veins, blood running in bright turquoise trails. You can't escape a color. And besides, I can't deny how majestic the temple looks against the bright sky. It seems at home, though it's not at home; it's so far from where it began.

You can't change the past, but it's infinitely reframeable. You can tell the same story over and over a hundred different ways, and every version is a little right and every version is a little wrong.

Maybe the show would air eventually, maybe the footage would leak, maybe there'd be a trial, maybe the trial of public opinion had already begun, maybe Jake Jackson's publicity team was already doing its work, because, haven't you heard? Raina had an affair. Ashlee is impossible to work with. Gretel is a liar. Ruby sleeps around. And didn't my lawsuit against Ashton's estate prove that I was in it for the money?

If our stories were up for public consumption, then the least we could do was tell them ourselves. I had the other women's blessings. I had some money coming in. I had to get to work.

Acknowledgments

Thank you to Jenni Ferrari-Adler, my agent at Union Literary, and Jean Garnett, my editor at Little, Brown, for their patience and support shepherding me through the overwhelming reality of writing a novel. Thanks also to Carina Guiterman, who acquired the novel and was an early champion, and to the entire team at Little, Brown who transformed this into a beautiful book.

The Norton Edition of *The Classic Fairy Tales* by Maria Tatar was my adult reintroduction to the world of fairy tales. This led me to the Carolyn Heilbrun essay "What Was Penelope Unweaving?" (from *Hamlet's Mother and Other Women*), which provided an epigraph and guiding light for this novel. I primarily used the Brothers Grimm and/or Charles Perrault fairy tales as a starting point for my own stories, though many anonymous people told versions of these tales long before they were collected.

Several *Bachelor* podcasts, among them *Bachelor Party, Chatty Broads*, and *Love to See It* (formerly *Here to Make Friends*), contributed to my understanding of reality TV production. The *Hallowzeen* project with Lulu Miller planted early seeds for this book, and flash-fiction versions of Gretel's story found a home in *Tin House*. The word-processing program Scrivener helped enormously with the task of organizing the novel.

Love and endless thanks to my family and friends, an embarrassment of riches. Thanks to my mom, Karin; my dad, Richard; my brother, Joe; my SIL, Sarah; my nephews and niece, Rasmus, Soren, and Thuri; and the entire Adelmann and Hansen families—aunts, uncles, cousins, and extended family galore. They make success sweeter and failure easier to take, and often make either a moot point. Thank you also to my many friends far and near, old and new, from Wantage, Ithaca, Charlottesville, Baltimore, Copenhagen, and beyond. Special shout-outs to Amanda, who always made a bad writing day better, Aunt Mer, who should probably get a cut as a book distributor, and Hester, who wins an Outstanding Roommate Award for being very quiet as I wrote much of this book in our only living space. Finally, Derek Denman experienced the ups and downs of this book along with me. He helped me to find sanity in the uncertainty and joy in the process.

About the Author

Maria Adelmann is the author of the short story collection *Girls of a Certain Age*, which explores the many impossible choices of modern girl- and womanhood. Her work has been published by *Tin House*, *n+1*, *Electric Literature*, *McSweeney's Internet Tendency*, *The Threepenny Review*, *the Indiana Review*, *Epoch*, and many others, and has been selected by *The Best American Short Stories* as a distinguished story. You can follow her on Twitter or Instagram @ink176. *How to Be Eaten* is her first novel.